Eden Forest

Part One of the Saskia Trilogy

Aoife Marie Sheridan

© 2012 Aoife Marie Sheridan

All rights reserved. Copyright Aoife Marie Sheridan 2012.

ISBN
978-1-908417-49-7

A catalogue record of this book is available
from the British Library.

Published 2012 by The Universal Publishing Group

This book is dedicated to:

Emmet Proudfoot

Prologue

I pull down my brown tunic to try and cover my ever-growing stomach. Sweat trickles down the back of my neck as the sun burns high in the sky, yet I have a sense of peace as I dig my hands into the cool soil that surrounds the flower beds. I close my eyes and inhale the beautiful scent of thousands of roses with lavender lady flowers and violets as their companions.

"Suis, could you fetch me a beaker of water?"

Suis jumps up off her knees.

"Of course, ma'am." She runs off along the path that winds through the rose beds.

I kneel back on my haunches while waiting for Suis to return. My mind wanders to the festival only two days away. I am excited, yet terrified. The festival is held every ten years for women of the age of twenty-five. The king and queen match us personally for our future husband or wife. I rub my belly gently; I have all I need for now.

"Here you are, ma'am." Suis hands me the water.

"Do you have a stomach ache? Because if you do, my mum always says rosemary leaves settle it."

A tingle of fear runs through me. I have to be more careful. If Suis saw me rub my stomach, then who else might have? I square my shoulders and take a deep gulp of water. "I will remember that. I actually grow some in my garden, but thank you for the advice, Suis."

Suis pushes the clay off her small hands, already forgetting about my stomach. She is only sixteen and my first apprentice so I am not entirely sure if my teaching is in any way good. The bell rings once, signalling it's time for lunch. We wash our hands by the fountain before making our way to a large barn where food is served for the gardeners. There is about twenty of us that are spread out amongst the four sections of the gardens. Each section holds different flowers and plants. The section that

I work in is S1. This is the smallest of all the sections; only Suis and I work here.

When we arrive at the barn, there is a large queue formed already, and I have to wait in line in the sweltering heat. It never bothered me before, but with swollen ankles and a sore back, it is getting harder. "Next," the server calls in a rough voice and slops soup into a wooden bowl, while another and equally rough server hands the man at the top of the queue a bread roll. I can't blame them for their lack of enthusiasm. Once we are finished eating, they have to serve all the workers from the vegetable and fruit gardens, and they exceed our numbers threefold. I take my soup and roll while thanking both men, but not receiving a reply. I sit myself at one of the long wooden tables that have been worn down from years of use. The cracks that run along the wood are wider, allowing me to see my toes peeking out of my sandals. Suis sits down beside me, glancing around the barn, looking terrified. "Why are the guardians outside, ma'am?" she asks with her eyes wide and innocent. "First of all, Suis, please call me Marta, and the guardians are always stationed here to make sure the work is done. If the work is done, then there will be no trouble." Suis looks into her soup. "And if the work is not done?" Her voice quivers a little. I can see by her face that someone has told her some nasty rumours; the children seem to think it fun to scare one another, but it's hard to make someone feel safe when they are so afraid. I pat her gently on the back. "The work is always done. Don't fret, child." Then I give her a square look. "And don't be listening to silly stories. Unless an adult tells you, always assume it is untrue." She relaxes her posture, relieved that everything will be all right, and she digs into her soup. Nicon sits down across from me. "Marta." He looks at Suis and acknowledges her with a nod. Then he raises his eyebrow in a question. *Is it okay to talk in front of her?* I give him a nod. "Any word on the supplies?" Nicon asks in a whisper so none of the guardians can hear. He is referring to wine I am getting him. It is a rarity here in Saskia, as the queen has banded all alcohol from our village, saying it's for our own good, but not everyone agrees. It is only allowed at times of celebration.

Dominic, my best friend's husband, knows people who know people. "Not yet, but soon," I whisper. He inclines his head and starts eating. He is a rather large man and with his build would be more suitable as a woodcutter, but he signed up to be a gardener. Everyone has called him small since we were children. He towered over all of us, but would never hurt anything. He is a gentle giant.

I eat my soup quickly. "See you, Nicon."

He sets his wooden spoon aside and drains his bowl by using it like a mug. He wipes his face with the back of his hand. "That was tasty. See you later," he says with a smile. I laugh, as he has bits of bread stuck in his beard.

Once back in the garden with Suis, I give her instructions to remove all the dead leaves. Then I return to my own work. After a few hours, I watch Suis from the corner of my eye. She is struggling, catching her hand on every thorn while trying to remove any dead leaves. "Ouch." She places another bleeding finger in her mouth. Her small face is scrunched up, making her features look smaller. "Suis, go wash your hands by the fountain and take a break." "Thank you, ma'am." She speaks with her finger in her mouth, making me laugh. "Call me Marta." She smiles, nods, and leaves to wash her hands. I return to my work, turning more soil. A shadow appears over me, a guardian. There is always one stationed at each garden, making sure the work is done. He is young so I know he will be harsher than other guardians. He looks at me with a scowl. "S1, where is your apprentice?" We are called by our sections. It is easier than names. I rise and incline my head with respect. "She has gone to the fountain to tend her wounds, sir. She will be back shortly." The guardian leaves without a second glance, his face stoic, and makes his way to the fountain to make sure I have told the truth. Suis arrives back shortly after the guardian is gone and looks at the rose bed as if in a challenge.

I say nothing of the guardian, as I do not want to upset her. It will only give her cause to worry. "Do you have an affinity, Suis?"

She looks at me, confused.

"Of course, everyone does."

"What is your affinity?"

"Why air, ma'am... I mean Marta." She gives me a shy smile.

"Then use it." She frowns. I walk behind her and place my hands on her shoulders. "Close your eyes." She closes them really tight. "Relax, Suis. I want you to reach out with your mind to the roses. Can you feel them?"

She nods. "Yes, yes, I can."

"Now feel along them until you come to a blank area. Can you see it?" She nods. "Okay, that's the dead leaves. Now send wind to knock them off." The rose bushes begin to rustle. "Gently. You only want to get rid of the dead leaves." one by one, the leaves flutter to the ground.

Suis opens her eyes. A smile spreads across her face when she sees all the dead leaves on the ground. When she smiles, she looks prettier. "No more thorns to poke at me," she says gleefully.

The bell sounds. It rings all over the village, sounding the end of the day. We put away our tools before leaving and head back for the village. The streets are full of villagers buying and selling goods. I have to squeeze through the crowded square to get to the other side where I live.

The village is encircled with large, round towers that house all guardians. From the square they look really small, yet their presence is felt always. They were built with black stone and a red slate that covers the circular roofs. The colours were a reminder that danger would never pass the guardian towers. Once, they had given comfort to the people of Saskia that we were been looked over and protected, but now they are a reminder of our darker days.

My small white cottage comes into view with its bright yellow straw roof. The village is scattered with small cottages for workers with no families. They are just sleeping quarters with a cooking and resting area. It is all I need. When I get to my bedroom, I gather the fresh garments and soap I have wrapped up on my bed and make my way to the spring to clean the sweat and soil from my body. The main springs are located beside the castle, but are always full with workers at this time of the day. I found a small spring not far from my home that was rarely used, and I love the peace and quiet.

On the way, I have to pass the memorial garden, just at the end of the village. I don't help maintain it, as it's too painful. My parents are buried there, along with other villagers. King Morrick came up with the idea that we should build the garden in memory of all the villagers who were wrongly accused of being traitors from the time Saskia was at war with the previous king, King Paulus.

I still feel angry, even though it has been over twenty years since the war. I was only five at the time and my parents were decapitated in front of me for sheltering wounded rebel guardians. They rebelled against King Paulus for his evil ways, as he had brought darkness and suffering to the Saskian people for almost fifty years. I shiver at the memory. But rumours were circulating lately that he still lives. Nobody ever found his body after the clean-up started, but we all hoped that he was so badly burned there was just nothing that remained. The rumours are starting to frighten people who fought and lived through the dark times. My parents faces come back to me, both of them on their knees as I was made watch. I wipe the fresh tears from my eyes. I am still amazed by how much it hurts after so long.

When I reach the spring, my stomach growls. I pat it gently. "Wash first, then food." I strip off my work clothes, a long brown tunic that has short sleeves just to the elbow and slits up the sides of my legs to allow flexibility while gardening. Brown is worn by all workers outside the castle, and blue is worn inside the castle.

I lace my tunic with soap and scrub viciously, making sure to get all the soil off it. When I finish, I hang it on a nearby branch of a tree. After I remove my sandals and undergarments, I let my hair down, removing all the pins. It falls just at my shoulders, a cascade of black curls.

There is a dip at the side of the spring that I use to lower myself into the water. It is warm from the sun's rays. The water splashes against my body, loosening every muscle. After lathering my hair with soap, I dip my head back and rinse. I stay a while longer than usual, daydreaming about what my baby will look like. I have only two months left, yet my bump is tiny. I thank God for small mercies. You can't take a lover before you are matched. It is against our rules. My stomach flutters with excitement and fear at seeing Morrick at the festival. I know we can't speak to each other, but just to see him will be enough.

I dry off and get dressed, returning to the village, greeting people as I make my way through the windy cobbled streets. "Marta." I turn around to see Corrona. "Come to mine. I made us supper."

I link my arm with hers. "This is why you're my best friend. You always know when I'm hungry." We laugh and talk about the festival over supper. Corrona's cottage is just like mine, except her resting area is covered in materials, beads, and pins, as she is gifted at dressmaking. She is making my dress for the festival, but it had to be altered several times for my growing body.

"So how do you feel?" Her eyes fall to my stomach. She is the only other person I could tell, besides Morrick, about being pregnant, but she doesn't know who the father is. It is for her own safety. I know what I am doing is reckless and stupid, but I love him.

She gives me one of her lopsided smiles. "Daydreaming again?"

I blush slightly. "No," I say while smiling. "How are you, more to the point?"

Corrona will be due any day. She is practically glowing and her smile couldn't get any wider. "I can't believe it, me and

Dominic having our own baby. I have waited so long for this." Her face becomes sombre. "But I'm afraid."

I sit beside her and wrap my arm around her shoulder. "It is going to be all right, Corrona."

I lay my head on her shoulder for my own comfort as well as hers. All baby boys are checked when they're born to see if they have an affinity for air, and if they do, the child is taken from its mother and reared in the castle to be a guardian. It's every woman's worst fear, but it only happens to about one in thirty. So I pray to God that Corrona and I will be one of the lucky ones, that either we have a girl or a son with a different affinity.

The next morning at work, Suis is all excited. "Morning, Marta."

I smile at her childlike expression. She reminds me of a mouse, a cute one. She is only sixteen so she still has time to bloom. "Morning, Suis."

She dances from one foot to another. "Do I get to use my affinity again?"

"For the next few days, yes. As you can see, the dead leaves are almost endless, but they will end all the same. Then you must use your hands."

Her smile falters only slightly. "Okay, at least I can use it for a few more days." She stands there smiling.

"You can start now."

"Oh, yes, sorry. Yes." And off she goes, full of enthusiasm.

The day goes by quickly and without problems. After work, I wash and dress quickly, as I am meeting Corrona tonight. There is a gathering in the main barn for all the ladies of the village to celebrate the matching festival that will be held tomorrow night.

The barn is lit by hundreds of candles, giving it a magical and romantic feel. I squeeze Corrona's hand with excitement. The barn has been lined with wooden benches with an aisle down the middle. Corrona and I squeeze into the second row.

"Hi, Marta." I turn around. Suis is behind me, looking pretty in a pink dress.

"You look beautiful," I say.

This causes a blush to rise in her cheeks. "Thank you."

A hush falls over the barn as Mirium the storyteller takes his place at the top of the barn. He is five hundred years old so he walks with a white staff. He has a long white beard and kind grey eyes. He swings his heavy gold tunic out as he sits down. Lots of people believe he is an oracle. Some girls go to him to see their future match and how many kids they will have, but it never interested me.

"Greetings, must I say, ladies, you all look glorious on this fine night." Giggles sound around the barn. I let out a sigh, causing Corrona to give me a harsh look. She is a believer. Then she squeezes my leg to let me know she isn't mad at me. Corrona couldn't get mad; she has a kind soul. That is one of the reasons I like her so much. Mirium starts with our history of how we came to be. It is one told to all girls before being matched. I heard it when I was younger, but this is tradition. He starts in a hushed voice. "A long time ago in heaven, there were four angels who did their best to always please God. God looked fondly upon his faithful servants. When the time came, the angels were sent down to earth to be born to the mortal world with free will. The four angels, Veronica, Lucian, Jeremy, and Sarra, watched as the other angels made their transition to life. The four angels talked about being mortals all the time, they did extra things to please God, yet they still remained angels. One day, Lucian convinced the other three angels to follow him, as he believed he knew how to become mortal without God knowing. Jeremy and Sarra were swayed by Lucian, but Veronica was nervous, as she didn't want to upset God.

"That day Veronica was bathing God's feet. God noticed the conflict within her soul. 'My child, tell me what troubles you.' So Veronica told him of Lucians plans. God was enraged by this betrayal. He struck the four angels down. He looked at each of their souls and he could see the greed to be mortals within them. So God banished them to a world parallel to Earth. He gave each of them an element. Lucian was given the ability to control fire. Veronica was given an earth affinity. Jeremy, the ability to control air, and Sarra, a water affinity. Spirit was God's. So each new generation was born with an affinity passed down by our ancestors. God gave them these powers so they could understand what he had created, and in time, he hoped they would understand the values of each element that he had given freely to the mortal world. He built a wall of fire to divide the worlds and gave them partial immortality so they could pay for their sins. And so forth, our world Saskia was created by four fallen angels." You couldn't hear anything in the barn. It was so quiet. Mirium rose. "That was twenty centuries ago and our founders have paid for their sins. God loves us, as we are as much his children as mortals are. We know he has forgiven us, as we can pass through the wall of fire to the mortal world." I felt as if Mirium was looking directly at me when he said this. Several people gasped around us, drawing Mirium's attention away. I believe in God, but not a world called Earth. It was a silly fairy tale. Mirium continued telling us about Earth, of its sheer beauty and of its wars. It made me think of our war against King Paulus and the question that was on everyone's mind. Was he truly still alive? If he was, would he seek revenge? I shivered at the thought. No wars had ever happened since King Morrick and Queen Bellona came into power. Punishment for crimes was not by public hangings or torture now. If a person committed a crime against another, they were exiled from their community and banished to the mountains. I heard tales of villagers seeing the exiles late at night, scurrying through the villages, scavenging for food. They say they are like wild animals, hunched over with black teeth and hollow eyes. People believe their souls have fled and all that is left is emptiness. A shiver of fear runs down my spine.

The king and queen have the final decision over Luxpagus, which is a village to the east of Saskia. Luxpagus was first established by a family with fire affinities and lots of people left the heart of Saskia and settled there. Aquaterra is another large settlement to the southwest of Saskia. The settlement is ruled by Musa, the tribe's leader, and he is very strict. Musa makes his own laws and deals with his own kind. They are left alone. The last main settlement outside Saskia is Humus. This is a community of people who follow the way mortals live and study everything about Earth. They control all of the south. They don't have a king or queen, but a committee voted by the people to make rules and keep everything in order. There are other small settlements scattered on the outskirts of Saskia, but these are the main three.

I continue to listen to Mirium's tales of the mortal world, of how mortals could live until eighty years old. We can live to about seven hundred. It doesn't seem fair for them to live such a short existence. When Mirium is finished, everyone applauds. Groups of girls whisper of Earth, of stories their mothers told them.

Corrona and I dance as soon as the music starts, but we exhaust ourselves too quickly, nearly forgetting we are both having babies.

Afterwards, we go back to Corrona's cottage. She pours out two cups of chamomile tea that she grows in her garden. I can tell by Corrona's face she wants to talk about something. "Marta, remember Mirium said we could pass through the wall of fire since God has forgiven the four angels?"

I shake my head. So this is what she wanted to talk about. "Corrona, you can't believe that."

"Marta, it is our history. Of course I believe it. I shouldn't be telling you this. I swore to Dominic I wouldn't tell anyone, but you're my best friend." She pauses. "Well, you know the horses Dominic takes care of?"

"What about them?" I say.

"Well, that's how they get through the fire."

"What! The horses will not get burned?" I am not smart with my reply, but it just doesn't seem logical. When I see Corrona's serious face, I decide to just listen.

"I am telling the truth. Dominic explained to me that the guardians, which all have air affinities, can create some kind of protection around them and the horses, which allows them to pass from here to the mortal world. The king and queen have been there, Marta, to the mortal world." I give Corrona a sceptical look, but she continues. "Look at it this way. Every baby is born with an affinity: air, water, fire, or earth." She doesn't add spirit, as only Queen Bellona seems to have that gift.

"Okay, what's your point?" I say.

"Well, the queen only takes babies with air affinities to become guardians."

I already know this, but it doesn't make sense.

"But you have an air affinity, yet you are sitting here," I say with a small smile to try and lighten the mood.

Corrona gives me a disapproving look, obviously not enjoying my humour. "Yes, I know. She only takes boys. Dominic said that's because they are normally stronger."

I sit there and ponder over what Corrona has just told me. It does answer the question of why every guardian has to have an air affinity, yet I just can't bring myself to believe in another world. I am not saying Corrona is being untrue. She truly believes in what she is saying, but I just can't accept such an explanation.I leave shortly after, but our conversation rattles around in my head. The village is quiet as I pass through the empty streets. I start to walk a little bit faster. I feel as if I am being watched. I glance around me, seeing nothing, yet the feeling of being watched doesn't leave. On the square, there are still a few lanterns lit, but the light doesn't touch the shadows.

"Aren't you pretty?" I turn around and have to crane my neck back to look up at a drunken guardian. Funny how he manages to get alcohol. He is over six feet tall and bulky. I turn to leave, but he grabs my arm. "Where do you think you're going?"

"I am going home." My voice shakes as I speak.

"Sir... That is how you will address me." He pulls my arm, dragging me behind him to a side street.

My stomach drops; panic sets in. I hit him with my free arm, making no impact. "Let me go!" I protest. He pushes me up against a wall of a house. I try to protect my stomach as best I can.

"You know, you have no manners. Maybe I should teach you some."

I am about to scream, but then Morrick is there, standing behind my attacker. He is over six foot tall with jet-black hair that falls just below his jawline. I can see a muscle tense as he looks at my attacker's back. His eyes shoot up to me, deep grey eyes surrounded by long black eyelashes that still take my breath away. I watch as he places a knife at the man's ever-paling face. "Taurus, release the lady at once."

Taurus raises his hands in the air. "Forgive me, your highness."

I move out from the wall after being freed from Taurus's arms. Morrick's hands are visibly shaking with temper. I can see the knife sink into Taurus's cheek as blood trickles down his face. "King Morrick," I say to make him stop, and he does immediately, sheathing his knife.

"Apologise to the lady," he tells Taurus through gritted teeth.

Taurus stands and faces me, all his drunkenness gone. "Sorry, ma'am, for my actions."

I harrumph. "Leave now," Morrick orders, but I can see he wants nothing more than to hurt him. Taurus bows and walks away. That just leaves me and Morrick, who does not come any closer, in case someone is watching us. "Are you hurt?" he asks while averting his gaze to my stomach.

"No, your highness, I am fine." I keep with the formalities also.

He moves beside me and his closeness makes me look around. He bends his head and whispers in my ear, "You look so beautiful with our child growing inside you."

I freeze with fear and excitement at what he is saying, but fear wins. I step back and bow. "Thank you, your highness, for helping me. Good night."

"You should be more vigilant this late at night. Be careful."

I look back over my shoulder, but he is gone. Walking briskly back to my cottage, I feel I am still being watched. Only after closing the door am I able to I relax. While trying to sleep, my mind will not stop thinking through all of tonight's incidents and remembering the festival is tomorrow, but I finally fall asleep.

Queen Bellona-Saskia

I look upon the paintings that hang in the library of all the people that went before us. Their stories never interested me, not even as a child. My father spent my childhood drilling stories of the past into my head. My hate for him pushed me to pray to God and ask him to take my father, but he never did. His fist was his way to discipline me.

My mother would clean my wounds after my father's rages. I could still hear her voice. "Oh why, Bellona, do you upset your father and force his hand upon you?" She would look at me with no remorse, only disappointment.

I hated her, but as always, I bit my tongue. "Sorry, Mother." It was just a whisper, as it was too painful to speak with broken ribs. For weeks after beatings, I was left to recover in my sleeping chambers. There were no children my age so the servants became my toys.

Shaking my head, I come back to here and now. I run my fingers along the spines of the books until I come across the one I want, the one my father used a long time ago. A shiver of pleasure runs through my body as the memories pour in. Her face frozen in a mask of pain. Her pleas for life. I was so young, yet every moment was truly enjoyable, watching her very soul torn apart. A smile plays on my lips just thinking about using the book again. Only this time, I know exactly what to do. I am not a frightened little girl anymore. I am the queen of Saskia.

Holding the book firmly to my chest I leave the library. Taurus, my personal bodyguard, is waiting for me outside to escort me back to my chambers. A small, fresh cut is on his face, something I must inquire about later, but not right now. I have too much to do. We walk in silence. The castle is empty, as everyone is preparing for the festival.

Reaching my chambers, I turn to Taurus. "I do not want to be disturbed."

He inclines his head. "Most certainly, my lady."

I close the door and cross the floor to my bookshelves that are mounted against the stone wall. Sliding the bible out causes a draft as the hidden door opens. I nearly laugh at the irony that my father used a bible as the passageway to enter such a dark place. I light the torch just inside the door and carry it down a winding stone staircase.

I remember the day I discovered the secret passageway. My father was raging, full of wine, turning over tables in the library. I had never seen him so angry. He tore the books from their shelves; pages fluttered around me. I was truly terrified. I knew what these books meant to my father. He crossed over to the mortal world, taking all kinds of books. He was obsessed with their world. He looked at me; the look of madness in his eyes terrified me. Racing towards me, he picked me up and threw me on the white marble floor, breaking my arm. A scream rose in my throat. "Get up. You disgust me," he said while moving towards me again. He tripped over an overturned table and fell. I got up and ran to my mother's chambers. Tears poured down my face as I cradled my arm. When I entered, my mother was lounging on her four-poster bed. She took one look at me and asked, "What have you done now?" At that very moment the realisation hit me. If he came after me, he would finish what he started, and my mother would not stop him this time. I ran and locked my mother's door. She got up off her bed. "Bellona, what do you think you are doing? Unlock that door at once." Placing the key in my dress pocket, I glared at her. "You won't hurt me any more." I could hear the venom in my own voice. Her face turned red with anger. "You spoilt little..." She never got to finish her sentence. Anything I put my hand on I flung at her. She screamed, startled. After emptying her dressing table, I moved around the room and started throwing books at her.

"Stop this at once—" She was cut off midsentence by a book I aimed at her head, but I missed. I reached to get another book and that's when the bookshelf opened. "Close it, and close it now, Bellona." Her eyes darted to the door. "Your father will kill you if you go down there." She actually looked frightened.

She darted across the room, but before she could reach me, I opened the door and closed it behind me. She was still screaming her protests from her chambers. I raced blindly down the stone steps until I ended up in a large, circular room. The room I stand in now. My father never knew I found his secret room and my mother never told him.

I place the book on the stone stand that is in the centre of the room. Opening the cover causes a breeze to flutter around the room, stirring the candle flames, making them dance wildly. I close my eyes and breathe in the musty smell of the book. A low sob pulls me back. Bethany, the servant girl, is curled up sobbing in her cage. I move towards her, making her move back into the cage. Her ratty, dirty hair covers her face.

"Oh, Bethany. Shhh! It will be all over soon." She looks at me and starts sobbing again. She has a poor existence. I am doing her a favour.

I prepare the altar by lighting candles and purifying the area for my sacrifice. Just below the altar, I place a large piece of black cloth for Bethany to lie on. Once Bethany is removed from the cage, I wash her down and remove her soiled clothes. She stands still, staring at the ground. The smell is becoming less intense the more she is washed. I hum a tune my mother used to sing to me at night time. It was one of her rare moments of kindness towards me.

"*Lorem*, my lady."

I hit Bethany across the face. "It is forbidden to use Latin. You know this." I inhale a deep breath to calm myself. Latin stirs too many awful memories. It was the tongue of my parents. When I came into power, I banished the language and enforced English.

Bethany holds her face. "Sorry, my lady."

I wrap her in a white silk robe and brush her wet hair from her face. Taking her bony hand, I place her on the ground in front of the altar. She keeps her eyes closed, but her body shakes with silent sobs. Taking my pendant off the altar, I place it around my neck. The purple stone starts to swirl.

Holding the black knife above Bethany, I start my incantation. Almost instantly, the energy in the room starts to rise, causing my hair to snap with electricity. I continue the incantation, saying it louder and faster, until I can't hear myself over the roars of the demons in the room. The demons circle Bethany and me in a large black fog. They move so fast a wind races through the room. The only thing you can see through the black fog is their red, greedy eyes. I thrash the knife into Bethany's heart.

Lightning strikes the floor beside the altar, opening up a hole in the stone floor. This has never happened before, but I ignore it and continue. Bethany's eyes shoot open and the roar that leaves her mouth is so filled with pain and horror it sets the demons off. Their dark forms cover Bethany. They slash at her flesh while sucking all the blood from her body. I place my pendant above her heart and the demons tear at her soul. Bethany's face is white and drawn, but she is still alive, still screaming. The colour of her eyes start to drain. She looks at me, horrified, trying to claw at her face, but the demons push her soul into my pendant. Bethany's eyes are completely white, her face frozen in a mask of anguish. The next part still shocks me. I can hear her bones crumbling. Her head twitches until all that remains is ash and hair. I close the ritual by thanking the demons, but they are already paid in blood and pain. The demons still linger in a circle around me. They normally leave after the sacrifice. Their unusual actions make me feel tense. The ground beside the altar starts to tremble. I get up off my knees. The hole that the lightning created is oozing with black liquid. The demons never move, but they all keep their eyes closed. I watch as a hand reaches out and grabs the side of the hole. Then a man climbs out with such ease and grace. When he stands, I can feel the power radiate off him. His gaze falls upon me. I inhale a sharp breath at the sight of his eyes.

His lip curls into a smile. "I seem to have that reaction from most people. Is it my eyes?" He laughs at his own joke. I have never seen anyone with red eyes besides the demons, but he is a man.

"Who are you?" I ask in a commanding voice.

He repeats my question back to me with a few of his own also. "Who am I? Where did I come from? And what do I want? They are the answers you really want to know." He raises an eyebrow. "Am I not correct, Bellona?"

My patience is running out. I turn to leave, but the man is right in front of me. "That's no way to treat a guest. Usually they would be offered a drink, maybe a seat." I am beginning to feel very unsettled with this man.

"You may sit, but I have nothing to offer you to drink."

He smiles. His teeth have reshaped from straight to long, black, pointed ones. "Oh, but you do." He springs and grabs my head, pulling it back as he sinks his teeth into my cheek. Pain shoots through my body, but I am unable to scream or move, which makes it more terrifying. Images start to play out before my eyes. A land on fire, the heat at boiling point. I can taste the hot air in my mouth, making it hard to breathe. People with hollow eyes and burnt skin, their bodies tied in chains while carrying large rocks in their hands. The weight of the rocks causes their backs to hunch over. It is an image of torment and pure horror.

The man pulls his teeth from my face. I fall to the ground. Blood still runs from my puncture wounds. I look up at him in shock. He licks his lips and kneels down beside me.

"I am Lucian, king of the underworld. This is the first time in twenty centuries I have stood on solid ground." He moves around the room, but it looks like there is an invisible barrier that only allows him to go so far. He doesn't look surprised by this at all; it is as if he were expecting it. I am unable to speak. The need to sleep makes my eyelids heavy. "Oh well, this will have to do for now. The day will come when I shall call upon you for one request that you must fulfil." He grabs my chin. "I want your oath, Bellona."

I try to speak, but can't. Lucian clicks his fingers and my mouth starts moving, my voice leaving, but it isn't me. I grab my throat to try and stop the words, but they just pour out. "I, Queen Bellona, give you, Lucian, my word that I will grant you one favour when ever you need it." He smiles and lets my face go. It rests on my chest. I don't have the strength to raise it. All I can see now is Lucian's legs as he walks away from me and returns to the hole beside the altar. "We will meet again." And at that, he leaves and the demons follow him. When the last one goes through, the hole in the ground closes up. My eyelids flutter and I collapse.

When I awake, the room is in darkness. My body feels stiff and sore. Grabbing the altar helps me steady myself and stops the room's spinning. I stumble up the stairs, inspecting my face with a shaky hand. It is crusted in dry blood. I hold on to the wall as I make my way back to my chambers. I stagger to my bed and collapse on it, falling into a nightmare of the underworld.

When I wake, I feel disorientated. I am lying on my bed in my gown. Raising my shaky hand to my chest, my fingers rest on my pendant. I let out a sigh of relief at feeling it under my fingertips. Moving my hand to my cheek, the skin feels rough. I rise on shaky legs and examine my face in the mirror. The left side from my cheek down to my neck is crusted in dry blood, but the puncture wounds have healed.

I have never encountered anyone like him.

Taurus is stationed outside my chamber doors. When I open them, he takes in my appearance. I can see he is straining to keep his face composed. "My lady?"

"Taurus, get Corrona to fill a bath for me and prepare my supper."

"Yes, my lady." Taurus leaves. I sit down on one of my armchairs beside the unlit fire. I have seen a lot in my hundred and fifty years, but never anything like Lucian, and to discover that another world exists... not a world I would ever want to rule. Corrona enters my chambers and her gaze falls on my cheek. She looks away quickly when she catches my eye, and starts filling my bath.

Marta -Saskia

The next morning, I awake to pounding on my door. Rubbing my eyes, I open it and Corrona bursts in. "Marta, how are you asleep? I have been awake since sunrise." Corrona is busying herself lighting a fire to boil some water for tea.

After shutting the door, I sit at the table. Corrona stops what she is doing and sits across from me, taking my hands in hers. "Are you feeling unwell? Is it the baby?" She places a hand on my forehead. "You feel a bit warm, but no temperature."

I flick her hand away. "Stop fussing. I am fine, just a bad night's sleep." Hurt flickers across her face. I never tell her about Taurus, because I know she will just end up worrying about me. "I am sorry. I'm just tired."

She gives me a lopsided smile. "All is forgiven. Now, we have to get you organised for the festival. Bethany is coming over to mine, as are you, and we will get ready together." Corrona's eyes are sparkling with excitement.

I can't help but smile back. "All right, but first I need a hot cup of tea to wake me up." Corrona pours out two cups of tea. I cradle mine in my hands. We still have three hours before the festival begins. Corrona is not coming, as she is married already, but she loves dressing me up. When we finish the tea, we leave my cottage and make our way to Corrona's. We chat while waiting on Bethany. She works with Corrona in the castle, taking care of the cleaning and running of it. The castle is divided into three sections—left, middle, and right. Both of them work in the left wing, and are called L1 and L2, as they are head maidens over several other girls. After an hour, Corrona gets up from the table. "I am going over to Bethany's to see what is taking her so long. It isn't like her to be late. She was so excited last week when we made plans for tonight."

I give Corrona a small hug. "All right. I will start getting ready." Corrona throws on her cloak and leaves.

Sitting in front of Corrona's dressing table, I start with my hair, releasing it from the bun I placed it in this morning. Curls bounce around my shoulders. I gather two small pieces from the front and tie them loosely, leaving my hair down, but keeping it off my face. As I sit sideways, my hair looks beautiful in the mirror. Some days from the heat, it would be frizzy, but today it is smooth and shiny. I lift my tunic and smile at my reflection; pregnancy suits me. I think I look beautiful with my bump. I go back into the kitchen and take a white rose out of Corrona's vase of flowers, placing it at the side of my hair.

Corrona arrives back then, her eyebrows set in a furrow. "She wasn't there," she says.

"Don't worry. She must have went to someone else's to get ready."

"Maybe?"

"Are you not going to say anything about my hair?" I ask while twirling around. "Oh, Marta, sorry. It is perfect." She comes over and twirls a curl around her finger. "It is perfect." She says sincerely. "Stop worrying, Corrona. Sometimes you worry too much." "You are right. She must have went to Ancellia's home… maybe…" Then she claps her hands together. "All right, let's get you ready." An hour later, after being pulled and prodded by Corrona, I am fully dressed in a beautiful blue dress. All the material gathers around my stomach to conceal my bump. It is perfect. I arrive at the main square of the village. While I stand there, I take in the transformation. I have heard it is one of the most magical nights, but have never seen it before. Everything is so exquisite. A large platform has been erected for the occasion for the king and queen to watch us. It is decorated in the finest silk of gold and reds. At each corner, there are fifty-foot sheets of white silk material billowing in a slight breeze. I pity whoever has to stand there for the night and use their air affinity, no doubt a woman.

I walk deeper into the crowd. Everyone is dressed in their finest clothes. The women gather on one side and the men on the other. The square is lit by lanterns and candles scattered all around. Large barrels have been turned upside down and candles are placed in the centre. Someone has spread rose petals on the ground to give it the illusion of a carpet. It is beautiful.

Goblets of wine are handed out by servers. A girl hands me a goblet while giving me a look of envy. "Your time will come. Don't worry," I say.

She gives me a disgusted look. "That's all right for you to say. I have another ten years to wait." She walks off, serving others begrudgingly. I hold the goblet and pretend to take small sips so nothing looks suspicious.

"You look stunning." I laugh as I face Nicon. And feel very shocked. He cleans up well. He's dressed in a black pair of trousers and a snow-white tunic. His beard is shaved, making him look younger, and his blue eyes are sparkling.

"Nicon, you will make some girl's dreams come true here tonight."

He laughs slightly, then kisses me on the cheek. "You are too kind, Marta."

Beating of drums settles everyone down, except me. The king and queen are arriving. My stomach tightens at the thought of seeing Morrick. "Ladies and gentlemen, bow for your King Morrick and Queen Bellona." The king and queen take their seats, both of them dressed in white robes with royal-blue trimmings, the colours that represent the matching festival.

Morrick stands then and walks to the front of the platform. "Rise." I look up and meet his deep grey eyes, causing my breath to catch in my chest. A small smile tugs at the corner of his mouth, but is gone as soon as it appears. His attention is now back on the crowd. "Ladies and gentlemen, tonight we will unite you together to live long and happy lives and create the next generation."

Everyone applauds, the men louder than the women. No doubt it is the last statement that makes the men happy. Everyone settles back down as the king continues to speak. "Once everyone is matched, we will celebrate with dancing and wine." Another roar goes up; then Morrick returns to his throne.

A small man with a large scroll takes his place at the front of the platform. He wears all blue down to his sandals. His nose is too big for his face, his eyes too small. He starts the list, letting the scroll unwind. It hits the wood with a large thud. He clears his throat and a voice erupts that doesn't match his face, much too deep and loud. "Felix is matched with Seth." And the list goes on.

After several minutes and smiling couples, Nicon's name is mentioned. I squeeze his hand and he smiles down at me. "Nicon is matched with Claudia." Claudia squeals with joy from across the stage and then blushes when Nicon smiles over at her. She is petite and pretty. I know her face from the gardens. She works the fruit and vegetable section. Her squeal of joy causes the little man to give her a stern look. He continues with more names, and more sounds of joy gush, causing his face to grow grumpier each time.

"Marta is matched with…" I hold my breath, hoping it is someone I can push away easily over time. "Taurus." I look up at the little man in disgust and can see Morrick staring at Bellona in shock as she smirks. Was I imaging that? I feel ill as the big brute comes towards me, grinning. I look the other way, pretending I don't see him. "Well, well, well. Aren't you a lucky girl?" The smell of wine hits my face. He seems to be always drunk and this infuriates me.

The music starts up then, signalling the beginning of the celebrations. I look up at Taurus with a show of disgust on my face. He laughs. "Do not be like that. I promise we will have lots of fun." He winks at me, pulling me into his sweaty body. I push him away. "I think I will wait another ten years." I storm off, pushing my way through the crowd, wanting to get as far away from Taurus as possible. When I reach the edge of the mass, I start to calm and watch all the new couples dance and talk. After an hour of standing alone, my mood darkens. I know Morrick can't be with me in public, but times like these make me feel even lonelier. I take the rose out of my hair and throw it on the ground and start walking back to my cottage.

A voice comes from behind me. "You dropped this." I freeze with fear. Has Taurus followed me? I try to muster up as much courage as possible.

"Go away." I turn around and am faced with Morrick holding my white rose.

I bow. "Sorry, your highness, I thought you were—"

He finishes my sentence. "Taurus. I guessed as much. Are you all right?" He places his hand on my elbow to help me rise and puts the rose back in my hair. "That's better. Now you look perfect." I smile. "I better go before anyone sees us."

He looks conflicted "I tried to make sure it was Nicon that you were matched with."

I look at Morrick, startled. "Nicon? And why would you do that?"

"I see how he looks at you, and he would have treated you well," Morrick says, looking annoyed.

This frustrates me. I did not want to be matched with Nicon. I wanted Morrick more than life itself, but this would never be possible. "Morrick, I don't want Nicon." I look away and don't say how I truly feel. It would be unfair.

But Morrick startles me with his response. "You have my word. I will find a way for us to be together." And then he is gone, back to the village.

Chapter One
Sarajane-Ireland, Present day

It's Sunday so I get muffled up and shove on my black wellies that are decorated with pink hearts. I smile to myself. Josh bought them for me. Josh is my best friend. We met when I was only ten years of age at our local beach, here in Blackrock, Co. Louth. From that day on, we never looked back.

"Sarajane, you can't keep doing this." My smile vanishes as Dad stands in the kitchen doorway. His face is drawn with sadness. I button up my army-green jacket.

"I can't stop, Dad," I say while pulling a black woolly hat down over my hair. A car horn beeps outside. I kiss Dad on the cheek without meeting his eyes. "Be back before dark," I say and stick my gloves in my pocket.

"Sarajane." I turn around and face him. "Please be careful."
I force a smile. "Always am, Dad."

Josh has the heater up full blast, as it is a cold morning outside. He's wrapped in a puffy black jacket, jeans, and heavy, black military style boots. His blond hair is tucked away under a black cap. "Love the boots," Josh says while he reverses out of the driveway of our two-story house. We live in a cul-de-sac with two other families. We keep to ourselves and so do they. I look back at the house and Dad is standing in the sitting room, looking out the window, wrapped in grief. I give a small wave and then we are out of sight. The drive is always silent as we make our way to the forest, my mind racing, praying today will be the day we find something.

Josh pulls in at a filling station. "Coffee?" he asks while taking off his seat belt. "Yes, thanks." His door closes and I watch as people go on with their daily lives. It looks so simple, no major complications. When my mother was around, I never realised how great my life was. Josh climbs back in, then hands me my coffee and drops a bag onto the floor on my side.

"What did you get?" I ask as he turns the key in the ignition.
"Your favourite. Tuna sandwich with lots of mayonnaise."

We leave the filling station and I wrap my hands around my coffee for extra warmth. We arrive at the parking lot just on the outskirts of the forest. I climb out, still clinging to my cup. We follow our usual trail. The ground is muddy from the rain. This causes my wellies to make squishing noises. Josh has nailed red pieces of cloth onto trees to help us remember the area we need to search. I send up another silent prayer that today I will find something, anything.

This area was the last place my mother was before she disappeared six months ago. She was out that day, walking Charlie, our dog. The Garda found Charlie dead, along with my mum's blue rain mac. That is all we have left of her.

It made no sense, her disappearance. There was no ransom. We weren't wealthy, just comfortable, so that was ruled out earlier on in the search. Also, my mother had no enemies. She was just a housewife.

We take opposite sides of our outlined area and comb the ground for clues. After two hours of coming up empty-handed, we return to the car. Josh gives me my sandwich and a bottle of minerals.

"Josh, do you think when someone dies, they would linger around?"

He takes a drink before answering me. "Yes, I suppose, if they have unfinished business."

I know Josh is just being kind. He really believes if you're dead, that's it, lights out.

"I don't feel her here," I say.

Josh places his hand over mine. "That's good, Sarajane." Pity fills his brown eyes, and it makes me angry.

I push his hand away. "She is alive."

He places his hands on the steering wheel, his knuckles turning white from his grip. I know he believes she's dead and that I'm in denial. "You can't keep this up."

I seal my sandwich, having lost my appetite. "Keep what up?" I ask, knowing fully well what he is talking about. I knew one day I would have this conversation.

Josh turns to me. "Sarajane, please. Searching for her in the same place for the last six months is not healthy."

My temper flares. "Sorry for taking up your Sundays." I jump out of his car, slamming the door, and return to the forest.

Josh follows me. "Sarajane, this is not about my time." I keep walking, splashing mud past my willies up onto my black jeans. Josh catches up with me. "Just stop." He stands in front of me. "I'm trying so hard to help you. You know I would do anything for you, right? I don't care about my time. I just worry about you."

I look away, shaking my head. Tears fill my eyes. "If I stop looking, it means I've given up on her." My tears spill over. Josh pulls me into his chest and lets me cry. Afterwards, I use my glove to clean my face and nose.

"I will come with you every Sunday forever, but I just think there is nothing to find here."

I look into his brown eyes. "I won't stop."

He wraps an arm around me and kisses my head. "Okay, we won't stop, then." We search for a few more hours, but find nothing. Josh drops me off at my house just as it's getting dark. Jessica and Dad are in the sitting room when I arrive home. "Sarajane, is that you?" Dad calls from the couch. "Yes, just getting changed." I kick off my muddy boots and leave them at the door. Then I race upstairs to change into my pyjamas and a T-shirt. I tie my hair up and splash cold water on my face before heading to the sitting room. I take a deep breath and plaster a smile on my face before entering.

A bowl of popcorn sits on the coffee table. I'm not hungry by any means, but I need to look fine. "Oh, popcorn!" I grab a handful and sit down beside Jessica, eating one at a time. We sit there and watch *It's A Wonderful Life*, Jessica's favourite film. It feels so depressing to watch it tonight. Once it ends, we all head to bed. I feel more down than I did earlier, and Jessica and Dad look no better.

BLEEP, BLEEP, BLEEP! My alarm clock wakes me out of a nightmare. I sit up in my bed and push my hair away from my damp forehead. The clock flashes seven a.m., plenty of time for a shower before work. Once showered, I pull on a clean pair of black jeans. I finish it off with a blue T-shirt and black boots. Scooping up my black curly hair, I place it on the top of my head.

"Jessica, it's time to wake up." I bang on my sister's door again. "Last chance or I'll come in there and pull you out of bed." A few seconds later, the door creaks open.

"I'm awake, okay, Sarajane, so stop bugging me." She rubs her eyes, squinting at me. "Since you're dressed, you can make me breakfast." While rolling my eyes, I head for the stairs. Jessica is normally a morning person, but since Mum's disappearance, it's taken its toll on us all.

I finish my breakfast and head for my car. It's an old Renault. My parents bought it for my eighteenth birthday, which was three years ago. I beep the horn just as Jessica is coming out the door with toast in her mouth.

"You need to learn some patience," she says with her mouth full.

Ignoring her statement, I pull out of the drive and make my way to Jessica's secondary school.

"Have a good day," I say just as she slams the car door and races over to her friends. I mumble to myself as I drive away. "Have a good day yourself, Sarajane. Oh, and thanks for dropping me to school."

I arrive at work with fifteen minutes to spare, so I head in to our local shop for a takeaway coffee.

"Morning, Sarajane, how are you today?" Mr. McCormack owns the shop. He's about seventy years old and has known me all my life, so I know his concern is genuine, unlike Mrs. Parkinson, who loves to gossip. She's the town's daily newspaper and I see her in aisle three.

"I'm good, Mr. McCormack."

"What can I get you, dear?"

"Black coffee, please." When he comes back with my coffee, I place the money in his hand and leave just as Mrs. Parkinson is making a beeline for me.

"See you," I call back to Mr. McCormack over my shoulder.

"Good bye, dear," he calls after me.

I cross the road and make my way into work. Susan and Christine are already in the bookstore, talking about Susan's new love interest of the week. "So who is the lucky fellow this time?" I ask while stashing my bag under the counter. Susan fumbles with the books in her hands while Christine makes herself busy.

"Oh, no one you know." Susan places the books on the trolley and starts pushing it down the aisle. I catch up with her, blocking her way.

"Why are you guys acting so weird?"

Christine stops what she is doing. "Susan, just tell her."

I place my hand on my hip, feeling irritated. "Tell me what?"

Susan lets out a heavy groan. "It's Max. Look, I know you guys had to listen to me after… well, you know, the last time, but he has changed. Really, Sarajane, he has."

Oh God, Susan is asking for trouble and she knows it, but I'm not her mother. "Whatever makes you happy, Susan, but please, be careful."

She gives me a smile. "He has changed. But what about Josh?"

"Don't worry. I'll talk to him and make sure he's at least pleasant." Susan looks so relieved. "But if he isn't, I really can't blame him."

Christine joins in. "Me neither, Susan. Josh really helped you out the last time with Max, and I don't blame him for hating the guy now."

Now Susan looks worried again, but she keeps defending Max, her ex, who hit her at a party. If Josh wasn't there, I don't know how far he would have went, but yes, he was really drunk and thought Susan kissed someone else, which she didn't, but in my mind, it was no excuse. I change the subject, much to Susan's relief, and we talk about the upcoming ball that is in the next couple of days. I didn't get tickets, but around our small town there's always great excitement leading up to it.

The day goes by quickly and I'm grateful. I don't know what Susan is thinking, but she really seems adamant.

After work, I head home and stick a lasagne in the oven. Food isn't great since Mum's missing and I was elected the chef. I tidy over as I wait for the lasagne to cook. My phone vibrates on the table. A text from Josh.

What are you doing tonight?

Sitting in with Dad and Jessica. I hit send and set the table. My phone vibrates again.

Want company?

Sure.

Two minutes later, another text. *See you at eight thirty.*

Okay.

Dad arrives home as I'm dishing out dinner. He lands a kiss on the top of my head. "Smells lovely."

I laugh. "Don't lie."

Dad smiles back, but it's weak. The circles under his eyes indicate weeks of barely any sleep.

"Any word from the Garda today?"

Dad sits down and removes his glasses, rubbing his eyes. "No, love, nothing, not a trace."

I squeeze his shoulder. "We'll find her, Dad. I know we will."

He places his hand over mine and pats it gently. "Yes... we will."

Jessica strolls into the kitchen. "Hey, Dad." She hugs him from behind.

"How was school, love?"

Jessica sits opposite Dad and starts at her dinner. "Boring."

"Your mother would not like to hear that."

"Yeah, well, she's not here." Jessica throws her knife and fork down.

"Jess, we're all upset," I say.

"Don't, Sarajane." She storms out of the kitchen and up the stairs.

"Sit down, sweetheart, and eat your dinner," Dad says, his voice drained. He gives me a small smile. "You know how she is."

I start eating my dinner, well, more like pushing it around the plate. Jessica is highly sensitive and seems to find it hard to control her emotions. When she's in a bad mood, she can drain a room, but in a good mood, she lights it up.

Dad and I finish dinner in silence, both caught up in our thoughts.

After dinner, Dad goes to bed so I clean over the kitchen and then curl up on the couch in the sitting room, flicking through the stations. I'm not even focusing on what I'm doing.

"Hey, Sarajane." Josh stands in the doorframe, nearly touching the top. He's over six foot tall and he's well built, as he plays rugby for our local team.

"Jesus, Josh, I didn't even hear you come in." I move over to make room for him on the couch.

"The door was unlocked. So what are you watching?"

I turn off the TV. "Nothing, was just flicking. So any news?"

He sighs. "No, work was slow and I just went to practice after." He gives a big stretch.

"Well, I had an interesting day at work."

He raises an eyebrow. "Oh, did some new romance novel come in for you and the girls?"

I hit him with a cushion. "You're funny."

"Yeah, I've heard that before." He grabs the remote and turns on some car show.

"Do you not want to know what happened?" He has the attention span of a flea when the TV is on. I grab the remote and switch it off, getting his full attention.

"Okay, I'm listening."

I go to the kitchen to get a drink. "Do you want a coke?"

"Sure," Josh calls after me. I come back with two cokes and hand Josh his. He doesn't open it straight away, but rolls the can around in his hands. "So tell me."

I get comfortable on the couch. "Well, Susan is back with Max." Josh doesn't respond. "But I know we'll bump into them at different times. So could you, like, try and be nice to him?"

Josh opens his coke and takes a long drink. "No." I give him an evil look, but he isn't giving in. "No way, Sarajane. That guy is a jerk, and to be honest, I don't care what Susan does. I don't want you around him." His words surprise me. Josh isn't one for telling me what to do.

"I am not allowed around him?" I say questioningly.

He gives me a look. "You know what I mean. He's bad news."

I tuck the cushion against me. "Well, I'll be nice to him for Susan's sake."

Josh turns back on the TV. "Suit yourself," he says and starts to watch the car show.

But my mind can't focus. It has gone straight back to Mum, wondering were she is now. Or what she's doing.

I can see Josh look at me from the corner of his eye and he lowers the volume. "You want to talk?" he asks. He knows the look on my face when I'm thinking about Mum.

"I miss her, so much, and I don't know how I'll cope if I never see her again. I keep telling myself that she's on vacation and soon she'll walk in the door and start fretting about the mess of the house and what meals we've been eating lately." I give a small laugh at the end, knowing she would be at her wits end if she knew we had cut out vegetables since she was gone.

I can feel the tears falling down my face. I didn't even realise I was going to cry. Josh hugs me and lets me cry in his arms. We stay like that long after I've stopped. It is such a comfort to be held. I rub my eyes.

Josh sits back. "Feel better?"

"Yeah, actually, I really do." I pick up a cushion and hug it to my body again. I always do this when I'm upset. "Thanks." I look at him. "I really mean it."

"What are friends for?" I roll my eyes. This is Josh's answer to everything he can't answer.

We talk for a while longer, losing track of time, but I don't bring the Susan thing up again. When I look at the clock; it's midnight. I stretch and yawn.

"Okay, I get the hint. You want to go to bed."

I give him a little smile. "Finally, you get the message."

He throws a cushion at me and stands. "Good night," he says while smirking. We say our good-byes and I head to bed, feeling a little better.

The next morning, the house is quiet. It's my day off, so Dad would have brought Jessica to school. I jump in the shower and wash the sweat from my body—another nightmare. I scrub shampoo into my hair. Maybe I should tell Dad about the nightmares. It's the same one every night. Then I decide against it. What good would it do?

I dress in my tracksuit, as I am going to my yoga class later on and just lazing around until then. I am heading for the stairs when I pass my parents' bedroom. The door is slightly ajar. I pause, then push the door open fully and walk in. The scent of my mother still lingers in the air. I close my eyes and inhale the trace of lavender. After a few moments, I go to her dressing table and run my finger along her jewellery box, hairbrush, and perfumes. Her silk scarves are wrapped around the end poster of the bed. I take one and sit on the edge of her bed while wrapping the scarf around my arm. "Mum, where are you?" I whisper, tears sting my eyes. I wipe them with the back of my hand. I know sitting here is doing me no good, so I start cleaning. First, the kitchen. The cooker has been used and neglected, so I pull on rubber gloves and start scrubbing with a Brillo pad, trying to get the burnt lasagne off the base of it. When I finish scrubbing the kitchen, I polish the rest of the house and put on a basket of laundry. My stomach grumbles so I make myself a sandwich. I check my phone. It's five o'clock. I head for the car.I arrive at our local community hall. Christine and her friend Laura do yoga with me. I see them going into the changing rooms. I keep going into our yoga room, not feeling very talkative. I roll out my mat and sit cross-legged. Everyone is chatting waiting on our instructor, Linda, to arrive. She's a very spiritual person, not in a way that she is religious; it's more like a different way of seeing and understanding the world. Most of the girls think she's really odd, but I like her weirdness. It's not something I can put my finger on, and she reminds me of the ballet teacher I had all through primary school. "Good evening, class." Linda arrives with a bounce in her step. She rolls out her own mat at the top of the class and sits down. She gives me a wink before she starts. "I want everybody to clear their minds and find your centre." I take a deep breath and try to empty my mind, easier said than done. "Now today, we're going to do something a little different. It's like meditation." I open one eye and look at Linda. She gives me a little smile and then closes her own eyes. "I want everybody to think of someone they love and try to picture them, maybe even try to picture what they could be doing right this moment."

My mother is the first person that pops into my head. I can picture her so clearly. She's smiling at me as she watches me blow out my candles for my twenty-first birthday. Her curls are loose around her shoulders, her eyes full of unshed tears of love. I can still hear her gentle voice. "Happy birthday, princess. Make a wish." My cheeks are damp with more tears. I don't open my eyes, just wipe my face and try to hold on to her image.

"Now try and imagine what that person would be doing right now." Linda's voice makes me lose concentration. My mother's face dissolves away. I open my eyes and Linda is watching me carefully. She gives me a sad smile.

After class, I stay behind as everyone leaves, whispering to each other how weird our class is. "Are you all right?" Linda sits down beside me.

"I could see my mum's face so clearly." I let my eyes wander to my hands.

"Did you try to picture what she could be doing right now?" Linda asks gently.

"No, I couldn't. Her image just faded." I look at Linda sideways.

She reaches across and takes my hand. "Why don't you try again? I will help you."

I take a deep breath and close my eyes. My mother's smiling face is there again.

"Can you see her?" Linda asks in her calming voice.

I speak quietly, afraid if I speak too loud her image will fade. "Yes."

"Try to picture what she could be doing right now." Her face becomes less clear, as if the channel is going out on TV. I concentrate harder. The colour is fading. My mother looks grey, her eyes empty. She is lying on a floor, smeared in blood, crying. My eyes shoot open and I gasp for air.

"It's okay, Sarajane. Relax your breathing."

I can't. I feel sick. It was a gruesome image. Where the hell did it come from? I run to the ladies toilet and bring back up my sandwich. When my stomach is finally empty, I stop getting sick. I wash my face with cold water. I look as white as a ghost in the bathroom mirror.

I can see Linda standing behind me. "What did you see? Did you see your mother?" I can only nod. Linda moves towards me and pulls me around to face her. "Where was she?" she asks urgently. She's starting to scare me. She must see the fear on my face, as she let's me go and relaxes her posture. "Sorry, I just... don't want to see you sad any more."

I shrug. "It was just weird. She was crying." I take a gulp of air. "And bleeding, lying on a floor."

"Could you see if she was in a room?" Linda asks. I shake my head. This is too much of Linda's weirdness for today.

"It was a stupid image I conjured in my head." I walk away. "I'll see you next week."

Linda doesn't answer, I'm not too sure if she heard me. She looks lost in thought, and I don't wait around to find out.

Chapter Two
MARTA-SASKIA, PRESENT DAY

The smell of dampness is overpowering. I open my eyes slowly. I am lying on a concrete floor, shaking with the cold. My wrists and ankles are badly bruised, my hair clotted with dry blood. As I start to get up, bile rises in my throat. Steadying myself against the wall causes the sharp, jagged stones to hurt my back. I stumble to the iron gate of my cell. My lips are cracked and dry; my throat feels like it is on fire. "Please, could I have some water?" I rasp. The guardian sits there, no reply. I can see the tattoo on the back of his neck. *Et Lux in Tenebris Lucet*: And Light Will Shine in Darkness. It has been twenty-one years since I have seen it. I know then I am back in Saskia. "I see you are awake," Clive says with a cruel smirk, descending the stairs. His blond hair and white complexion look paler under the lights, giving him a ghostly air. I retreat farther into the shadows of my cell. He turns the key in the gate and enters slowly. His crystal-blue eyes never leave my face, soaking up my terror. I back into the wall and my panic rises. I know Clive is just like his mother, Bellona. Cruelty seeps from his every pore. I want to scream, but know it is pointless. Tears stream down my face. Please, God, keep my daughters safe. I know I will never see them again. Clive circles me with his hands grasped behind his back. He throws his head back and starts laughing. "So you are the whore who was sleeping with my father? A peasant with a king." His face twists with rage and disgust. Clive pounces, grabbing my hair. I scream. The cut already on my head starts to bleed again, and blood trickles down my face. He throws me viciously to the ground. "You won't escape this time." I curl myself into a foetal position. Clive withdraws his leg and aims for my stomach. I can't stop him so I just lie there, letting my mind slip to happier times. Memories pour in. My and Morrick's first kiss at my door. The first time we secretly met at the Amour Caves. Falling in love with him was so easy, but now I would pay the ultimate price.

I blink. Pain runs through every part of my body. I look around through swollen eyes. I am on my own again with the same guardian on guard. I try to speak, but every part of my body is too sore. Darkness overtakes me.

The next time I wake up, Clive and the Queen Bellona are standing over me. She looks at me with distaste. Her snow-white, hard face shows no other emotion. A white gown flows all around her, the ends soaking up my blood pooled around me on the floor. She doesn't seem to notice, or maybe she doesn't care. "Taurus, lift her up. I have many question's to be answered," the queen says in a monotone, as if this is wasting her time.

Taurus steps forward, a smirk on his face. "Hello again." He lifts me up. The pain is too much to bear, and I let out a screech before the darkness takes me yet again.

I open my eyes, but the light hurts. I close them again and can hear Bellona and Clive arguing in the hall. I can hear Bellona's voice rising. "Are you pleased with your handiwork?"

"Yes, Mother, I am," Clive says with self-satisfaction.

"You are just like your father, stupid and weak." Clive tries to answer, but Bellona cuts him off with a slap. "Now listen to me. I need her alive, and beating her to death will not get us answers. Am I not correct?"

"Yes, Mother." Clive sounds like a five-year-old boy being reprimanded.

Footsteps sound down the hall. When the queen speaks, she sounds irritated. "What, Taurus?"

"Sorry, my lady, but the king is looking for you."

The queen lets out a sharp breath. "Clive, stay with her. He does not know she is here, and I do not need any more problems."

"Yes, Mother."

Footsteps sound at my door. I keep my breathing even so it looks like I am asleep. A chair creaks beside me. After a few moments, I open my eyes and Clive is looking at me. There's a handprint on the side of his face. "Do you know the day my mother told me about you and my... father I didn't believe it?"

I turn my head away from Clive. I just can't listen to him. Morrick told me how cruel his wife and son were, how they would manipulate situations. Clive grabs my face roughly. "You will look at me when I speak," he roars into my face, covering me with spit.

The door opens then and Ancellia, a servant girl I had only met a few times before, comes in. She bows to Clive, but her eyes never touch me. "Prince Clive, I have come to bathe Marta as requested by the queen." He flicks his hand towards me and Ancellia enters the room.

Clive rises from his chair. "I will return later." He looks at me and leans in close to whisper in my ear. "When I get back, you better give me answers or I will kill you." He stands straight and leaves the room.

Once he is gone, I turn to Ancellia. "Where is Corrona?" Ancellia ignores me. "Please, Ancellia."

She looks at me with anger. "You have dragged enough people into this. You will not drag me in as well." She pushes me over roughly, hurting my side, and bathes my wounds. After she leaves, I lie there thinking of Corrona and the day I decided I needed to get out of Saskia.

Corrona and Dominic were blissfully in love. She sat in her armchair beside the fire, rubbing her very large belly, while Dominic rubbed her feet. I sat and watched them and wished I could be normal like that with Morrick and not always hiding our love. My stomach fluttered thinking of him. Even though we had been seeing each other nearly a year, I still felt nervous around him.

Corrona's voice snapped me out of my thoughts. "Marta, go get the maidens. I think my baby is coming."

Dominic stood up, his eyes wide. "Now, right now?"

Corrona looked up at Dominic with a smile on her face and nodded. Then her attention turned to me. "Hurry." She twinged with pain. I left and ran to the castle and placed my hand over my own stomach and smiled. Butterflies erupted in my belly.

I reached the castle and raced across the courtyard, but just before I knocked on the large wooden door, it opened. I was faced with Bellona. She arched an eyebrow. "Yes?"

I bowed. "Sorry, my lady, but Corrona needs maidens. She's going into labour."

"Very well." The queen beckoned two maidens and headed for Corrona's cottage. Taurus followed just behind her and me after them. I felt sick the whole way back. I didn't think Bellona would come also.

When we entered, Dominic stood and looked at the queen in shock. "My lady."

"Please, do not rise." She sat on the armchair that Corrona had vacated.

Corrona lay on her back, sweat running down her face. The two maidens placed damp cloths on her forehead and face. The small cottage now smelled of sweat. I knelt down and took Corrona's hand. Dominic held her other hand while telling her he loved her. Corrona's swollen belly started to ripple. She screamed between pushes.

"Shhh, child, there is no need for that. Be quiet," the queen said, irritated. I looked at her and she smirked back at me, making me drop my gaze. Did she know about Morrick and me? No. I would be dead by now.

Corrona continued to push as the maidens directed her through her pain, and then the room was filled with the cries of a baby boy. The maidens handed the baby to Corrona. "Oh, my precious baby." She placed a kiss on his head and cradled him to her chest. The room buzzed with a newfound happiness. Dominic was looking at his wife and child with pure love, tears sparkling in his eyes.

"Marta, isn't he perfect?" Corrona asked me while counting his toes.

I laughed through tears. "Yes, he is."

Corrona looked up at Dominic. "I love you so much."

"I love you too." He kissed her and then his son.

The queen stood over Corrona. "May I?" She reached out her hands for the baby. Corrona and Dominic both looked up, startled. They had forgotten about the queen, as had I. Corrona hesitantly handed her baby to her. Tears ran silently down her face. The queen usually visited in the first month of a boy's arrival, not straight away after the birth.

Dominic rose; Taurus stood in front of him. We all watched as the queen placed a beautiful pendant with a purple stone in the centre of it over the baby's head. Its little eyes followed the movements. I looked at Corrona. She was holding her breath. "It's good news," the queen announced. We all let out a sigh of relief. Taurus moved away from Dominic. "He has an air affinity." The words slipped so calmly from her mouth. Corrona started screaming. She tried to get up to plead with the queen, but she was too weak to lift her own body. Dominic's face turned white. "Give me back my son." The queen looked at him with a scowl. "Taurus." She turned to leave. Dominic pulled a small knife from his sleeve and ran at the queen. Corrona screamed when she realised what Dominic was going to do. Taurus swung the blunt end of his sword at the last minute, hitting Dominic in the side of his head. He fell to his knees, blood running down his face. I rushed to him. Corrona was still screaming, her arms outstretched, pleading for her son.

The queen opened the cottage door to leave, but before she did, she turned to Dominic. "You are lucky I do not have you exiled for that." She paused. "But I am a forgiving queen and since emotions are running high, I will let this pass." Then her gaze fell on me, yet she was still talking to Dominic. "I will not be so lenient in the future." And at that, she left the cottage with the maidens and Taurus.

Dominic pushed me away and crawled to his wife. He held her in his arms, whispering over and over again. "I am sorry. I am so sorry." But Corrona was inconsolable. I sat on the floor and cried for them. I cried for my own faith. I knew I had to protect my baby. I had to leave.

Now back in the room, I wipe tears away. The memory still feels so fresh. No one comes back that night. I fall into a restless sleep.

The next morning Taurus wakes me. "Get dressed. The queen is waiting for you."

My stomach tightens. I get dressed while Taurus watches me with a look of hunger in his eyes. I dress as quickly as I can so his eyes won't be on me too long. He marches me in silence to the main library where the queen sits, waiting on me. "Thank you, Taurus."

Taurus bows and leaves, closing the double doors behind him.

"Marta." She gestures her hand to a chair beside her. I approach slowly and sit, feeling sick in the pit of my stomach. "I was given"—she pauses—"shall I say, orders to retrieve a person from a specific area in the mortal world, and to my surprise, what is brought back to me? You." She raises an eyebrow as if I can explain further. I only believed I was brought here to face charges for betraying her with Morrick, but I didn't say this. I just kept quiet. "You see, the person I was ordered to retrieve was meant to be very powerful." She looks at me questioningly. "Are you powerful, Marta?"

"No, my lady."

She nods her head. "I didn't think so. But you must have found a way to gain more power. Is this correct, Marta?"

"No, my lady."

She turns on me, her face fuelled with anger. "Do not lie to me!"

I cringe back in the chair. "I am not, my lady. I only have one affinity."

She looks at me with her cold eyes. "We will see about that." She rises. "Taurus," she calls and he enters. "Take her to my chambers. I will be there shortly."

Taurus escorts me to Bellona's chambers. I have no idea what is going on. I stand in her room, waiting for her arrival, while Taurus stays outside the door.

When Bellona comes into the room, she takes me through a bookshelf and down a flight of stone steps into a stone chamber. "Since you will not tell me the truth, you will tell Lucian." She smirks and kneels, cutting her palm with a knife. Then she starts speaking in a language I don't understand. I stand frozen with fear as the room temperature drops and a feeling of foreboding touches my very soul. A man appears out of a black fog.

Bellona is still on her knees and drops her head. "My king." But his red eyes stay on me. I feel stripped in front of him and it is hard to meet his eyes. I can feel nothing but evil in the room.

After a few moments of silence, Bellona rises off her knees. "Is this the one you seek, my king?"

He places a finger with a long black nail over his lips to silence her and moves towards me. I stand frozen with fear. He runs a nail along my face, causing my blood to rise to the surface. He licks it with a long, pointed black tongue. I sob with fear, but cannot physically move. He tilts his head back, closing his eyes. Bellona is watching with a look of anticipated fear.

"She is not the one." Lucian speaks clearly and turns on Bellona.

"But, my lord... she was there... where you said she would be." She stutters through her sentence.

Lucian tilts his head to the side. "She is not the one." I can see Bellona, her face stretched with fear. Lucian walks towards her like a lion approaching its prey. I am afraid for Bellona, which is something I never believed I would feel for her. "But she is the reason the one exists. Go back and retrieve her."

"Yes, my king." Bellona looks eager for this to end.

"Bellona."

She's terrified now. She can't speak, just nods stiffly.

"Don't disappoint me again or your heart will not beat much longer." Then he looks at me. "Keep her alive; she will be useful." And then he vaporizes into the black fog and is gone.

When we are back in Bellona's chambers, she paces the floor. "Why did you leave Saskia?" She stops pacing.

"I was afraid." I didn't feel as afraid of Bellona now after seeing Lucian. He said the one he wanted existed because of me. That could only mean one thing—my daughter. And I would never tell her, even if she killed me, but I needed to warn someone so they could protect her.

"Afraid of what, Marta?" Bellona is getting annoyed.

"You," I say.

She laughs. "Why? Because you defied me by sleeping with Morrick?"

I knew she had to have known, but hearing her say it causes my breath to catch in my chest. I try to look calm. "Yes."

"Taurus." He enters. "Take her to the chambers. Have Clive make her talk. I am too tired."

Taurus takes me to the chambers where Clive is waiting for me. I can see the excitement in his face. He is no more than a bully.

Chapter Three
Sarajane -Ireland, Present day

I wake for work the next morning with a pounding headache. I feel groggy all morning.

"Are you all right? You didn't look good after yoga," Christine says.

"Yeah, just a headache. I think I might have the flu or something, just don't feel so good."

Christine doesn't look convinced, but leaves it alone. "Okay, well if you want to talk, you know..."

I give her a little smile. "Yeah, I know. Thanks, Christine."

Susan is in bad form also, but I don't ask her what's wrong. More than likely, it has to do with Max and that is a conversation I can really take a pass on.

Work drags by and when half past five comes, I am truly grateful. I drive home with my wipers on full to keep the rain off. Irish weather, we have, like, seventy percent rain most of the year. W

hen I pull into the drive, I notice another car parked outside our house and someone is sitting in it. I run for the front door, but still get soaked. Rooting around in my bag for my keys, I hear the other car door slam.

"Sarajane." Linda, my yoga instructor, is walking up the driveway with no jacket on. The rain is already dripping down her face. She has never come to my home before.

"Linda, hi. What are you doing here?" I can't help but ask.

"I needed to speak to you." I get the key in the door. She stands in the rain looking at me.

I pull the door open. "Come in." I grab a towel from the bathroom and give it to her in the hall so she can dry herself off.

"Thanks," she says while rubbing her face with it.

"Go on into the kitchen. Just let me change. I'll just be a moment." She nods and heads in the direction of the kitchen. I run upstairs and change out of my wet clothes. When I return to the kitchen, Linda is sitting down at the table, drying her hair with the towel. I fill the kettle. "Cup of tea or coffee?" I ask.

"Coffee, please, three sugars."

"Three sugars, not worried about the calories?" I joke. Linda looks like she works out all the time. She is muscular for a woman. Not as in she has massive arms, but nothing moves and it goes beyond being toned.

She smiles at me. "I love sugar." I make two coffees and sit down beside her, pouring milk into mine. I offer her some, but she shakes her head. "No thanks, I like it strong."

"So is everything all right?" I ask.

"Of course. I just wanted to make sure you were okay. You just seemed upset when you left last night." She takes a sip of her coffee.

"Yeah. Sorry about freaking you out." I give an embarrassed smile. "I just got upset, but I'm fine now... Well, except for a severe headache I had all day."

She puts her cup on the table and joins her hands together, looking very serious. "I need to ask you something about what you saw when we meditated last night."

I was not expecting this and my headache was getting worse. "Look, Linda, I'm not being rude or anything, but my head is pounding. I would prefer to forget it."

She reaches across and pats my hand, looking truly concerned. "Did the headache start after you left last night?"

I try to think back to last night, but the pounding in my head is getting pretty severe. I stand and stumble against the table, spilling my coffee everywhere. I jump back just before it hits the floor.

Linda's voice sounds like it's far away. "Sarajane, are you okay?"

I feel like I'm going to get sick. She grabs both my hands to steady me. I close my eyes against the nausea that's clawing up my throat. A haze starts to fog my vision, and everything becomes confusing. There's a man's face that I can see. He has really long white hair and wears a long blue cape. He looks like a wizard from a kid's storybook. He opens his mouth and speaks, making me jolt with shock. Linda clenches my hands tighter.

"Adora, I have tried all day to communicate with you."

Linda responds by speaking, but this is all going on inside my head, only Linda's voice is coming from in front of me where she stands. I keep my eyes closed.

"Sorry, Mirium, to worry you, but I did some mediation with Sarajane, and then I couldn't contact you. I don't know what happened."

Mirium frowns. "She is with you now? You know this is dangerous." Mirium lets out a heavy sigh, as if disappointed with Linda. "We will deal with it another time, but did you find out where Marta is?"

Then the image of my mother is there. Mirium is watching it carefully. Then it's gone.

Linda speaks. "Is it enough to find her?"

Mirium doesn't answer straight away. "I think so. So this is Sarajane?" He says this with a kind smile.

"Yes, this is her," Linda replies with relief in her voice, to hear he isn't mad at her.

My headache starts to reside, the grogginess leaving. I'm becoming more aware of everything and starting to freak out. As if Mirium picks up on my feelings, his smile fades and his face becomes serious.

"*Vale*, Adora."

"*Vale*, Mirium."

Then everything is gone, and I'm standing in my kitchen, looking at Linda, who just stares back at me, still holding my hands.

I push her away from me. "Get out." I point at the door with a shaky hand. Linda doesn't move, just looks at me as if I just slapped her.

"Sarajane, there is so much you don't understand. There is no need to be afraid."

I look at Linda, disbelieving. "You are a freak, Linda, if that is even your name. Now get the hell out of my house!"

She gives me a sad look. "One day you will understand."

Before I can say any more, she leaves. I sit down, trying to breathe. What the hell just happened? I run to the bathroom and throw up. That is twice now she's made me hurl. What did she do to me? What did she do inside my head? I'm freaked. I text Josh and ask him to come over. Dad and Jessica have gone to the cinema to see the newest release of the *Twilight Saga, Eclipse*, so I'm alone. I change my jeans that are soaked with coffee. It must have spilt all over my chair that I sat on.

Twenty minutes later, the front doorbell rings. I'm still sitting in my bedroom, trying to get my head around what just happened. I go downstairs and open the door to Josh.

"Are you all right? I came as soon as possible."

I wasn't even too sure what to say. "Yeah, come on in." We climb the stairs to my bedroom. I plonk down on my bed. Josh studies all the photos on my wardrobe door, a lot of them of us since we were young. He laughs at one of me when I was thirteen. He had covered me in mud and I was fuming.

"I remember that day. It was a classic. You were so mad." He's still smiling when he sits down on my computer chair, but his smile fades when he sees the disquiet on my face. I can't hide it any longer.

"Linda was here," I say.

"Linda, as in your yoga instructor?" he asks, looking confused.

"Yes, that Linda, or should I say Adora."

Josh moves to the side of my bed. "I'm lost, Sarajane. Start from the start."

So I do. I tell him everything from the start and leave nothing out. When I'm finished, we sit there in silence.

"So do you think she can see things?"

I get off the bed, feeling irritated. I asked myself the same question several times. "I don't know. I mean, of course not." I look at Josh. "Right? Like, those things don't exist."

"Look, you're very stressed and it's been a really hard time on you—"

I cut him off. "I know what I saw, Josh." I can feel the tears rising. "And it really scared me."

Josh pulls me into his arms. When he leans back, his face is thoughtful. "So what are you going to do?"

"I need to see Linda and get some answers off her," I say, full of determination.

"I will drive you over to the hall."

I shake my head "No. This is my problem. I'm doing this alone."

Josh is getting annoyed; I can see his nose flare. "Sarajane, no. I'm bringing you or you're not going at all."

I know when Josh gets like this there's no way to get around it. I put my hands on my hips to let him know I'm so not happy with him. "Fine." He smiles with smugness. I grab his keys as I walk out the door. "I'll drive since I can't go on my own." That takes the smugness off his face. It gives me a few moments of satisfaction, which doesn't last long.

Once we're near the hall, I start chewing on my lip. "What if she denies everything and says I'm crazy?"

Josh has been quiet in the passenger seat for the whole drive. "Just ask her what exactly happened."

I pull into the hall and get out of the car. Josh climbs out after me. "No. Stay in the car."

"What if she attacks you?"

I roll my eyes. "Oh, for Pete's sake, Josh, she's my yoga instructor, not an axe murderer."

"Fine, but if you need me just scream. I will stand outside the car," he says in a stern voice. I don't know why, but I feel like laughing. The smile is wiped off my face as I walk towards the building. I look back at Josh who gives me an *I'm right here if you need me* look. I take a deep breath and pull the door. It's open. I enter the hall. It's eerily quiet, or maybe it just feels like that because I am nervous and freaked.

"Hello," I call and then feel silly. I don't know what I'm going to say to her. A part of me wants to turn on my heel and leave and pretend this never happened, but the more determined part of me says I need answers. Someone touches my shoulder. I swing around and scream in alarm; Linda screams back.

"Sarajane, you scared me."

I laugh nervously. "You scared me too, Linda." Right on cue, Josh comes through the doors like a bull let out of a field. He looks at Linda with hate. "Josh, it's fine. I just didn't see Linda and I got scared." God, I sound pathetic.

"Are you sure?" Josh asks, still looking at Linda as if she were the devil.

I move my eyes towards the door to give him the hint to leave. "Yes, I'm positive." He leaves hesitantly, sending glances back at me. I clear my throat. "Sorry about that," I say.

Linda looks annoyed. "You told him, didn't you?" It isn't really a question, more of an accusation. What the hell did she expect?

"Yes, you, like, freaked me out completely, Linda... or is that even your name?" I ask, irritated now.

Her face becomes a little more sombre. "No, my name is Adora, and I know right now you want answers, but I'm a bit busy."

The cheek of her. "Busy? Linda, I mean Adora, I need some kind of explanation. You did something to my head. Who the hell was that man?"

Linda starts walking back towards the room where our yoga classes are held. I follow her. I'm going to call her Adora again and then feel silly. "Look, I'm not leaving until you tell me what the heck happened."

She continues walking, but calls back to me over her shoulder. "I know you won't leave it. You're just like your mother."

Her statement stops me in my tracks. "What did you just say?"

Linda stops and looks at me. I can see by her face that she wishes she hadn't said that. "Look, I'm not like normal people and neither are you." She enters the hall. There are bags lined up on the floor.

"Where are you going?" I ask.

She picks up a bag. "To my car."

I give her the dirtiest look I can muster. "You know what I mean."

She lets out a breath of exasperation. "I'm going home, Sarajane, and what happened in your kitchen was real." She walks past me as if the conversation is over. I grab the strap of her bag to stop her.

"What are you?"

She looks at me with dry amusement. "Not mortal, anyway. I can communicate with certain members of my tribe telepathically, but somehow when I meditated with you, it caused some kind of interruption and I was finding it too difficult to communicate with them. So that's why I went to your house, to see if I tried again with you, maybe I could get it back. And as you saw, I did. Now I really have to go if that is all you wanted to ask."

I let her strap go and stand there dumbfounded. When she is out the door, my mother's face springs into my mind. I chase her out to the parking lot. I can see Josh ready to intervene, but I shake my head, letting him know not to move. "Linda, I have only one more question and then I'll let you get on with your packing."

She throws the bag in the boot. "What, Sarajane?" I can't get over her tone of voice.

"Why did you want me to picture my mother?" I can see her back tense as she closes her boot.

She takes her time facing me. "You're not the only one looking for her."

"What do you mean by that? Do you know where she is?"

Linda walks to me and takes my bewildered face in her hands and kisses my forehead like a mother would a child. Then she looks me in the eyes. "I don't know where she is, and I just want to help you find her. But in order to do that, I must go. Please try to understand."

I can't answer her. Is she saying she's helping me find my mother?

"We will meet again, Sarajane." She enters the hall again to retrieve more bags.

Josh is beside me once she's out of sight. "Well, how did it go?"

"I'm more confused now than I was before we came here."

I get Josh to take me home. I should have forced Linda to answer my questions properly, but at that moment, I honestly wasn't able. I was confused and too upset to listen to any more of her weirdness. But for some reason, I felt a lot of truth in what she said. It made no sense to me, but it felt true.

Chapter Four
BELLONA- SASKIA, PRESENT DAY

I pace my chambers, waiting on Clive to arrive. He enters wiping blood off his knuckles. "She knows nothing. No one could take that pain without talking." He sits down at the small table and chairs that I have in my chambers for breakfast. I sit opposite him.

"If she doesn't know, maybe she is not the reason the one exists, but Lucian would not be wrong." Clive looks at me in puzzlement, but I don't explain any further, and he knows better than to ask. I start to pace again. "We need to find out why she left. I feel like it is the key to all of this." I glance over at Clive from the corner of my eye. "She is still alive?"

He shrugs his shoulders indifferently. "I think so."

"You cant do anything right, can you? I told you we must keep her alive." My patience is coming to an end. I grab his face. "She better be alive for your sake." I let him go forcefully.

"What about her friends? Have you questioned them?" he asks with annoyance in his voice, rubbing his face.

I stop pacing. Why had I not thought of her friends? Maybe Clive is useful after all, but I would never tell him that. I wave my hand in the air. "Maybe. Leave me now. I must think of how to clean up your mess *again*." Clive leaves, his shoulders hunched. He hates disappointing me. He is like a dog—pet him too much and it becomes soft.

"Taurus," I call, and he enters my chambers.

"My lady."

I approach him with a suggestive smile and run my finger along his hard, muscular chest. "Remember that silly girl who was a friend of Marta's? The one who was pregnant."

"Yes, my lady." He grabs my buttocks, pulling me into him.

"What was her name?"

"Corrona, my lady." He starts nibbling my ear.

I swat him away. "Focus, Taurus." He becomes alert again. "Bring her to me," I command.

"Yes, my lady." He turns to leave.

"Oh, Taurus, don't forget I want you here tonight."

"Of course, my lady." He gives me a sensual smile and leaves.

I sit down on an armchair beside the fire with my back to the door. A knock sounds. "Come in."

Corrona appears in front of me and bows. I know it isn't out of respect, more like fear. "My lady." She is frail looking with dark circles surrounding her eyes.

I smile at her. I could make all her worries go away. "Please, sit." I gesture to the armchair across from me. She sits, nervously fumbling with her hands. "How are you, Corrona?"

She looks up at me, startled. "I am fine. Thank you, my lady."

"Corrona, I know losing your baby caused you a lot of pain." I pause and let the sorrow cross my face. "But it causes me great pain, too, to upset such a valuable member of the castle."

She doesn't look at me and when she speaks, her words are clipped. "I am sorry to hear you are in pain, my lady." So she is still upset, stupid girl. She is already getting on my nerves, but I don't let my irritation show.

"Well, I would say you are wondering why you are here, so I will get to it. Why did your friend Marta leave Saskia?" Before she answers, I raise a single finger. "And more important, who helped her? Because we all know she did not get across by herself."

Corrona looks down at her lap. I can see the tension in her paling face. "I don't know, my lady."

"Corrona, look at me." She does with pure fear in her eyes. "I know whoever helped her would be banished, but I am considering to overlook that. If you answer just one question. And also I will give you something in return. I will give you your baby boy back."

Tears run down her face. She whispers, "What is the question?"

Good, now we are getting somewhere. "Why did Marta leave Saskia?" Corrona starts crying. I look in the fire and inhale a breath, letting her know that my patience has run out. I am not one to bargain, so she knows this is not an offer I shall make twice. "You can leave now. You must not want your son back." She stands up, still crying. "And if guardians come to your door and take Dominic, don't be surprised, since you helped a criminal."

She is nearly at the door, but her footing falters. She pauses. I smile. I will get my answer after all.

"I will tell you."

I stand and face her. "Go ahead. I am listening."

She wipes away her tears. "You must give me your word first, that I will get my baby back."

Clever girl. In Saskia, if we give our word, we must stick by it, so it is never given lightly. I don't need the child for anything. There are plenty more. "You have your queen's word."

Corrona's eyes fill with tears again. "She was pregnant."

It all makes sense now. I knew she was secretly meeting Morrick. I could see it from the day of the festival, the way he looked at her, so I spoke to Javan to make sure Marta was matched with Taurus so I could keep an eye on them. But since Taurus told me she didn't want him and Morrick's disappearing acts, I knew they where meeting. So Morrick was the father. Was this why the child was so powerful? Clive or Luna are not powerful. Yes, they have an affinity each, but only one, nothing like what Lucian is looking for. It doesn't matter. At least I know now what I am looking for.

I look up at Corrona. She is still standing there. "Taurus." He enters. "Could you bring Corrona to the maidens' quarters? I have given her permission to take her baby back." He bows and leaves with a guilty-looking Corrona.

I pace my chambers, thinking of how best to deal with this. Taurus re-enters. "It is done, my lady."

"Taurus, can you arrange for Clive, Felix, and yourself to go to the library? I will meet you there shortly."

We gather around the library table and I tell all three of them of their tasks. Clive is getting upset again. "He has another child?"

"Clive, not now. Look at the overall picture."

He stalks towards me, his anger nearly visible around him. "Mother, he should be exiled to the mountains for his crimes, like all the other criminals over time."

He is lucky he is my son or I would have silenced him already. "Son, we will deal with that later, but first we need to retrieve the child." Clive knows not to push me any further, so he sits down with an angry thud. I ignore him and turn my attention to Felix. Part of Felix's job is to study the mortal realm and all the differences between both. "Felix."

"Yes, my lady."

"What is the time difference in the mortal world to here?"

"One day here is equivalent to one month in the mortal world, my lady."

"So Marta was gone for... nine months. What is the age of the child we are looking for?"

"Twenty-one years of age, my lady."

"Very good, Felix." He smiles in self-satisfaction. "So I need that child, or should I say woman, and please..."—I look at Clive when I say the next part—"without as much as a scratch on her."

Clive rises then, visibly irritated. "What do you want the girl for, anyway?" His tone is high pitched and too questioning. Even if he is my son, it is not something I will tolerate. I think the words in my head, but I can see from Clive's frozen face he knows he has overstepped the line.

Spirit, come to me. I can feel it dance around me. *Brush his heart; make it skip a good few beats,* I whisper in my mind. I let the thought skitter over to Clive. He grabs his chest. His face is nothing more than a mask of shock that I would hurt him. Pain runs across his expression at having his heart stopped. He falls to his knees and then gasps for air once I release him.

My guardians stand perfectly still. Taurus has a little smirk on his face that he is trying to contain. I know he is glad Clive is suffering. It makes me feel angry towards him, but I can't hurt Taurus. There is too much at risk. "Get up and do not ever question me again."

Clive gets off his shaky knees while nodding his head. The smell of urine hits me then. I look at his trousers. They are stained all down his leg. When he follows where I am looking, his face turns red with embarrassment and anger.

"Now saddle up the horses and go get me that girl." Taurus and Felix move to the door. Clive is frozen, looking at his trousers. "Clive, clean yourself up." He walks past me with angry tears in his eyes, ones I hope he will not shed and make a bigger fool of himself.

"Taurus." He pauses before closing the door.

"Yes, my lady."

"How long will it take to cross over?"

"One full day."

"Well, then, I expect you back here in three days." They leave and I pour myself a goblet of wine, feeling satisfied with myself.

Marta-Saskia,

Present day

I open my eyes. I am back in the cell. Tears break through the crusted blood around my eyes, making my tears flow red.

I think I am back in the cell a day. I try to move, but the pain shoots through my body. A choked sound escapes my lips. I can hear the rattle of my cell door. Then footsteps approach me. I close my eyes tight and pray it will be over quickly. I know I will not live through another beating. I am not afraid of dying; I am afraid of not living.

I can hear the shuffle of clothes as someone kneels down beside me. "Drink some water." I open my eyes and look up at a guardian with a pitcher of water in his hands. I don't answer, just nod my head. He lifts me up and brings the pitcher to my lips. It could be poisoned, but I don't care. It will make my death come faster. I take a deep gulp of water. It tastes so good. When I have my fill, I look up at the guardian who is studying me. He has piercing green eyes that really stand out against his tanned skin.

"What is your name, guardian?" I ask through cracked and dry lips.

"Tristan, my lady." I recognise his name. He is Morrick's head guardian. "Can you stand?" he asks while scanning my battered body.

"No, I don't think so." I move to try, but he stops me.

"I will carry you."

"Carry me where?"

"I am under orders from King Morrick not to say."

I feel sick. Morrick knows I am here. "How did the king find out I was here?" I ask in a whisper.

"I don't know, my lady." I don't get to ask anymore. He lifts me effortlessly. Then he looks down at me in his arms. "We must be quiet, but darkness has fallen so we should pass unseen." I just nod my head. He carries me up the stone steps and pauses at the door, listening.

"What about the queen's guardians?" I ask, feeling afraid now that I might be saved. The fight to survive comes surging back. He gives me a small smile; the corner of his lip turns up slightly. "I have them kept busy with a fire in the stables." Is all I can say to this is "Oh". Listening at the door, he moves when he thinks it is safe. He carries me through the village. I can see the red glow in the night sky from the fire. We keep to the shadows in the village, moving slowly. It feels at times like we are waiting forever, while villagers get water from the well and run towards the stables. I can hear the panic of the horses. I hope they all get out unharmed. As if he can read my mind, Tristan answers my unspoken question. "Don't worry. The horses are safe. They are just playing up, creating a lot of noise." As we move through the village and into the outskirts, I black out a few times with exhaustion. Soon I can feel the movement of a horse underneath us. I didn't even remember saddling a horse. Tristan must have saddled one while I was out. I try to open my eyes, but they are too heavy to open. After a while, the horse slows down. When I open my eyes again, we are at the Amour Caves. We enter the mouth of the cave, Tristan still carrying me. Five men could stand on each other's shoulders it is that high, though it reduces in size to about nine feet the farther in you go, so it is comfortable at all times to stand in. The torches are lit along the cave walls. Tristan walks down the hall of the cave until it branches off to the left. I know the room he is taking me to. It is the room where Morrick and I used to meet in secret. Now it feels such a long time ago. We enter the large room. Flames from the small fire dance along the walls. Tristan moves straight across the room and places me on the ground gently as he pushes the correct stones in to reveal the hidden door. When a breeze flutters into the room, his arms are around me again. We make our way down a cold tunnel. It is lit up with torches placed every few feet. The tunnel opens up into the main room, which is finished luxuriously. A large fire burns in the centre of the room; smoke billows out through a pipe that has been drilled through the ceiling. The flooring is bare, but the furnishings of large armchairs are placed all around the room. The walls are covered in large paintings of royals and draped with beautiful red material that makes the room feel warm.

Tristan lays me beside the fire on a large couch covered in sheepskin. I search the room for Morrick and my stomach tightens when my eyes fall upon his face. He is sitting in a large armchair in the corner of the room, still as handsome as the first day I set eyes on him. He looks at Tristan and beckons him just outside the room entrance. They talk in hushed voices. The longer they are gone, the more nervous I feel. I don't know what to say to Morrick. I never truly believed I would see him again.

As I wait, my eyes become heavier and I finally fall asleep. When I wake, Morrick is dishing out a bowl of soup from a large pot set over the fire. My movements alert him.

"How do you feel?" he asks while topping off the bowl. Just hearing his voice makes me want to cry, but I have to be strong.

I push back the layers of blankets that are on top of me. "Sore." I start coughing and it feels like I have not used my throat in a long time. It is dry, as if my mouth has been filled with sand. Morrick comes to me with water and lifts my head while I drink greedily from the goblet. When I finish, he studies my face, running his fingers along my cheekbone.

"Did she do this to you?" he asks, his voice full of torment.

"It does not matter. I am safe now."

He holds my face with both hands. "Nobody will ever hurt you again." He stands then and brings me a large bowl of soup. It is in a porcelain bowl, something I have never eaten out of while in Saskia. I am accustomed to wooden bowls and spoons.

"Eat. It will help your strength." I do as I am told, as I am starving. I eat two bowls of soup. When my belly is full, I lie back down and the heat of the fire sends me off to sleep.

I am awoken a short time later by voices. I feel a lot stronger. We heal quickly, so I am very lucky. Being part immortal has its benefits. Any mortal would have died a long time ago. Tristan, two other guardians, and Mirium are sitting around the fire with Morrick. They all sit on large armchairs with high backs. They must have taken them from around the room.

Morrick rises when he sees I am awake. "Marta." Pushing the blankets back, he helps me to the fire as Mirium places another chair in their circle. "Marta, this is Legis and Liber, my men." I acknowledge them both with a nod.

"And you have meet Tristan."

I give him a grateful smile. "Hello."

"And you know Mirium."

I do, but I can't understand what the oracle is doing here. His eyes are alight, as if he knows a secret I have not yet discovered. More than likely, he does.

I incline my head with respect. "Greetings, Mirium."

He looks amused. "Greetings to you, Marta."

"Marta." Morrick's voice makes me look away from Mirium. "Tristan is the best man we have here in Saskia and I trust him. So he will retrieve our child from the mortal world."

He goes to speak again, but my breath catches in my chest as the memory of Lucian wanting my daughter rushes back. "What do you mean retrieve our child?"

Morrick looks aggravated. "To protect our child. I can only protect it here, with me."

I stand then, even against the dizziness. "Don't you dare go near her. She has no idea."

Morrick stands too. "Her? So I have a daughter." His anger pours out. "Why did you leave? You took my child from me." His voice gets louder and harsher as he walks towards me. "You broke me."

Mirium interrupts us then. "Morrick, you know why. This will do no one any good."

Morrick swings around, his shoulders held straight with anger. "I want to hear it from her lips," he says while pointing an accusing finger at me.

I try to get my own anger under control, but I know my own words are laced with it. "Morrick, I had to protect Sarajane. I did what was right." His face falls; he just looks devastated.

Morrick and Mirium share an unspoken understanding. What the hell is going on? But I never get to ask.

"Sarajane, what a perfect name. Princess Sarajane." His voice now sounds gentle. "What is she like?" I don't think I can feel any worse. Morrick just looks lost, not a look I ever thought I would see on a king's face.

"Morrick, I am so sorry. I had to protect her."

He clears his throat. "It does not matter why. Now we must just keep my daughter safe."

"She is safe. No one knows. I told them nothing. I know you're hurting—"

He cuts me off. "They know, Marta." He comes to me and holds my arms. "Corrona told Bellona."

I push Morrick away. My anger flares. "Why would you say that? She would not do that to me."

"Marta, she told me herself. How do you think I knew where to find you?"

"No." I couldn't believe this. "Why would she?"

Morrick's face was torn with sympathy. "Bellona gave her son back." I know then what he is saying is true.

I push past him and run down the hall of the cave. I have to get to Sarajane. I stumble against the walls as the dizziness washes through me. Morrick grabs me from behind. "Let me go," I roar.

He holds me until I calm down. "We will get to her. She will be safe."

My body goes limp against him and I cry. "My baby girl," I say through sobs.

Morrick strokes my hair. "We will get her. *Amour meus aeternus.*" I am taken aback by the Latin. It is not used anymore, but the meaning startles me even more. *My eternal love.* So he still loves me after all this time. I straighten up and walk back with Morrick to the other guardians and Mirium. Pulling myself together, I sit down around the fire once again. Morrick explains his plans to retrieve Sarajane.

Tristan lit the fire in the stables for two reasons. One, to draw attention away from me so he could get me out of the cell, and two, so the horses would be unsettled and Dominic would take his time trying to settle them down. So the queen's men could not leave until morning. Dominic, the horse master, has a way with the horses. I don't know if it is a gift, but they do as he tells them. So it gives Morrick's men a head start.

"Morrick, there is a man looking for Sarajane also." I look into the fire as I speak, even though I can feel all eyes on me. I don't want them to see my fear. "Bellona took me to him." I look up at them, but it's Mirium's eyes I hold. "He was not from this world or the mortal world. He said I am the reason the one he seeks exists." Everyone looks at me patiently. "His name is Lucian." A look of recognition passes through Mirium's eyes. "Do you know him?" I ask him directly. "This is worse than I thought," Mirium says. I stare at him, waiting for him to continue, but he doesn't and Morrick doesn't push for an answer either. "What do you mean worse than you thought?" Mirium looks at Morrick before speaking to me. "I am sorry, Marta, but this is something I can not discuss yet." Morrick's hands touch my shoulder, telling me not to question this any further, and he changes the subject. "We will get her, Marta. It will take a full day to cross over to the mortal world, so Tristan and Legis will leave tonight, retrieve Sarajane and bring her back to Saskia. Liber will stay behind to protect you when I am unable to be here."

After Morrick finishes he sits back down. "Explain what she looks like and a bit about her to Tristan so he knows what to look for."

So I do. I explain of my daughter's beauty, her long, black, curly hair, slightly tanned skin, five foot seven inches. Then I look at Morrick. "She has your eyes." He doesn't respond. "She is very strong willed." Tristan just nods. I know she will find him very attractive.

"Does she know anything about us or herself?" Morrick asks.

"No, she has no idea, but on her twenty-first birthday she released a lot of magic. I felt it and it was strong, but she wasn't aware."

Tristan rises. "Morrick, there are rumours that King Paulus is making his way to Hummus. I think it would be best if I resumed my search for him while Legis and Liber go to the mortal world to retrieve the girl." I can see by Tristan's face he thinks this is all a waste of his precious time. My gratitude towards him drops.

Morrick is silent for a moment. "Tristan, this is my daughter and I want her brought to me safely by you and Legis. That is not a request."

Morrick looks as annoyed as they stare at each other, but Tristan composes his face. "Yes, my lord." Yet his body language still says he thinks his efforts could be of better use elsewhere.

"I do not want her told anything, as I think it will be best coming from me and Marta." I nod in agreement. Morrick stares into the fire and a silence falls around the room. "Does she think I am dead?"

I swallow a lump in my throat. This is the part I am so worried about. I have just found him again; I can't bear losing him twice. "No. It is complicated, Morrick." My eyes wander to the ground. I am too ashamed to look at him. "I have been gone for twenty-one years. I never believed I would see you again." I look up at Morrick, and actually feel like I am going to get sick. "I have a second daughter… with a mortal." Hurt races across his face. I want to explain more, but Morrick rises. Mirium looks at me, not in disgust, but with pity.

"You need food and rest," Morrick says as he turns away from me. I don't blame him. I find it hard enough right now to look at anyone without feeling ashamed. "Tristan is all ready?"

"Yes, my lord."

He places his right hand on Tristan's shoulder. "*Et Lux in tenebris Lucent.*" Tristan smiles at Morrick fondly and leaves with Legis. Morrick explains to Liber his duties and then leaves with Mirium by his side.

I follow them to the mouth of the cave and call after Morrick. "I am sorry." But he keeps walking.

"You must rest my lady." Liber speaks from behind me. He leads me back to the couch and hands me a fresh bowl of soup with a large piece of bread. While I eat, he just sits there and stares into the fire. "My lady, may I ask a question?"

I sit up fully on the couch and turn to him. "Of course, Liber."

"How did you cross to the mortal world?"

"The same way anybody crosses."

"I know, my lady, that you used the horses, but who actually took you across?"

I don't like the way he asks. "I am sorry, Liber, but I can't." I am not going to let him know about Corrona and Suis's involvement, even tough Corrona betrayed me. I can imagine I would do the same if Sarajane were taken from me and then offered back. It does not matter, though. I still feel angry.

I try to sleep, but I am restless. I lie on the couch for an hour or so, staring at the ceiling. I look over to Liber, who is asleep by the fire. It is smouldering now. I leave the room and grab a torch from the wall, taking it with me outside. There are no stars in the sky. I am so used to mortal skies that it seems unnatural to have a plain, black sky. We have a moon, but ours shines red at night. I miss the beauty of the moon and stars in the mortal world.

I lie awake nearly the whole night, worrying about Sarajane and Jessica. I wonder what John is doing right now? And if things will ever be the same again...

A day has passed since I have seen Morrick. Liber has been with me the whole time. We barely speak; he just watches my movements. I feel like a prisoner. I have nothing to do but wander through the tunnels that branch off into more rooms. There are several sleeping quarters and a small library. I find nothing of interest there and even if I did, I know I would be unable to focus. A small writing room is filled with scrolls. The farther I move down the tunnels, the barer the rooms become and the torches are more spaced out. I wonder why these rooms are here.

I make my way back to Liber in the main room and lie back down on the couch. I have too much time to think of everything. Like when Clive was questioning me in the cell, pushing me for information about how I found a way to enhance my magic, which was rubbish. One of the times when he had beaten me nearly unconscious, I heard him mumbling to himself, saying maybe Bellona was wrong, maybe she sent them to the wrong area. But I knew it was Lucian looking for answers.

The thought of Lucian sends another shiver down my spine. What would he want with my daughter? I feel like I might go crazy with all of these thoughts going around in my head. I don't voice my worries to Liber. I just don't trust him; he feels wrong to me.

Later that day I can hear hooves pounding into the ground. I jump up.

"Stay here. I will see if it is safe," Liber says and leaves. I sit up on the couch, unable to relax myself. Footsteps sound down the cave and into the room.

"Who was it?" I ask while turning around. I am faced with Morrick. "Hi" is all I am able to say.

He comes over and sits beside me and takes my hands. "I have missed you so much, Marta."

I hug him and start crying, feeling nothing but pure relief. "I've missed you too."

He holds me like that for a long time. " I know why you left." I pull back and look into his grey eyes.

"You do?"

"Yes. Corrona told me everything. But I wish you had trusted me enough to protect you and Sarajane."

Looking in his eyes, I can see how much pain I have caused him. "I am sorry, Morrick. I truly am, but how was I to know that you would protect Sarajane and me? And if it were a boy, would you have broken your own laws for me, a servant?"

"You're not a servant to me, Marta. I love you. And yes, I would have broken the law no matter what the consequences were."

I start to cry again. "I have made such a mess. I have a family back in the mortal world." Morrick looks away from me, visibly displeased. I knew this would be hard on him, but I feel like I need to explain. He paces the room with his hands behind his back; he looks like a king at that moment, causing me to smile sadly.

"Do you love this mortal man?" He stops pacing and looks directly at me.

"John is a good man. He took Sarajane in as his own, and we have a daughter together."

"So you do love him?"

I approach Morrick and lay my hand over his heart and place his hand over mine. "I love you, Morrick. Our hearts only ever love once. It is not possible to love twice."

He pulls his hand away, his face conflicted. "Maybe you stopped loving me, or never did?"

"There wasn't one night that I did not cry for you. I needed you to hold me and kiss me because I still love you. I always have and I will never stop."

Morrick looks at me then with a guilty look on his face. "I know you did."

I am taken back by this confession. "What do you mean?"

"I watched you from a distance, just to make sure you were safe."

I am baffled. "You watched me, but never said anything?"

"I could not. Mirium said it was the way it was meant to be, so I crossed a few times in secret to see if you and Sarajane were all right."

My heart skips a beat at the mention of our daughter's name. "You knew it was a girl all along?"

"I wanted to hear it from you. I did not want to assume anything." I feel ill at such a betrayal, but have I not betrayed him?

Morrick pulls me to face him. "I love you. I will never stop, but I also had no choice but to watch." His words are full of passion and I know he is speaking the truth.

"Why could you only watch?"

Morrick lets me go. "Mirium said it was the will of the gods."

"That was it? No other explanation?"

"No." I know he is lying, but before I can question him, Morrick pulls me into his embrace and kisses me passionately.

I have waited for this for twenty-one years and it feels so good that I let myself melt into him. He carries me down to one of the sleeping chambers and lays me down on the bed where we make love. We lie naked in each other's arms afterwards.

My mind returns to Sarajane. "Do you think Tristan found her?" I ask, looking up at Morrick.

"Yes. He is the best man I have." He kisses the top of my head. "Please do not worry. She will be with us shortly."

"He would not hurt her?"

Morrick looks at me seriously. "Never. Don't ever say that." His face softens then. "If she looks anything like her mother, I would only worry that he would fall in love with her." He gives a little chuckle.

"She looks like both of us, but she has your strength; she is strong willed." Morrick lays his head back down, looking up at the ceiling. I lie on Morrick's chest, his arm tightly around me.

"Sleep, my love. You must be exhausted." I smile into his chest, feeling happy for the first time in years.

"I love you, Morrick."

He kisses the top of my head. "I love you too."

Chapter Five
Sarajane -Ireland

The next morning I have work. I wake with no headache, thank God, but just a lot of confusion. I don't have time to think too much, as I'm already pushing it for time. I get dressed and skip breakfast. Jessica's sitting in the kitchen, finishing her breakfast with a puss on her face. I don't ask what's wrong. More than likely she wouldn't say. So I drop her off at school and head into work.

Christine and Susan haven't arrived yet so I open up and start tidying over. The bell over the door rings five minutes later and Christine arrives.

"Hey, Sarajane," she says while taking off her coat and hanging it in our little canteen.

"Hey, Christine," I call after her. When she arrives out on the floor, I ask, "Where is Susan? I thought you always gave her a lift?"

"Yeah, she got a lift with Max." Christine leaves it at that. Susan arrives then and her face is glowing. Things must be going good. She spends the whole day talking about how great Max is and how he has changed so much. Christine and I nod and smile when necessary. I really hope he's changed for her sake.

When I get home, Jessica is doing her homework with a few friends. I stick my head through the sitting room doorway. "Hey, guys." I get a few low mumbled hellos. I don't feel like cooking, so I order pizza and run upstairs to change. When I'm coming downstairs, Dad arrives in the front door. "Hi, Dad, how was work?" I ask. He looks terrible, but it's nothing new. He looks like this since Mum went missing. "It was busy, sweetheart." Dad has his own real estate agency. He helps people find rental or sale properties in the area. That's how he and Mum met. Mum had just moved back from somewhere in Europe. She was vague on details, as she had travelled a lot. Her parents had just passed away in a car accident and she had no other family, so she decided she would build a new life in Ireland, and the rest is history.

Dad throws his suitcase and jacket on the chair in the hall. I can hear Mum now, getting on to him about hanging it up. He seems to think the same thing, as he stops and picks up his jacket, hanging it on the rack. I start setting the table and Dad sits down heavily on one of the kitchen chairs.

"What's for dinner?" he asks, trying to push some enthusiasm in his voice, which fails.

"Pizza." Before he can start, I feel the need to explain. "I know, so not healthy, but I had a stressful and busy day at work too."

"Why are you stressed?" he asks. Well, at least I get away with the pizza.

"Oh, girl stuff." His face brightens a little. I want the ground to suck me up when I see the questions running across his face. "No, Dad. Susan, my friend, she's having some problems."

Relief washes over him. "Oh, all right, love." In other words, case closed.

I clean up after everyone has pizza. Josh arrives then. The sitting room is full so I head for the stairs with Josh. "Going to my room, Dad."

He leans back on the kitchen chair and removes his glasses. Dad could spend hours going through the newspapers he buys on a daily basis. I say it's an addiction, but he says it's an interest. "Hello, Josh"

Josh gets on well with Dad and is always very respectful. "Hi, Mr. Anderson." I roll my eyes and start up the stairs.

"Leave the door open," Dad calls after me. That deserves another eye roll.

Josh looks around my room as if he's never been in it before while I sit crossed-legged on my bed. He doesn't look at me, just keeps looking at all my photos on my wardrobe again.

"Josh, is there something wrong?" I ask. He's too quiet and his recent attention to my photos is something he never bothered with before.

He finally turns around then. "Sorry, I have things on my mind." He sits down on the side of the bed and rubs his face. He looks very stressed.

"You know you can talk to me." Josh normally is happy-go-lucky and he always listens to me so it would be nice to return the favour, even if it is just this once.

"I'm in love with someone and she has no idea." He gives a little sarcastic laugh and continues to look at the floor with his elbows resting on his thighs. He gives me a quick sideward glance. I feel like laughing, but think better of it when I see how serious he is. He looks embarrassed and a bit awkward.

"Have you tried to tell her?" I ask gently, knowing this is a big deal for him to talk about his feelings.

"No." He starts rubbing his hands together. "It just never feels like the right time."

A feeling of sadness comes over me at the thought of losing him. "Well, I can assume it isn't... Who was last week's girl?"

He gives a heartfelt laugh. "Siobhan. God, no. I don't know what I was even thinking. I thought she was different. I made it clear it was just a bit of fun and she was all up for it and now she's acting crazy." Josh gets up and opens my bedroom window, letting in a cold breeze. I'm only wearing a string top, and goose bumps pop up all over my arms. When Josh notices me rubbing my arms, he closes the window. "Sorry, just feel really warm." He is only in a T-shirt.

"It's fine." I grab an old black V-neck jumper that has been around for years. "I'll just throw this on."

Before I have it on, he stops me, taking the jumper from my hands. "What do you see when you look at me, Sarajane?" He asks this in a tone that suggests the answer is very important, so I take the question seriously and answer honestly.

"I see a good person with a big heart. You're funny and caring. You're Josh." He doesn't look satisfied with my answer and he's starting to worry me. "Josh, what's wrong?"

"I am..." A knock sounds from my bedroom door and my dad sticks his head in. "Tired," Josh finishes.

I look at him "What?"

"I'm tired," he says again.

"Oh, all right."

"Are you kids all right?" Dad asks, while giving me a look that says, *Your bedroom door was meant to stay open.*

Josh puts on a smile, but it is clearly strained. "Yes. Hmm... I was just leaving. See you tomorrow." He doesn't even meet my eyes.

"Okay, bye." I call after him.

Dad gives me a kiss and says his good nights to me and then I hear him going into Jessica's room. I lie on my bed, worrying about Josh. I wanted to talk about Linda. I roll over to turn off my bedside light just as my phone vibrates. I flip it open. A message from Josh flashes up on the screen.

Sorry about tonight. Just really tired. See you tom

I smile and write back. *Sleep well, Josh. X*

Then I fall asleep.

Chapter Six

SARAJANE -IRELAND

The next day at work we sit around mostly and have girl chats. At eleven o'clock, Christine joins me for a coffee in our small canteen.

"Has she said anything to you?" I ask her.

"No, she just seems happy. Best to leave it alone."

I sit down on one of the stools. "You're right. I just worry for her." Christine pours out two mugs of coffee and hands me mine. "Thanks."

"Yeah, I know, me too, but she is big enough to make her own decisions."

Susan enters the already crammed canteen. "Talking about me?" she asks, but there is a smile on her face.

"No, we're not. Oh, I brought in that dress you asked me for. Let me grab it." I leave and rummage under the counter for the bag.

A few minutes later, Susan comes out, handing me my phone. "Its been ringing and guess who it is?" she says with a smile.

I take the phone from her. Two missed calls from Josh. "Susan, we're just friends."

She gives me an innocent look. "Of course you are." She goes back to the canteen, winking at me before closing the door.

I roll my eyes and call Josh back. "Hey, sorry I missed your calls. I was busy."

"No worries. I was going to meet you for lunch, if you want?"

"Yeah, one o'clock, meet me at Bites," I say.

"Okay, see you then."

When I go back inside the canteen, two sets of smiling eyes look up at me. I finish my coffee as they giggle. "You act like you guys are five," I say playfully before I finish off stocking the history section.

Bites is my favourite place to have lunch. Well, to be honest, there isn't much of a choice. It's Bites or Tracey's and there's more grease in her hair than on the pans. I spot Josh at a back booth. He's in his work clothes, ripped jeans and heavy brown boots. He works in the wood mill not far outside town. I slide in opposite him.

When he sees me, he raises an eyebrow. "Hey how's work?"

"The usual. You know, two five-year-olds working with me." Josh looks confused and I laugh. "Never mind." I pick up the menu and glance through it, even though I already know what I'm going to order.

Rachel arrives then to take our order. "Hey, Sarajane, what can I get you?"

"Hey, Rachel. Could I get bolognaise and a glass of coke?"

Josh orders a burger and chips with a large glass of milk.

"Have you heard from Linda since?" Josh asks.

"No, it's been two days and nothing. But maybe it was all a trick. I wasn't feeling well and you know Linda is weird anyway."

Josh gives me a little smile. In other words, he's not convinced. I think I'm trying to convince myself, because if I let my mind believe what I thought I saw is real, then what else was possible, and that's a scary thought.

Our food arrives and it smells lovely. I dig in to my bolognaise, my favourite dinner of all time. It isn't a meal you would have for a first date, but Josh is used to me getting it all over my mouth. "So I got two tickets to the ball," Josh says while taking a large bite out of his burger. I roll my eyes. "Why do you even go? You hate to dance." He smiles slightly. "The things I do for you." I laugh at his boyish grin. I've gone to the ball with him every year for the last three, but it doesn't feel right now that Mum is missing. Nothing feels right, no matter how hard I try to get on with things for Dad and Jessica's sake.

Josh speaks as if he's read my mind. "I know you don't want to go anywhere with your mum... you know, but I think it would be good for you."

"Can I think about it?" The brightness leaves his brown eyes. I know he's disappointed, but he tries to hide it by gobbling down a few chips

"Yes, but it's tomorrow night."

I nearly choke on my bolognaise. Oh God, he's right. It is that close.

Josh gives me a little smile. "I wanted to give you the tickets the other night, but it didn't feel like the right time. You know, with Linda and..." He trails off. A feeling of guilt rises in my stomach. I know the tickets aren't cheap.

"All right, count me in." His whole face lights up, his brown eyes sparkling.

Going through the list in my head of things I need to do for the ball distracts me while I finish my food. When I look at my phone, I realise the time. "Christ, I'm late!" I grab my bag, but Josh makes it to the counter before me and pays for the food. "Thanks."

"No worries. So I will see you tomorrow night, say seven-thirty?" Josh says with excitement in his voice.

"Yeah, see you then."

I cross the road and head back to work. "Sorry, I'm late."

Christine peeps her head out from under the counter. "Hey, it's grand. Susan went for hers ten minutes ago. I think she's meeting Max."

I say nothing about that. "Could I finish up around three tomorrow?"

She gives me a smile. "Sure, what are you up to?" Christine is my sorta boss. Her mother owns the shop, but she's in her late eighties and isn't able anymore. She hasn't handed the shop over to Christine yet, but lets her run it. The woman just couldn't let go.

"Josh is taking me to the ball." I raise my hand before she can say anything. "As a friend."

"I wasn't going to say anything, only that Susan is going with Max too."

"Oh, well, we'll just have to get along."

Christine looks sceptical. Honestly, I don't feel too optimistic myself.

When I arrive home, I change into something more comfortable for shopping. "Jessica, Jessica?"

She pops her head in my bedroom door. "Yes?"

"Will you come dress shopping with me?"

Her eyes light up. "Yes. Where are you going?" She sits down on my bed as I tie up my hair.

"Josh is taking me to the ball and it's tomorrow night."

"You're going to marry Josh."

I look at her through the mirror and laugh. "He's my friend, Jessica." I turn around. "Boys and girls can be friends."

Parking on the main street is easy as there are no cars around. Jessica and I enter the Red Ribbon dress shop. It's the only shop that sells ball gowns in town, and it is still open. The owner must have been aware there would be last minute shoppers. The bell rings overhead as we make our way inside. A glamorous woman in her late sixties, with short blond hair, approaches us. "Hello, can I help you and your friend with anything?" she asks. "She's my sister and it's just me looking for a gown." I can see why she wouldn't think we were sisters. Jessica has dead straight, jet-black hair and green eyes, and she is very petite. My five foot seven inches is tall compared to her five foot three. My hair is curly and my eyes are a grey, unlike both my father and mother. So basically, we look totally different. "Okay, any colour or style in particular?" the lady asks. I give her an apologetic smile and shrug. "That's okay, dear. With your figure, you will look beautiful in any dress." She ushers me forward and starts picking up several dresses. "The fitting rooms are to the back." She hands me the pile of dresses, which I have to push down with my chin in order to make it to the fitting rooms without falling over. I look at Jessica as I pass her and mouth *HELP!!!* She starts laughing.

The first dress is red in a boob-tube style that goes out in a poof from the waist down. When I come out of the fitting room, Jessica is lounging on a black leather sofa. There are mirrors around me and I can see myself from every angle, which is not good, as I look like a big red cake. Jessica starts laughing and can't stop. The owner gives her a sharp look that shuts her up quickly.

I walk straight back into the fitting room and try on four more dresses. They are nice, but none of them really stand out. The last dress is black, which is my favourite colour. I slip it on over my head and tug it down, adjusting it until it falls to the ground. The material is heavy and tight against my upper body, showing off every curve. Then it swirls just at the thigh and flows to the ground. It is stunning. I walk out of the fitting room, and Jessica sits up straight.

"Sarajane, it's amazing."

I smile. "I think so too."

The owner comes over with black high heels with a simple de Monte design on the front of them. I slip my feet in. "Now you look perfect, dear" she says. I pay for the gown and shoes, three hundred euro for all, but I have to say it's worth every penny. I take Jessica out for food afterwards to thank her for helping me. It's after eleven o'clock by the time we arrive home, and Dad is in bed already.

The next day at work goes by quickly, as Susan and I talk about our dresses for the ball. Christine listens enthusiastically, but I feel sorry for her. "Are you sure you won't come with us?"

Christine gives me a look. "Really, I prefer some wine and a good romance novel. Not looking at all the couples hanging all over each other."

"Well, if you change your mind, you have my number."

Christine gives me a hug. "Thanks."

When three o'clock comes, I get my bag and jacket from the back and say good-bye to Christine and Susan. Susan is staying on until four so at least Christine only has an hour and a half without us.

I drive home and start getting ready. First thing, I jump in the shower and take my time with my hair, especially making sure I condition it really well. Once I'm dried, I slip into my nightgown and head downstairs to blow-dry my hair only slightly, just to take the heaviness out of it. After that, I go back upstairs and put on my dress and shoes. I check the time on my phone. Still an hour left. So I take great care applying my make-up, foundation, some simple lip-gloss and tint of a blusher along my cheeks, eyeliner and finally, mascara. Done. I check myself in my full-length mirror attached to my bedroom door. I look beautiful.

Leaving the mirror, I go downstairs to the sitting room, where Jessica and Dad are waiting on me. Walking in, I give them a twirl, causing the bottom of my dress to spread out.

"You look like a princess," Jessica says while rising off the couch to come over and inspect me further.

My dad smiles, but it is a sad smile. He is thinking of Mum. "You are beautiful, darling." He lands a gentle kiss on my forehead. Tears prickle my eyes. Mum should be here.

The doorbell rings and Dad volunteers to get it, anything to distract him from this sad moment. I clear my throat to pull myself together. Looking at Jessica, I can see the sadness on her face. "I miss her too," she whispers, barely audible. I hug her so tightly she squeals slightly.

Josh walks in the door then and I have to say he looks so handsome. He's in an all-black suit with a white shirt, making his tan stand out. His eyes are practically sparkling. "Wow, you look stunning," he says while leaning in and giving me a kiss on the cheek.

"You don't look too bad yourself."

Jessica inhales a sharp breath. "Don't be so mean, Sarajane."

When I look at my little sister, she looks truly angry. I turn to Josh and roll my eyes. "You look dashing, Prince Josh." Jessica is still angry, as she knows I am being sarcastic.

"Okay kids, stand together for a photo."

Josh places his hand around my waist and gives it a little squeeze. I look at him with a smile, but his face is so serious that my smile falters as it feels his brown eyes are searing into my very heart. I know Josh cares for me, but there is so much more then care on his face right now. Then I hear the click of the camera.

Dad lowers it. "Come on, kids, smile." This time we both do, but I know our smiles will be strained when we get the photo developed.

I give Dad a kiss and he hugs me tightly. "I love you. Have a great night. You deserve it."

Tears fill my eyes. "I love you too."

We reach the ball fifteen minutes later. We don't speak on the way, which leaves me feeling awkward.

The room that the ball is being held in is already full with couples. The room is lit by hundreds of fairy lights. No overhead lights are on, only the fairy lights and small tea lights on all the tables. The music is soft. It's spectacular and everyone looks amazing.

We descend the stairs and enter the ballroom. Josh gets us drinks, his mood picking back up a bit. I stand just by the stairs, clutching my purse. A few ladies give me scowls as their partners eye me up. I feel such relief when Josh returns and hands me a glass of champagne. Now a lot of girls are giving looks, and it's not because their men are looking at me. It's because they're looking at Josh and wishing they where with him.

"To us. May we have a wonderful and magical night." I click my glass with his, causing his face to break into a smile. The smile I return is genuine, as I feel happy that he's back to himself again. Maybe I misread the look he gave me in my house and he feels awkward that he gave me the wrong impression.

The music picks up tempo and I'm eager to dance, but Josh isn't eager at all. "Come on. We'll sit down and talk." Josh takes my free hand, moving me through the crowd until we come to a small table and two chairs. We sit down, admiring all the talented dancers.

Josh takes my hand in his, drawing my attention away from the dance floor. "I need to tell you something."

Just then a tall shadow looms over our table. "Excuse me, would you like to dance?" asks a husky voice. I look up and into the eyes of a gorgeous guy. He must be in his mid-twenties. My stomach gets all nervous. He's tall with broad shoulders and his eyes are a piercing green. He has shoulder-length black hair tied at the nape of his neck. His jawline is strong and defines his full lips.

Overall, I'm speechless so Josh speaks for me, with a serious tone. "No, she would not. Can't you see we're talking or did you miss that?"

The guy averts his eyes to Josh. "I was not speaking to you. I was addressing the lady."

I finally find my voice. "No, thank you…" I pause.

"Tristan. My name is Tristan."

"Okay, no thank you, Tristan." He tilts his head in a bowing motion and cuts Josh a hard look before he walks away.

Josh is smirking at his back. "Fool," he says in a sneery tone, but when he looks at me, his face falls. He can see the anger on my face.

"Josh, don't ever speak for me again. I can answer for myself."

"Oh can you? You were doing a great job. Sitting there with your mouth hanging open." His own anger flares across his face.

I grab my purse. "You are a jerk sometimes. I'm getting another drink." I walk off to the bar. Regret washes over me as soon as I reach it. I shouldn't have called him a jerk. I *was* sitting there with my mouth hanging open. My stomach flutters thinking about Tristan. He is like nothing I've ever seen before. The tingle of breath upon my shoulder makes me go still.

"May I get you a drink? Or should I consult with your jealous escort?"

"He is my friend, and yes, a glass of champagne." I look up at Tristan, his green eyes studying my face. He turns towards the barman and orders two champagnes. "Thank you." I take a sip, not too sure what to do now.

"What's your name?" Tristan asks.

"Sarajane Anderson." When I say my second name, it seems to surprise him. Don't get me wrong; he's not overly surprised, but his eyebrows rise ever so slightly. It would take a lot to make them go really high.

"Anderson? That is interesting."

"Why?" I ask, but before he gets to answer me, Josh is there. He hasn't noticed Tristan or maybe he's just ignoring him.

"Look, Sarajane, I'm really sorry. It's just I really…" Then he notices Tristan. "You again. Can you not take no for an answer?"

Tristan places his untouched glass of champagne on the counter and enters Josh's personal space. "You are beginning to annoy me, boy."

I squeeze in between the two of them before it gets out of hand. "Stop acting like two kids." Two sets of eyes shoot down at me, as both of them are taller. Josh looks annoyed while Tristan's face remains expressionless. So I take my fury out on Tristan this time. I hand him back the champagne. "Thank you for the drink." I turn my back on him and take Josh's hand. "Dance with me," I say.

Josh steps on my toes several times. "I told you I couldn't dance." I laugh. Josh lays his hand on my face "You're beautiful."

"Oh, I know I am," I say with a big smile and swat his hand away.

"I'm serious." He places his hand back on my face. "I'm in love with you, Sarajane."

It feels like time has frozen and only Josh and I exist. I can see by the way he looks at me that he means it. God, how did I not see this coming? I really care for Josh, but I don't love him. Josh speaks then, as if he knows how I feel. "I know you don't love me, but in time, you will grow to." And then he kisses me, gently at first, and then he deepens the kiss. When I pull back, we are both a little breathless.

"Josh, I really had no idea."

He laughs and it's full of joy. "I know. You can be so blind at times." He pulls me into him and circles his arms around my waist. "I have always loved you."

"Sarajane." I turn out of Josh's arms and am faced with Susan, who is in a flood of tears.

"Jesus, Susan, what happened?" But I already know. The look of hurt on her face makes my stomach tighten.

"Susan, did he hit you?" Josh asks while scanning the crowd for Max.

She gives a bitter laugh. "You warned me, but I wouldn't listen." I hug her, feeling so sorry for her. "I have to go," she says, panicked.

"No, wait, I will come." But she leaves straight away. I race after her. Josh grabs my hand.

"I'm coming with you."

I kiss his cheek. "Not this time."

I follow Susan. She's sitting on the curb outside the hall, crying. Her shoulders shake with sobs. I sit down beside her.

"You have to forget about this guy."

Susan cuts me a dirty look. "It's easy for you to say. I love him, Sarajane."

I can't believe I'm hearing this. "He hit you twice now, Susan. He will never change." I can see the conflict in her eyes, but then they shadow over with anger.

"He didn't mean it." She storms off.

"Susan, wait up." She starts to run, and I give chase after her, but in high heels, it's really hard. By the time I reach the end of the street, she's jumped into a taxi. When I stop to catch my breath, I notice the streets are deserted. I wrap my bare arms around myself and start walking back, glancing over my shoulder every few seconds. The noise of my high heels echoes off the pavement. I start to walk faster. Someone grabs me from behind, roughly. I swing my hands around, clawing at my attacker's face. "Let me go," I yell. Adrenalin pumps through my body, along with fear. With all my might I draw back my leg and kick with the heel of my shoe. I can feel the spike make contact with flesh. I gag. My attacker roars in pain, causing his hold to falter while allowing me to twist out of his grasp, and I run blindly. My hair is whipping in my face, unshed tears causing my eyes to blur. I push my body until my lungs burn. A quick look behind confirms no one is pursuing me. Branches whip at my clothes and face, making me slow down. When I stop to catch my breath, I take in my surroundings. I'm in the woods, the opposite side of town, about five minutes from the hall. I didn't realise I ran that far. "Shit." How stupid could I be to run into the woods? But I panicked and just ran. It's so quiet;

the only noise is from the inhabitants of the woods. I stand still. The only thing I can hear now is my blood pounding in my ears. My breathing and heart rate begin to slow. That's when I hear a twig snap off to my right. My head shoots in that direction, but I can't see anything. Quietly, I remove my heels and carry them. My black dress is now dragging along the ground, but I can't do anything about it. Leaving my bag behind me on the bar counter leaves me with no cell phone to call for help. I'm not even sure if it would work out in the woods anyway.

    I slowly move around a large tree, keeping my back to it. A hand clamps over my mouth and Tristan is standing in front of me. I pull his hand off and relief washes through me. "Oh, thank God. There is a man chasing me. Well, I don't know if he still is, but he was." I want to throw myself into his arms with relief.

    "Sarajane." I hear Josh's voice. "Sarajane!"

    I run towards his voice while calling his name. "Josh!" Then I can see him.

    "What are you doing?"

    I throw myself into his arms. "Someone was chasing me, but it's okay. Tristan's here." I let go of Josh and turn around, but he isn't there. "Tristan?" I call. I hear a thud behind me, causing me to jump nervously. Josh is on the ground and Tristan standing over him.

    I kneel down beside Josh. He's breathing. "What the hell did you do that for?" Was it because of what happened at the ball? Before I can ask, I can see another man coming towards us, the man who attacked me.

    "Tristan, that's him." I can hear the fear in my voice, but Tristan just stands there doing nothing.

    The man approaches us. "You got her?" he says to Tristan. I was so foolish to trust a stranger.

    Looking down at Josh, I can see he's still breathing, but he's unconscious. My anger flares. "You asshole." I stand and push Tristan away from Josh. He doesn't even blink a cold, green eye.

    My attacker walks up to me, visibly angry. "How dare you put your hands on him!" I scream at him.

Tristan speaks then. "Legis, stop." He turns to me. "You, move." The stiffness and coldness of his posture makes me realise how stupid I was to fall for his charming act at the ball. Anger bubbles up inside me. "Like hell I will."

Tristan comes right up to me, his cold gaze intent on my face. "If you don't, I will carry you, princess."

Chapter Seven

SARAJANE

It's so dark I can barely see two feet in front of me. Tristan walks behind me, and Legis leads the way. I don't know where they're taking me. Or what they want. Neither of them has said anything since taking me.

Legis stops abruptly, causing me to smack into his back. He swings around, grabbing my arm to steady me. These guys move unnaturally fast.

"Legis, what is wrong?" Tristan asks from behind me.

"Sir, I need some light." He looks back at Tristan as he speaks.

"I shall lead and you stay behind her." Tristan pauses as he walks past me. "Don't try to run. I am in no mood to chase you." He takes his position in front of me. Tristan does not move straight away. Instead, he holds out his hand in front of him and whispers, "Lux." I can see a light radiate in front of him. I jump back, slightly startled.

"Lets move," he commands. Legis nudges me on. We start walking again. I'm trying to peer over Tristan's shoulder to see where the light is coming from, but he's too tall, so I just stare at his back. After a few moments, Tristan makes a hand motion for us to stop. Then the light goes out. He swings around and places his hand over my mouth, startling me, while pulling me back into his chest. Legis stands as still as stone, not even blinking. We wait. I can't hear or see anything, only Tristan's heart beating fast. I am too close to him for comfort. I can feel his muscles tense in his chest and stomach. He makes a hand motion to Legis to get down. Then slowly he lowers himself and me to the ground, never taking his hand off my mouth. He lies down on his side right against me and pulls my hands to his chest, holding them with his other hand. The heat radiates off his body against mine, making my back feel cold. I can now hear the shuffling in the distance. Maybe it is Josh.

I try to scream, but my sounds are muffled. Tristan whispers in my ear. "Stop or we all die, you stupid girl." I try to scream again and pull my hands free, but I can't get them out of his iron grasp. So I bite his hand until I taste blood. He doesn't even flinch. I know it's hopeless.

The movements pass us and I can now hear there's more then one person. Tears roll down my cheeks when I realise I will not be heard or rescued. Tristan looks at me, his jaw muscles tensing. It feels like forever we lie like this; then Tristan speaks. "I am taking my hand away." I look up into his eyes and know straight away I shouldn't have, as my stomach flutters. I drop my gaze and manage a nod of my head. Tristan removes his hand slowly, but he still holds my hands against his chest. He doesn't say anything, just watches my face. His green eyes have softened. A blush rises in my cheeks. I can't take much more of his closeness.

"What are you staring at?" I'm getting annoyed now. Well, I'm uncomfortable with this gorgeous guy staring at me. He lets go and stands up.

Legis moves up beside us. "Was it Clive?" he asks.

"I think so. It sounded like there were three of them. It must have been Taurus and Felix, also." Tristan looks down at me still on the ground and grabs my wrists roughly. I'm about to protest when he pulls me off the ground.

I look at his hands still on my wrists. There are no teeth marks. "I bit you. I... I tasted your blood."

He withdraws his hand. "We need to move now."

"But I bit you." Tristan ignores me and starts walking away.

We come to a clearing where two huge horses, black as coal, are waiting. They don't stir when we come closer, just stand there obediently. "I'm not getting on that horse until someone tells me where I'm going. And why." They both ignore me. Instead, Legis retrieves a leather roll from behind a tree and unravels it, revealing three black cloaks. Legis and Tristan put theirs on and fasten them around their necks. I start to panic. These guys are lunatics.

While their backs are turned, I slip off my high heels and move quietly away. My heart is racing now. My mind is screams, *Run!* So I do. The minute my feet hit the woods' floor, noise rises, alerting Tristan. I run and don't look back. I can hear Tristan calling my name as he takes chase after me. The rocks and sticks dig into my feet, but I ignore the pain and push my body harder. I can hear Tristan behind me, his heavy boots breaking every twig under them. He reaches out to grab me. I try to pull away but fall awkwardly, taking him down also. I land beside the trunk of a large tree, slamming my side into it before falling onto the ground. I let out a whoosh of breath.

Tristan rolls off his back and comes over to me. "Move your hands. I need to see if you're hurt badly."

I move away. "Don't touch me."

"Fine. Get up, then, and walk." I stand using the tree for support. My side is burning, but it doesn't feel as if anything is broken, just a lot of bruising.

"You're an asshole." Legis comes rushing through the forest, a little out of breath. "You got her." Tristan just nudges me on. "Move." We make our way back to the clearing. Since they grabbed me from the ball, neither of them have hurt me or threatened me, and Tristan only knocked out Josh. Which meant, more than likely, they wouldn't hurt me. But why take me? We reach the clearing again. Tristan comes towards me with the black cloak and places it around my shoulders. As he ties it at my neck loosely, I watch his hands. Definitely no teeth marks. I don't know why, but tears run down my face silently. Tristan's hands pause and he tilts my chin up so our eyes meet. His gaze is soft, concerned, and my stomach flutters. I feel so angry with myself—that I can find him so attractive under the circumstances. He lets my face go abruptly, the coldness seeping back into him, and he jumps up on the horse and stretches out his arm for me to take. I could run, but he would just catch me, so I have no choice but to take his hand. Tristan pulls me up on the horse as if I weigh nothing.

"Hold on tight," he commands.

"Why?" I ask. He kicks the horse and we launch forward. I grab his waist tightly.

"That is why," he says.

I don't reply. I'm just praying I don't fall off. We dodge trees so closely I can see the veins on the green-brownish leaves. My heart is in my mouth. I close my eyes tight. My stomach isn't holding up well. Maybe not seeing every tree in such detail will help. We come to an abrupt stop, and I open my eyes. We're fifty feet from the cliff.

Tristan speaks in a language I don't understand. He says a few sentences gently, but his body is tense.

Just then, the ground trembles under us.

I grab Tristan tighter. "What is happening?"

Fire shoots up through a long crack that has opened just at the cliff's edge. It roars up into the air. Tristan kicks the horse and charges for the wall of fire, Legis beside us. Just as we hit it, they both say *"Aeirus"* in unison, while I scream and shut my eyes tightly. My ears pop as if I'm on a plane just at take off. Now I can't hear anything at all. I feel the sensation of flying. *Have we gone over the edge?* It doesn't feel like falling, and I'm still holding onto Tristan's waist.

I open my eyes slowly and wish I hadn't. We're in a large bubble, the two horses side by side. When I look down, their hooves aren't touching the bubble, but floating. Outside, the fire rages all around us. It looks like we're moving at an incredible speed by the way the fire licks past us so quickly.

I start hyperventilating. *Oh God, what is keeping the fire away? What if it breaks?* My breathing becomes harder.

Tristan's voice is strained as he calls to Legis. "Can you hold it? She is panicking."

"Yes, sir," Legis replies. Their voices seem far away and everything is turning dark. Tristan swings himself around and grabs me before I fall off the horse. He places me in front of him so I'm facing him. His lips are moving, but I can't hear anything, and then I black out.

In my dream, faces of tormented people race through the fire, reaching out for me to save them. The smell of burnt flesh makes me gag, and I recoil. As the hands come through the bubble, reaching for me, all the flesh melts away, leaving only bones. I scream and fall off the horse into the waiting hands of the dead.

I wake with a thud. My eyes shoot open. I'm lying against Tristan's chest, his arm firmly around me. His other hand holds the reins. I can feel the horse beneath me slow down. Tristan relaxes his grip around my waist, and I look up at him.

"Let me off now." He stops the horse immediately. I jump down, clumsily landing on sand, white sand. I look around me. There's nothing but sand for miles. *Oh God, I feel sick*. Tristan jumps down and walks towards me. "Stay away from me," I roar.

Tristan stops abruptly. "I know you're upset." But the way he looks at me says he doesn't care. He holds out his hands in front of him, as if he's trying to calm a wild animal.

"Upset? Upset? Not even close. Where the hell am I? And what was that… fire?" I ask.

Tristan approaches me slowly with his hands still outstretched. "We need to move now." His voice is full of irritation.

I let out a roar. "Like hell I will. Answer me now. Where am I?"

He looks at Legis who says nothing. "I will tell you where you are, but then we have to move." I don't answer him. He comes right up to me then, still taking caution not to get to close. "You're in Saskia and the wall of fire is the passage to get here." I don't even know how to respond. Maybe all this is one big nightmare. I pinch myself hard on the arm and let out a little squeal. I'm not dreaming. I take some deep breaths to calm myself. "Okay. Okay, so I'm in Saskia… And why am I here?" I can hear the hysteria in my own voice. "I can't answer that." I let out a roar of frustration. Tristan uses this opportunity to grab me and throws me over his shoulder caveman style. "Let me down now." He climbs up on the horse and places me in front of him. I try to wiggle out, but he restrains me with his arms. "I told you we need to move. So calm down and soon all your questions will be answered, princess." He spits out the last word. He kicks the horse and off we ride. "How far back do you think Clive and the others are, sir?" Legis asks. "They would still be looking, so if we make it to the first resting area in the next hour, we will be a day ahead of them." An hour later, night has fallen completely. This world is weird. There's not as much as one star in the sky, even though it is clear and the moon is red. It's not creepy the way you would think. It's breath-taking. We slow down. Tristan helps me off the horse. "We rest here." I don't have the energy to argue. So a nod of my head is all the reply he gets. Not that he notices. Tristan and Legis are pushing sand back with their hands and pulling out of the ground what looks like large rolls of leather. Legis rolls his out. It is full of blankets, wood, a hammer and a few large pieces of paper wrapped around something the size of a large stone. Tristan's holds similar things, but also glass bottles along with what looks like strings of leather. They set to work. They have tents up within the hour. I have to say I'm impressed by their skills. I pull back the flap of the tent that Legis has erected. There are blankets all over the ground, giving it a cosy feel, yet it's spacious enough for all three of us to sleep in. I really hope that is not the case or I'll just sleep outside.

Tristan starts setting up a small fire. I sit down beside him. "Is this a different era?"

He pauses what he is doing and considers my question. "In a way, yes. Saskia is very different from your world… I am not knowledgeable enough of your world, but Legis would gladly tell you."

I look at Legis. "What do you want to know?" he asks while kneeling down on the opposite side of the fire, as Tristan continues setting it up. I feel like saying I want to know everything, but I think about the most basic question I want to ask.

"What is this place? Is it all sand?" I hope the answer is no to my last question.

"It is a world parallel to yours and in ways no different. The outskirts of Saskia is sand, but that is as far as it goes."

Okay, next question. I'm watching Tristan from the corner of my eye as he lights the fire. He has no lighter or matches, yet the flames begin to build. "How does he light the fire?"

Tristan looks up at me. Legis speaks then. "In our world, we are born—"

"Legis, enough," Tristan says, then rises. He lifts the brown paper parcels and opens them, handing each of us bread, cheese and one of the glass bottles. I look at mine. The bread is as thick as three slices of normal bread and the cheese is cut generously. *Is this our dinner?* "Eat," Tristan says while tearing his own bread. A perfect gentleman. "No butter. A bit of coleslaw maybe?" Legis laughs. "Sorry, but this is it. One of the differences in our worlds. We eat to live, but in your world you live to eat." I don't like the statement even if it is partially true. Tristan ignores us and eats his own. He seems to have no social skills. I can't eat anything. My stomach is still unsettled, and as much as this chat seems normal enough, these guys have just kidnapped me. I open the bottle. It has a corkscrew on hinges as its seal. I take a sip first, testing it. It's wine, white wine, tasty. I take a deep gulp and then reseal it.

"So do you have cities or towns like us?"

Legis looks at Tristan for approval. A nod of his head allows him to answer. "I would not say we have cities, because you will think of large metal structures. Ours are more like large villages. The central point is the castle."

"A castle. So do you have, like, a king and queen?"

Once again, Legis looks to Tristan for approval and receives it. "Yes, we do." I sit there and try to picture this village with its big stone castle in the centre. Legis interrupts my thoughts. "We live very simple lives here compared to your world."

I never would have guessed, but I don't voice that. Instead, I go right back to the start. "So are you going to answer my first question? How did he light the fire?" I look sideways at Tristan; he's looking directly at me. I blush. Thank God it's dark. "How did you light the fire?" I ask him directly.

Tristan comes over and sits beside me. "Before we go any further, I need you to understand I am not your friend and I don't have to answer your questions." He looks me straight in the eye. "Understand?" His words are cold and harsh.

"Yes, I understand." My voice comes out in a whisper.

"I am going to scout the area," Legis says and leaves.

Tristan rises, returning to the opposite side of the fire. "Get some rest. We have a lot of ground to travel tomorrow." He throws me a leather roll. "Wear these tomorrow," he says while looking me up and down. "They are far more suitable." Taking the roll, I walk to my tent. This guy really hates me and I don't know why. I push Tristan to the back of my mind. I have more important things to think about. Like why I'm here. But I know at this stage they will not tell me anything.

I lie down on all the blankets. It's really comfortable. My mind wanders to Jessica, Dad and Josh, wondering if they're looking for me. Poor Dad—first Mum, now me. What if they have my mum here in this world? But it makes no sense.

I stay in the tent for a while, unwrapping the leather roll. It contains a white tunic, trousers, socks and boots. I start to change straight away, but keep my cloak on over the outfit. I can hear Tristan telling Legis he is on guard and then Tristan goes to the other tent. I lie there biding my time. I don't have many options. Only when they are asleep, I will escape. Going back the way we came is not an option, but at this moment, I just need to get away from Tristan and Legis. After waiting another two hours, I creep from my tent. Legis is asleep by the fire. Carrying my boots in my hand, I pass Tristan's tent and hold my breath. As I tiptoe past, sweat gathers on my neck. If he wakes, what would he do? Kill me? Fear makes me move faster. Once I pass, my speed picks up. When I glance back, the glow of the fire is far away. Now I only hope that Legis told the truth about this place not being all sand, or I will die of dehydration. But I'll take my chances. After my boots are on, I stand still to let my eyes adjust to the dark. The red moon casts only a small amount of light. The temperature drops the farther I go into the desert, causing me to wrap my black cloak tightly around my body. West seems the best direction to go; it's far away from Tristan and Legis. I just hope it will not take too long to come across normal ground, and then I can figure out how I'm going to get out of this mess. The first hour I gain a lot of ground and am feeling positive about the decision I made, but as the hours slip by and sand is all I see, my thoughts turn to fear of never seeing home again. This god-forsaken desert could take my life yet. My thighs burn; my throat is dry. *How long have I been walking?* Looking up at the sky tells me a few hours. It's starting to get brighter and the temperature has risen. When I turn away from the sky and try and focus on my feet again, dizziness washes over me, causing me to stumble and fall face first into the sand. The need to sleep pulls at me; my body feels exhausted. *When was the last time I ate?* Saliva flows into my mouth at the thought of food. I swallow it to try and tame the dryness in my throat, but it does little good. I once read that you can drink your own urine only once in a dire situation and it would not poison your system, and this definitely qualifies as a dire situation. The thought of that makes me get up on to my feet and walk, my steps slow and clumsy. Movement in the distance makes me stop. I squint but my eyes can't focus properly. The dizziness settles as I stand still for a few moments. I refocus. Nothing, no movement. So I keep pushing further with the feeling of dread. Catching movement again, I stop. It's closer now, but it doesn't seem possible, unless whatever it is, is moving at an incredible speed. A horse? No, no dust or sound. Tristan? I freeze. No, he would be coming from behind me. At this thought, I turn around and laugh at the emptiness I'm faced with. God, I feel as if I might lose my mind out here. The cloak on my shoulders feels as if it weights a ton. I strip it off with no energy to carry it and dump it on the sand, hoping a wind will rise and cover it over, hiding the path I have taken. Maybe being in the tent with water and food wasn't so bad. Then I scold myself for such weakness. "No, he took you from your home." My newfound anger pushes me on. The movements are all around me now, but it must be my imagination, as they seem to move when I move. Noise comes from my left, no my right. I strain to listen. The noise comes again. It's like a hiss of a snake, only louder. Then it's all around me. I turn in a full circle but can't see anything. My head spins, causing me to fall onto the sand again. Closing my eyes, I try to let the dizziness pass. I roll over on my back, keeping my eyes closed. *Keep it together, Sarajane*, I tell myself, but the prospect of dying makes laughter bubble in my throat. I let it out. My laughter soon turns hysterical and I feel like crying. I open my eyes and every part of my emotions turns to fear. A white grotesque face looks down at me. It shimmers as I try to focus. I question what I'm seeing, if it is real or not. The creature hisses at me, showing off a long black tongue that slides between black pointed teeth. Eyes that are hollow and empty stare at me. Fear runs through me as more faces appear around me. I shut my eyes and pray for this to stop and repeat to myself *This is not real* over and over again. But when I look up, they are still there, staring at me with hungry black eyes.

Digging my elbows into the sand I push my body up. The creature closest to me rises off his haunches and places his foot on my chest, pushing me back down. His body is human-like only hunched and twisted. The others start to look impatient. Growls rise deep in their throats. I hold my breath, afraid to breathe. *What are they?* Frozen with fear, I don't move as much as a muscle. The creature's inhuman growls start to rise.

One of the creatures moves closer to me very slowly. As he moves, he keeps glancing over at the one who pushed me down, so I assume he's the leader. It licks its lips. A whimper of fear rises in my throat as it reaches me. My noise attracts the attention of the leader. He grabs the creature just before it touches me and throws him on the sand. The creature slams its fists into the sand while looking at his leader. It points at me. "Eat."

My mind goes frantic. *Eat, as in eat me? Get up!! Get up!!!* I scream in my head. Rising on shaky limbs, I get to my knees. Sweat gathers on my forehead from exhaustion. When the creature sees me trying to get up, a high-pitch squeal leaves his throat and he charges. The others are pounding the ground with their feet and fists while screeching. He is an inch from me, his eyes wild with hunger, but that's as far as he gets. An arrow is embedded in his neck. Blood splatters across my face as he crumbles to the ground. There's an eerie silence amongst the creatures as they focus behind me. I look around just as Tristan and Legis move forward. The leader of the creatures digs his feet into the sand like a bull, causing dust to rise, and throws his head back, letting out a deafening screech. They charge. Tristan takes three of them out with arrows in a matter of seconds, while Legis fights on the ground with two swords, decapitating anything that moves. I stay on my knees, too shocked to move. It's over in minutes. Only one lives—the leader—but he has a long gash down his torso. Tristan places his foot on his chest, the same action the creature did to me. *Had he been here that long?*

Legis brings water to me. I gulp it down as Legis looks at me with disappointment. "You could have died," he says. I ignore him and pour water all over my face, feeling a little more alert. He helps me rise on shaky legs. My attention returns to the creature under Tristan's boot. Tristan has his sword pointed at its chest.

"Exile, you are a long way from the mountains." His tone is harsh.

The exile looks at me. "Smell."

This causes Tristan to sneer cruelly. "You lie." And he slices off the creature's hand. It goes berserk under Tristan's foot, but doesn't get loose. "Why are you here, exile?" Tristan's voice is even harsher than before.

The creature is squealing in pain, but he manages one word. "Smell," he says again. Wrong answer. Tristan slices off his other hand. Oh God, I feel sick. The creature is screeching in pain. It sounds like a dying cat. Two pools of blood stream from his wrists where its hands once were.

"Stop it, Tristan. This is cruel," I shout at him. He looks at me but keeps his foot on the creature's chest as it trashes under him.

"Be quiet. I will deal with you later." His tone is deadly; his eyes are filled with anger. Feeling very afraid, I take a step backwards. His attention is back on the creature again. "Last chance, exile." He raises his sword.

The creature looks afraid, shaking its head in a pleading gesture. Just before the sword reaches him, he speaks. "King Paulus." The blade pauses at his throat.

"Where?" Tristan asks.

The creature's features take on a resigned look. I think he is done talking.

Tristan pushes the blade harder. "Where, exile?" And then to my amazement the creature throws his head forward, pushing the blade into his own neck, killing himself. Blood gurgles in its throat.

Bile rises in my throat, and I look away as Tristan pushes the creature off his blade using his foot and wipes it on his trousers. He slides the sword into the holder on his back. Then his intense gaze turns on me. My muscles tighten as he moves towards me, breathing heavy with anger. He grabs both my hands, pulling them together without speaking, and from his belt extracts rope that he uses to tie my hands together. "I'm sorry," I say in a panicky voice, but he keeps tying knots in a complex way. I yank my hands to try and stop him. "I said sorry. Please don't." He shoves cloth into my mouth, cutting off my protests, and ties a piece over it to keep the gag in place. I'm still protesting, but nothing I say is understandable. "If I have to tie you to me, I will." He shakes me. "Do you understand?" I nod my head as tears fall from my eyes. Tristan's face softens slightly. Hating to show him any weakness, I look away from his gaze. He places me in front of him on the horse and Legis mounts his own. We make our way back to camp. I try to keep my body straight, but I'm too weak and I slump from exhaustion. I start to drift off but panic every time I see the creatures in my mind. "Sleep. You are safe now," Tristan says and wraps an arm around me so I wont fall off. He holds the reins in his other hand. The warmth from his body and his heartbeat lulls me too sleep. I feel safe with his strong arm around me. I just wonder what price I'll pay for his kindness, and then my thoughts are no more as I fall asleep.Waking up some time later, I'm lying on my side. I smile with warmth and contentment. There's a heavy blanket over me. My hair is loose, and a curl falls onto my face. I raise my hand to push it back and that's when I feel the rope biting into my wrists. My hands are tied. Sitting up too quickly sends a rush of dizziness through me. I regret the action straight away, as my head is spinning. It slowly resides and all last night's events come back to me—trying to escape, the creatures, Tristan's anger and his kindness. A blush rises in my cheeks when I think of his arm around me. Struggling to my feet is harder then expected without the use of my hands. It's hard to balance, but I make it upright and steady myself. Tristan and Legis's voices make me pause.

"Why would King Paulus want Morrick's daughter?"

"To use her against him," Legis replies.

Tristan lets out a heavy breath of frustration. "King Paulus is smarter then that. If he wanted to get at Morrick, why not take Clive or Luna? Morrick does not even know her."

"Maybe Paulus knows something we don't," Legis says, but doubt clouds his voice.

What are they talking about? The creature mentioned this King Paulus. My stomach growls, reminding me it has been nearly a day since I have eaten anything. I leave the tent.

Legis is turning a rabbit over the fire, and he looks up at me. "Good morning." I'm surprised he has spoken to me after last night's events.

"Legis." I sit on the log across from him. Tristan gets up and leaves without a word. So he's still angry. Legis focuses on the rabbit. When he feels it's done, he takes it off the stick that has been pierced through its body and starts cutting it up with a small dagger. He places three large leaves—they look like dock leaves, the ones you use when you get stung by nettles—on the log beside him and equally divides the rabbit meat between the three of us.

He hands a leaf across to me. "Thank you, Legis." I raise my tied hands since he obviously missed that small detail. "Could you untie me?"

"You will have to wait for Tristan to come back." Legis doesn't meet my eye; instead, he starts eating his own.

"I haven't eaten anything in two days. Untie me, please."

His face darkens. "If I were you I would stay quiet." So he hadn't forgotten last night after all.

Tristan returns from wherever he was a half an hour later. All of Legis's food is gone and mine is cold at this stage. Tristan looks at the two leaves on the log and then at Legis. He kneels down in front of me with a small dagger. "If you try to escape, I will tie your hands and legs every day. Understand?" When he looks up at me with his green eyes, my breath catches in my throat. This close, I can see flecks of gold around his iris. Also, a few days' growth of stubble has started to appear, giving him a rugged look.

His eyes search my face. "Do you understand?"

A blush creeps into my cheeks. *How long was I staring at him?* I drop my gaze and lift my up my hands. "Yes, I understand." He cuts the rope. Rubbing my raw, red wrists gives me some relief. Tristan hands me my leaf of rabbit meat. I take it and start eating immediately.

"I never heard you in the desert." I was more thinking out loud. It was something that had bothered me—two horses coming through the desert, yet they were silent.

"You were ready to collapse when we found you," Legis says, causing me to look at him.

"Yeah, I was." But I should have heard them.

Legis turns to Tristan with a look of surprise and curiosity on his face.

Chapter Eight
SARAJANE -SASKIA

We set off on the horses again, until the sand under their hooves gives way to green grass. There is dew on the grass, giving it a frosty effect. The sun is high in the sky and there isn't as much as a small breeze now. Sweat has gathered all over my body. We push on through the green grass. My hands are still tied, so there isn't much of a chance to escape. If I had just waited until we were out of the desert, I might have gotten away.

"We are close to a spring, if you want to get washed before we arrive." Tristan's breath brushes my hair as he speaks, making me shiver. A wash sounds perfect, but I'm not taking a wash in front of Tristan and Legis.

"No, I'm Fine." I know I smell anything but fine. I smile, a little payback.

We rest after two hours of heavy travelling. The horses need water and a break. Tristan helps me off the horse and releases my hands while giving me another warning before giving me water. As if I could run with both of them watching me.

I sit down in the long grass. The sun hasn't dried off the dew. It soaks into my trousers, but what does it matter? I could be dead in a few hours. Trees spread evenly apart, letting enough sun in, yet offering shelter. The shape of the trees reminds me of hands spread out facing upwards. It's a little creepy that I haven't heard as much as a bird since I arrived in this world. I watch as Tristan rubs his horse down, whispering to her about what a great girl she is. He's better with the animals than humans. We arrive at a large cave. Its mouth looks daunting. This is where my life ends. Tristan helps me off the horse with a gentleness I haven't felt before. Could he sense the turmoil within me? Gazing into the depth of his eyes tells me he feels guilty about how afraid I look. *Why feel guilty?* I don't let these thoughts linger; they could end up being my downfall. To trust someone or even care for him would be a mistake.

I drop my gaze and take in my surroundings to distract my active mind. The area is barren. A few bushes rustle in a slight breeze that has started to blow, yet the sky is cloudless. *Is this the last time I'll see the sky?* Home has never felt so far away. Taking a deep breath, I try and steady myself and follow Tristan into the cave.

Inside, the cave is lit up with torches attached to the walls all the way down the long corridor. I keep on Tristan's heels until he makes a sharp left turn into a large room. A fire burns in the centre, outlined with rocks that are blackened from constant use. Other than the fire, the room is empty.

The sound of stone grinding makes me look away from the flames. My eyes don't adjust straight away, as sparks still dance in front of me. They're soon replaced with Tristan pushing in stones on the cave's wall. A click sounds; the part he was pressing on slides back, letting in a draft of air that makes the flames dance wildly along the cave walls. A tunnel all lit up with torches stretches out before me. I can't see what's at the end, as it curves to the right. Tristan waits patiently for me to step completely into the tunnel. My fear of small spaces has rendered me frozen in the secret doorway, but a gentle nudge from Legis pushes me on. I take another deep breath to steady my frantic heartbeat. I glance at Tristan to try and read his face for to expect, but it shows me nothing, perfectly blank. Legis joins us and the door slides shut with a thud that feels so final. Light from the torches gleams on the dagger that Tristan holds in his right hand as he approaches me. Panic rises. *Why kill me now?* I move back, but am held still by Legis. Now I am face to face with Tristan. I close my eyes and await my fate. The sound of rope hitting the stone floor and the free feeling in my wrists makes my eyes flash open. There's a glint of amusement in Tristan's eyes and then I'm faced with his broad back as he walks on down the tunnel. I follow as I rub my raw wrists. Every step makes me more nervous. Tristan steps through an archway into another large room. He steps aside and I'm faced with six people, but it's only one that makes my heart race. My mind isn't sure if what I am seeing is real. "Mum?" I whisper.

She holds me in her arms as I let my emotions free and cry. The smell of freshly cut grass and lavender encircles me, turning my cries into low sobs. She brushes my hair with her hand, relaxing my body. "I can't believe it's you," I say while taking in my mother's appearance. She looks the same, but there's a sadness wrapped around her, giving her appearance a grey shadow. I'm startled by my own analysis, but she kisses my forehead, wiping these thoughts away and replacing them with joy.

"Yes, it is me, love. Are you hungry?" She turns on mother mode. My mother takes me by the elbow and through the room that seems to serve as a sitting room and a kitchen. The floors are bare, just concrete, but they're swept and free of any dirt. Large red armchairs are positioned around a fire in a large circle; a couch lies behind them, covered in sheepskin. There are large paintings of what look like kings and queens, framed in gold. Red material is held onto the walls and draped down to the floor.

My mother leads me to a large table that could hold up to fourteen people. The chairs look heavy with tall backs and are covered in a royal blue lush fabric. I'm surprised when I sit to feel cushion under me. I was awaiting hard wood. I can see my reflection in the perfectly polished table. I look exactly how I feel—bewildered, confused and tired. Large dark circles have formed under my eyes; my hair looks like a crow's nest. A bowl of soup slides in front of me and I can no longer see myself, thankfully.

My mother hands me a spoon. "You are safe now. We will talk later, but first, eat and then we will get you cleaned up." I squeeze her hand just to make sure she's real. She watches me as I eat. Every time our eyes meet we smile at each other. The others are talking, but I don't strain to hear their conversation. I just focus on my mother. She introduces me to Alana, the maiden, after I eat my soup.

"I am Alana. I have a bath ready for you, my lady." Alana is beautiful with strawberry-blond straight hair and a full fringe that draws you to her eyes. They are a deep blue, but her left iris is circled in an unusual gold band. Her tall, slim figure would be suitable to the catwalk, and her pale complexion doesn't make her look ill, just flawless. I dislike her already. She smiles at me self-assuredly and escorts my mother and me to what Mum calls my sleeping chambers.

The furnishings and material are something you might expect to see in a castle. The first thing my eyes take in is a huge four-poster bed that dominates the room, covered in snow-white linen. A heavy chest rests at the foot of the bed. Alana removes a full-length, simple purple dress and lays it on the bed carefully. The floor has a royal blue carpet that my feet sink into. A large bronze bath is placed to the right of the bed and steam billows from the boiling water.

"Alana, could you help me?" my mother asks. Alana bustles across the room to where my mother is standing beside a large mirror. The mirror is framed in gold wide enough to reflect five people standing side by side. They push it farther down the room, revealing a fire that is already stacked with logs, and my mother lights it. There are no windows in the room; the only light comes from the torches along the walls placed about five feet apart.

After I gape at the room, my mother helps me remove my clothes. Her hands linger on my wrists and anger radiates from her. "Who did this?" She meets my eyes with the fierce stare of a mother frightened for her child.

"I tried to escape." I take off my tunic to avoid any more questions. She helps me with the rest of my clothes, her anger still covering her like oil poured on water.

The water is hot, but I lower myself slowly, letting my body adjust to the temperature. I close my eyes and try and relax. I can hear my mother gathering my dirty clothes.

"Why did they not just tell me you where here?" I ask.

She meets my gaze with sadness. "Would you have believed them?" She lets the question linger, but when I don't answer, she picks up my boots with her free hand and turns to Alana. "I will be back shortly." She smiles at me and closes the half-circle door as she leaves.

I sink farther into the bath. I wouldn't have believed Tristan, not in a million years, if he told me he was taking me to my mother. She knows me so well.

"My lady, I will wash your hair." Alana holds a jug and small bottles of what I presume is shampoo.

Feeling exposed in front of her causes colour to creep into my cheeks. My embarrassment turns to anger. "Don't call me my lady," I snap.

"Shall I call you princess?" Her voice holds a hint of laughter. She's making fun of me. My face reddens.

"No. Sarajane."

"Very well, Sarajane." She gives me a little curtsy, smartly. *What's with this girl?* Her hands move expertly across my scalp, massaging the shampoo into my hair. It smells like coconut.

Stepping out of the bath, I am then wrapped in a towel that covers me from my shoulders to my feet. Alana lets me face the mirror as she combs through my tangled hair. My mother returns. Between the two of them, they dress me and tug at me. The girl that looks back at me is a princess. I smile at her, causing her to smile back.

My mother meets my eyes in the mirror. "Purple suits you, love." She's right' it makes my grey eyes look more unusual and my tan sets the dress off nicely. The simple gold sandals on my feet are easy to walk in. It's a little bit of heaven.

When we return to the main room, it's empty and Alana serves us tea while we sit in the large armchairs beside the fire. I take a sip and it leaves a funny taste in my mouth.

"I don't know where to start," my mother admits.

"Mum, it's okay. You're alive. That's the most important thing. Dad and Jessica will be ecstatic." My mother's face grows more worried. This must be bad. We sit looking at each other for a few moments and finally she tells me, "This is my home." Not what I was expecting, but I try to keep my face neutral. "I was twenty-five and pregnant with you. At the time there were rumours of trouble brewing so I left and crossed over to the mortal world."

I don't respond. All I think of is that I'm from this world. That begins to sink in and then my mind is in overdrive with questions that I never get to voice. My face must relate my conflict. "Love, this is a lot to take in, so that's enough for now." I go to speak, but she gives me her *don't cross me* look. "It is all going to be fine. Now we will eat." Right on cue, Alana appears and starts stirring a large black pot that sits above the fire. It reminds me of a witch's cauldron. My mother sets the table for seven people. I stay in my armchair, lost in thought, trying to piece this together. I have so many questions. Three guards and a powerful-looking man arrive then. I scan their faces for Tristan and a pang of disappointment touches my chest when I don't see him. The powerful-looking man sits on the armchair that my mother vacated. I study him. He has black shoulder-length hair that frames a strong face and alert grey eyes . He wears all black—a simple plain tunic, black trousers and boots, but it doesn't take away the air of power about him. He reaches out his hand towards me. His fingers are long and look like he's never done a hard day's work in his life. "I am Morrick." I take his hand and am surprised by the callouses that push against my palm. "Sarajane." My mother is watching us from across the table. She smiles and then busies herself helping Alana serve the three men who are now seated at the table. I drop Morrick's hand realising I've been holding it far too long. He gestures to the table. "Shall we?" The food is great, a stew made with vegetables, some I recognise and some I don't. Morrick introduces me to the three men. "These are my guardians." Then he gestures to the one nearest to him and introduces him as Kiar. Kiar has blond hair to his ears and puppy dog brown eyes. There's softness in him. He's broad and tall, just like the next man I'm introduced to. His name is Liber. He doesn't smile, just nods. He has a plain face and expression. The last man is the odd one out. His name is Neve. He's thin and pale, with a shiny bald head and a crooked nose that looks like it was broken repeatedly. His expression is open and a wide smile greets me. I like him already.

We all eat after the introductions. Neve and Kiar are best friends since childhood and they tease each other playfully, making everyone laugh. Kiar seems to be the older of the two and the smarter one, as Neve is not the sharpest tool in the box.

"Neve, remember the time you were trying to impress Gem," Kiar says already laughing.

Neve grumbles, "Leave it out, Kiar."

But Kiar launches into the story. "He was trying to impress Gem with his fire affinity, saying it was a level three." I notice a stiffness has fallen around the table, but Kiar doesn't seem to pick up on it. "And he burnt all his hair and eyebrows off; none of it ever grew back."

I can't help but laugh at the mental image of Neve with his hair on fire, but no one else seems to find the story funny. "Mum, what's wrong?" I ask.

Her smile is strained. "Nothing, love." Everyone becomes very focused on their stew.

"What is a fire affinity level?" I ask Kiar. I've never heard of it before. Maybe it's a different way of explaining sticks on fire in this world.

My mother answers. "I don't want to overload you with information, but since Kiar mentioned it…" Kiar gives a sorry look. "We are all born with an affinity, which means we have the ability to control an element—fire, air, earth or water. And the level is how good you are. It's just one through three."

Wow, this is scary, yet amazing. "What do you mean by control? Do I have one?"

My mother looks relieved at my response. "Control isn't the right word, really. It's more like working with it, and you should have one."

This was all very hard to believe. "What can you do?" I ask her.

"My affinity is fire." She raises her hands. "I promise I will show you tomorrow, but for now you need to rest." Disappointment courses through me.

I'm ushered to my room. My mum tucks me into bed like I'm five. I don't mind her fussing over me. I fall asleep to her humming a haunting yet beautiful melody that could only belong to this world.

Chapter Nine
BELLONA

I am expecting Clive, Taurus and Felix back soon. I pace my room, waiting for their arrival. Excitement courses through my body. Soon I will have the girl in my grasp and then immortality will be mine. I examine my face in the mirror. Lines have started to show around my mouth and eyes. Ageing in not something I take in stride. Beauty is youthful. I grin at my own reflection.

"I will fix that for now."

Locking my chamber door and retrieving my pendant from its box, I kiss the purple stone, then let my breath linger on it, causing the stone to come to life. The purple stone starts to swirl as if a tornado has erupted inside. Bethany's soul swirls with the vortex, her face still frozen in horror. I place my lips around the stone and inhale deeply, feeling Bethany's soul coursing through my body, my blood, making me look and feel more youthful. I open my eyes and walk back to my mirror. Raising my head, I examine my face more carefully this time. Yes, I look younger—no lines just a flawless face. My sacrifices are paying off, but they only last so long and then I will show even more signs of ageing again. I smile. Soon I will not have to worry about that. A knock at my chamber doors pulls me away from my reflection. I open it and Taurus is standing there. "We have her, my lady." I pull the door open fully for Taurus to enter. "Where are Clive and Felix?" He gives me a wicked smile. "I told them to guard the girl while I debrief you." He reaches back and locks the door. I clip off the silver broaches on my shoulders that hold my dress up and let it fall to the ground. I can see by the hunger in Taurus's eyes that he is pleased. My breasts are firmer than before and my buttocks tighter. "Make your queen happy." Taurus crosses the room and lifts me off the ground with one strong arm while placing me on my bed.

He strips off his armour, black tunic and trousers. He is all muscle—a real man.

I dig my nails into his back until I draw blood and he gasps in pain. He likes rough sex, as do I. He bites my shoulder, pain shoots down my arm, and then he takes me. Giving me all of him, he thrashes hard, making my back arch. Afterwards, I dismiss him. "I will be down shortly. Have the girl ready for me."

"Yes, my lady." The sex is great, but the company boring. I sit at my dressing table and brush my hair out. It is almost white, but not with age. I was just born that way.

I leave my chambers and proceed to the holding cells. Clive is walking towards me. "Son." I kiss both his cheeks. "You have made your mother very happy."

Clive tilts his head back, hunger for approval in his eyes. "I only live to please, mother." I incline my head towards him and hold out my arm for him to take.

Taurus and Felix stand on either side of the gate while Clive remains by my side. The girl is tied in the centre of the room to a large wooden pole. She sits on the ground, her eyes alert, fear visible in them. Yet she just studies me as I study her. She has long, jet-black hair with a full fringe, large green eyes and full lips. She looks like Marta. This is the girl.

I move around her in a full circle, saying nothing. Images of my childhood flash in my mind, stopping me in my tracks. Then they're gone. I look at the girl. Sweat is trickling down her face as she concentrates. *Is she making me remember? Impossible.* My mother's face is there then, humming a song as I look up at her craving for attention. I close my eyes. "Stop it."

Taurus is beside me then. "My lady?"

I walk to the girl. "Stop it now."

"I don't know what you're talking about," she says while giving me a look that tells me she knows exactly what I am talking about.

"What are you?" I have never seen a gift like this.

The girl's face softens and she looks lost. "I don't know." She is telling the truth.

"What is your name?" The girl closes her eyes as if in meditation. Lucian's face flashes in front of me. The image widens. I can see myself and I look petrified. He throws me on the ground and the image ceases.

The girl's eyes shoot open. "What do you want with her?" Her voice is full of emotion as she pulls against her restraints.

Taurus moves to silence her rage, but I stop him. I am not sure if she can harm us. I look at Clive. "Make sure she is tied correctly I don't want her getting loose."

Clive sneers. "Yes, this little girl could harm us."

I give him a look of ice that silences him. "Check it now, Clive." I watch as Clive strolls towards the girl, smirking. He moves around the pole that she is tied to.

Kneeling down, his face stiffens with anger; then he looks at me. "She nearly has them off."

The girl's eyes are closed, her face relaxed. I am not too sure what she can do, so I take a small step back. Clive is struggling, trying to retie the knots, even though he tied them in the first place. I can see the girl stretch out her fingers, but before I can warn Clive, her fingers brush his. Clive howls back in pain, holding his side. We all jump. It is over after a moment. Clive is panting, staring at the girl with wide eyes. She is covered in a layer of sweat, her energy drained.

"Taurus, tie her."

Clive starts to protest, but I cut him off. "She has no power left; she is drained." Taurus reties the girl as instructed.

Clive gets off the floor. "You knew she would hurt me?" He questions with hurt in his voice.

"Don't be so petty, Clive. Is there a mark on you?" He lifts his top, examining his side that is untouched.

"Taurus, lift her top up."

The girl's eyes flutter open, the exhaustion visible on her face. "Please" she pleads. When Taurus lifts her top, I know exactly what I will see. Her swollen skin is black and blue with bruises.

The door leading down to the cell opens and Taurus leaves to see who it is. When he returns, his face is sombre "Sorry, my lady, but you have a guest waiting in your chambers."

I raise an eyebrow to invite Taurus to continue. He doesn't respond. It can only mean one thing, at last.

I leave and return to my chambers. "Ah, Liber"

He bows. "My lady."

"Sit." I gesture to the armchair beside the fireplace and sit across from him. "You are late."

"I know, my lady, but I was unable to leave," he says.

"Proceed."

"I was at the Amour Caves, guarding Marta."

My face twists with disgust. "I knew he took her." But I didn't need her now anyway.

"My lady, Tristan and Legis returned from the mortal world with the child, Sarajane," Liber says.

I rise abruptly. "That is not possible. Do not lie to me, Liber."

His face freezes in terror. "Never, my queen."

I go along with it, not sure what to believe just yet. "So tell me about her?"

He swallows. "She is unaware of this world or her magic, but she is indeed Marta's daughter. The resemblance is visible.

"Stay here, Liber. I will be back shortly." I leave and return to the cell.

The girl is still tied to the pole, her eyes closed. She must be still drained. I kick her awake. "What is your name? And don't push me, child, or you will live to regret it."

Her eyes drop closed. She is unable to keep them open, but her cracked lips open slightly as she gives me her name. "Jessica." It is barely audible, but it is enough.

"You fool, she is not the one."

Clive's face turns a crimson red. "She is, Mother."

I strike him with all my force across the face and he lands against the wall. Blood trickles from a cut at the corner of his mouth. "Do not lie to me," I roar. "Taurus, explain." I look at him from the corner of my eye; he is still standing beside Clive.

"Sorry, my lady, I have no excuse." He doesn't flinch away from me. I leave and return to my chambers. Liber is still sitting there. I start to pace the floor.

"My lady, she—"

"Hush, Liber. Leave." He bows and leaves. I don't need to hear his babble. I have too much to do. I am leaving for my secret chambers when a knock comes to the door and my daughter Luna enters.

"Darling, what a lovely surprise. But I am very busy." I try to keep the irritation out of my voice. I never know when she may come in handy.

"Mother, I will make it brief. Where is Father? I have not seen him around the castle." She blushes slightly. "It is just... I need to speak with him."

"He is gone on business and will be back shortly. Is that all?" I raise an eyebrow.

She curtsies "Yes, Mother. Sorry for disturbing you."

I enter my secret chambers from the winding stairs. Suis is asleep in her cage. I don't need her now, but she still might be of some use, and she helped Marta escape so punishment is all she deserves. I light all the torches, waking Suis.

"Bellona, please, I know nothing else." I know she doesn't; she told me everything.

"Hush, I am busy."

"Please."

I kick her cage, making her jump back. "Be quiet, child, or I will feed you to the demons."

Her eyes widen with fear, making me laugh. I spread a large piece of cloth in front of the altar and kneel down with the knife in my hand. A bowl of water sits at my knees. I start my incantation for calling Lucian.

The first time he came to me was an accident. I had called upon the demons, but Lucian showed up instead. I knew the moment I saw him that he was very powerful.

I slowly slice my left palm and watch as my blood falls from my open hand into the bowl of water, each drop causing the water to turn red. On the sixth drop, the hair rises on my neck. He is coming. He always scares me, but I hide it as best I can.

I place my hand in the bowl to quicken the healing of my palm. Lucian loves blood and I don't need to entice him.

"Bellona." A shiver of fear and pleasure runs through my body as he speaks my name.

I fall on my hands, bowing. "My king." His long black tendrils lash out and grab my wrists, pulling me up. When he retracts them, slime is all over my arms. Lucian laughs when he sees the distaste on my face. He is in spirit form tonight. Sometimes he takes human form and he is quite tasty to look at, but his eyes are always blood red. He reaches out and wraps his tendrils around my body, pulling himself towards me. His red eyes move closer. I can hear Suis whimper with fear in her cage. I don't blame her. Lucian is terrifying. He has shown me what he can do.

When he is beside me he flicks out a long black tongue that is pointed at the tip and runs it along my face, cutting me. He starts to lick the blood off my face. I try to stay as still as possible. When he is finished tasting my blood, I can see it trickle into his eyes. "So what news do you bring me, Bellona?"

I clear my throat. "My king, I know where the girl is. I will capture her soon and bring her to you."

"Soon. I do not like that word. You see, I have waited for centuries for this and yet you come to me with delays."

I look at Lucian, feeling afraid. "My king..."

"I need that girl, no matter what force you must take," he says.

"Yes, my king" I start to feel a bit braver. "Why, if I might boldly ask?"

"To ask is very bold of you, Bellona." He takes human form, shocking me at how quickly he changes. He grabs me by the throat and lifts me off my feet, cutting off the air from my lungs. My legs dangle in the air. I am going to black out. Lucian throws me on the ground. "Do not disappoint me again." I lie on the ground, gasping for air. He kneels down beside me. "I will not kill you, Bellona" I just look at him, still trying to catch my breath. "I will strip your flesh from your body and let you scream in agony. Just before you die, I will let your flesh knit back together and then I will start all over again. So you better do as you are told." I rasp "Yes, my king,". Lucian's head jerks towards Suis, who is wide-eyed with fear. "You brought me a gift. How thoughtful." She screams as Lucian disintegrates into a fog and floats through the bars of the cage. Once inside he takes human form. Suis screams again. Lucian laughs. "Scream for me, child. Scream." And then he tears into her flesh. I turn my head away as he rips out her throat. The sounds of him tearing her apart make me gag. I lie there until the noise is gone. When I look over at the cage, Lucian is no longer there, but Suis's organs are dripping from the cage bars. I vomit on the floor, my throat now raw. Once I make it back to my chambers, I wash and change my clothes while putting on my pendant. I notice my hands are shaking. I pour myself a goblet of wine and drink it in one gulp while trying to calm myself. I can't show signs of weakness.

I leave my chambers and find Taurus in the library. He rises when I enter "My lady."

"Sit, Taurus." He sits back down. "I need you to get Clive and bring him here. Also, make sure Felix keeps an eye on our guest." Taurus rises and inclines his head in acknowledgement. "Oh, I don't want her harmed."

"Yes, my lady." After he leaves, I have a few moments to sort through how best to deal with the situation. The girl will be heavily guarded. I need to flush her out.

"Mother, you asked for me?"

"Sit, son. There is something I need you to do in a week's time. I need you to go to the Amour Caves and scare Sarajane. Tell her you are her brother and Morrick is her father. Also tell her what her mother has done." Clive smiles. I can see the wheels turning in his head so I have to give him a reward. "You can hurt her." His grin spreads. "But don't kill her."

"Yes, Mother." Then his grin fades. "Why a week? Why not now?"

"Because it would look suspicious if you arrive when Liber leaves. We need to keep him. I will have Liber leave messages that will help you convince her that Morrick doesn't want her around. And then I will swoop in and be a forgiving queen and take her under my wing." Clive takes out his dagger a smile spreads on his face. "Clive." I give him a cold gaze that wipes the smile away. "If you kill her…"

"I won't, Mother." His smile reappears. "I will just have a little fun."

"You are dismissed, Clive."

He saunters to the door, still playing with his knife. "How do I get there?" he asks from the door.

"Don't worry. When the time comes I will show you." There are underground tunnels that connect the castle to the Amour Caves, in case the castle is ever ambushed again. Morrick was so stupid to bring her there. He knows I am well aware of the tunnels. I just hope he hasn't blocked them.

Chapter Ten

SARAJANE

The next morning, I change into travelling clothes. I overheard Morrick and my mother arguing last night. She wanted me and herself to go off and spend some time together away from here, but Morrick argued over our safety. He said leaving the confinement of the caves wasn't safe, as he could not protect us elsewhere. My mother won in the end.

I tuck my trousers into my boots as my room door opens. "You heard about this last night?" she asks as she examines my travel clothes with a hand on her hip.

"The caves carry sounds," I say while straightening my tunic and wrapping my cloak around my shoulders. "Ready?" I smile.

My mother is dressed the same as me—black pants, boots, white tunic and a black cloak. We both look like spies. "Ready," she replies, smiling back. As we pass the main room, Mum picks up a leather bag and we make our way out of the caves. The light outside is blinding. The air tastes like a fine wine. I drink it in deeply. I have only been in the caves one day, but in the small space it feels like it could have been days.

"So where to?" I ask.

"Take this and keep it in your boot." I raise my hands as my mother hands me a dagger. I can't carry a dagger around. More than likely I would end up hurting myself. "Sarajane, we can't go any farther unless you take it."

I take it hesitantly. It feels light as I weigh it in my hands. The blade is covered in a leather holder, the handle white pearl. I slide it into my boot; it feels uncomfortable against my ankle. My mother gets down on her knees in front of me and extracts the dagger. "In the side of all boots there is a holder for any dagger. It's aligned with your ankle." She slides the knife back in. It feels better, but I'm still aware it's in my boot. Maybe it takes time to get used to it.

We move at an easy pace, crossing the barren landscape that surrounds the mountains. Mum asks about Jessica and Dad.

How they were the last time I saw them, and about Jessica's school and Dad's work. For the next hour, the conversation feels easy and normal. I can hear the sound of gurgling water nearby.

"We will stop soon and have food," my mother says while linking her arm with mine. We settle near the stream, and I take off my boots and socks. I dangle my feet into the rushing water and let the sun wash over me. My mother settles beside me, handing me bread and cheese. My mother throws me a sideward glance as I eat. When I continue eating she laughs to herself.

"What?" I ask around a full mouth.

"I really thought you would plague me with questions."

I finish my bread and wash it down with water. "I have lot of questions, but I thought you could start at the beginning. Like how you ended up back here?"

Removing her own boots and socks, my mum dips her feet in the stream and relaxes her posture while closing her eyes. "When I left, I truly believed I would never see Saskia again. So I never told you of it." She gives a small laugh and glances towards me. "Would you have believed me if I told you this existed?"

"No. I guess seeing really is believing." My feet start to get cold so I pull them out and let them dry in the sun's rays.

"I was out walking Charlie when I was taken. I recognised Taurus, the queen's guard, and knew I wouldn't be able to escape. I thought I knew why they had come for me, but it turned out differently." My mother falls into silence, but I'm holding my breath.

"Why?" I whisper.

Her eyes are pleading, asking me to understand. A tear slides free down her cheek. "I can't lose you, Sarajane." The fear on her face makes me hug her.

"You will never lose me, Mum. I promise."

Kissing my forehead, she wipes her tears away. "In Saskia, we are matched with our husband or wives at the age of twenty-five. Until then, you can't take a lover."

I want to laugh, but don't. My mum's face is pale now. "That's ridiculous."

"It's our way, but I broke the rules, as I was already in love and pregnant with you." I feel sorry for her. "So they brought you back here because you fell in love before you were allowed to. And did you bring me here in case they tried to take me back also?" She swallows and meets my eye. "Yes" was her reply, but her eyes say no. I don't push her; she looks too distraught. I wonder who my father is. It doesn't matter. Soon we will go home, and in my eyes, John is my dad. Panic boils in my stomach. *John isn't my dad.* And then a calm washes over me. *Everything will be okay,* I tell myself, but thinking of John gives me a pang of homesickness. "When are we going home?" I ask. "Morrick is sorting out a few matters. It could take another two weeks." My eyes widen in alarm. "Two weeks?" I put on my socks and boots roughly. *Two more weeks.* "Sarajane, we don't have a choice." I exhale, my anger resides and a calm falls over me again. "Sorry, I-I just miss home." She embraces me. "Me too, love." When we gather everything up, we continue walking. "I want to show you something." We walk through long grass that brushes our knees. There are trees every fifty feet. It's not like a forest, as the trees are too spaced out. As the sun shines, it gives a golden light to our surroundings. It is beautiful. The colours are so bright and strong and there isn't a cloud in the sky. We start to climb uphill and when we reach the top, the view takes my breath away with the sheer beauty of it. No painting or picture could do it justice. There are loads of trees but they have thick brown trunks about the width of five men. They shoot up into the air at a magnificent height. All the leaves are snow white; they flutter to the ground, giving the illusion of falling snowflakes, yet the trees never go bare. Under the trees sit snow-white wolves. You would not notice them if not for their bright blue eyes.

"Will they harm us?"

My mum glances at me. She is in awe of what she sees too. "No. As long as you do not harm them." I have to laugh at the stupidity of attacking a wolf.

We walk down the hill and as we come to a slight bend, a spring comes into view, set into the side of a large red bank. Water is pouring from above and sparkles, crystal clear. I stand there and just admire it.

"I have never seen anything so beautiful," I say, mostly to myself.

"Our world is full of beauty. One day you will see it all."

We turn back to the wolves and make our way across the grass. As we get closer, the wolves became very alert. They all rise, their blue eyes fixated on me. It's a terrifying and amazing moment, to capture the attention of such creatures.

Mum seems taken aback also as she stops in her tracks. "I have never seen them behave this way."

"Maybe they know I'm a stranger?" It sounds like a weak excuse. Maybe they're hungry. The thought sends a chill down my spine. I start to get nervous, fiddling with my hands.

Mum notices and reassures me. "It is all right. I would not let anything happen to you."

We move slowly under the trees. Mum sits down, pulling me gently with her. The wolves are huge up close. Their coats look so soft and shiny. They all fall on their front legs as if in a bowing gesture and their eyes are all set on me. One by one, the wolves rise. It is the most unnerving moment of my life. They gather around me and one of the wolves reaches me and lies down, placing his head in my lap. I hold my breath.

"It is all right; you can touch him." Mum assures me, yet her face says something else. She looks confused. "I have never seen them like this. It makes no sense."

I reach out with a trembling hand and let my fingers sink into the wolf's fur. "Wow." He doesn't even move. I let out a sigh of relief. "This is amazing. I've never seen a wolf before, let alone touched one."

I look all around me. There are wolves under every tree, their blue eyes staring at us. This all feels so surreal. "Why do they sit under the trees?" I ask Mum.

"They protect them. The trees are known as weeping willows... The story goes that a man named Willow lived out here on the outskirts by himself. He didn't want to live amongst us. To the villagers, he was odd as he always had a pack of wolves with him. He was known to have a very powerful earth affinity. They say he created the spring you just saw by reshaping the landscape."

"Wow, that seems hard to believe."

"Willow was intrigued by the mortal world, but he felt very sorry for them, as their lifespans were so short, so he started planting trees in their memory." Mum moves her hand around us, motioning to all the trees. "So for every leaf that falls, a soul has passed from the mortal world, but the trees will never go bare, as mortals will always reproduce and exist. So when Willow died, they say he whispered into the wolves' souls and made them promise they would always guard his trees. They have never left the trees unguarded since Willow died. They are friendly as long as you mean them no harm, but they would kill in an instant if you posed a threat to them." I sit there thinking about Willow speaking to wolves, whispering into their souls. It all seems like something from a fairy tale, this world was so full of magic and beauty. "Why did Willow feel sorry for us?" I ask. "Because an average mortal lives between seventy and one hundred years." I roll my eyes and point at myself. "I know. I'm a mortal, but everyone dies, right?" Mum begins to look uncomfortable. "Yes, of course everybody dies, Sarajane, but you are just like us, part immortal." She rises abruptly, startling the wolf that looks up at her with sharp eyes but then just strolls away sensing no danger. "We must return."

I pat the wolf on my lap and say my good-byes before leaving. I follow Mum. She is walking very fast now, making it hard to keep up with her. "What's wrong? What did I say, Mum?"

She stops. "You are saying nothing. That's the problem. It... It's just not like you." She walks back to the caves. I don't understand what she means, yet a voice in the back of my mind tells me I understand her perfectly well.

By the time we arrive, it's getting dark. The main room is alive with laughter. Kiar, Neve and Alana lounge on the chairs.

When Alana notices us, she jumps to her feet. My mother stops her. "Stay, Alana. I am going to lie down for a while."

"Are you all right here?" she asks me.

"Yes, I'm fine."

Neve pipes up. "I will mind her." He winks at me playfully. I roll my eyes.

Kiar and Neve become my friends over the next couple of days. My mother is never around, always off with Morrick. Tristan and Legis are off on a secret mission nobody will tell me about, and Alana avoids me like the plague. When she's around, she's just plain nasty.

I explore the caves with Neve and Kiar whenever we are left alone, which seems like always lately. The cave tunnels are a maze and I would get lost if I were on my own.

One of the days, I ask Neve about his fire affinity. "Could you show me?" Neve and Kiar exchange looks and both of them answer in unison with a big grinning yes. We find a small room and place our torches in holders on the walls. Neve takes centre stage and tells Kiar and me to stand back, which deserves an eye roll. Neve and drama go hand in hand.

"Welcome, all."

The annoyed look on our faces makes him less dramatic. "Fine. Fine. Okay." He holds out his hand, palm up, and spreads his fingers. "*Lux*," he says. A small ball of fire hovers above his hand. I stumble back in astonishment. Kiar steadies me. Neve is delighted with himself. "I can't believe I did it on the first go."

Kiar answers my confused look. "He is not very powerful with fire. Air is his main affinity."

"I can be good with fire. Watch," Neve says, self-assured.

"Neve, don't," Kiar warns. But it is too late. The room becomes engulfed with flames. The flames cling to the walls and ceiling, sweeping through the room.

Just before it hits us, Kiar grabs my hand and pulls me into his chest. "*Aeirus*," he roars, and then the heat is gone. I stand out of Kiar's arms but still hold his hand. We are in an air bubble. I can see Neve in his own bubble of air, but sweat soaks his clothes.

"He is hurt," Kiar says while pushing our air bubble through the flames as we make our way towards Neve.

The fire is circling around the room. It reminds me of our log fire at home. Dad would have it roaring on cold winter nights. The doors of the fireplace have glass so you can see inside . The flames cling to the roof of the log fire, but that's because no air can get to it. When Dad opens a little vent, the air rushes in, and the flames return to normal.

"Why are the flames not leaving the room?" I ask Kiar as we continue to make our way over to Neve.

"Because Neve called it here." Kiar is sweating by the time he reaches Neve and engulfs him in our bubble. Neve collapses to the ground; his hands are badly burnt. I drop to my knees. "Neve, can you hear me?" No reply. I check for a heartbeat. It flutters under my fingertips. He is unconscious. "We need to get help, Kiar," I shout up at him, starting to panic.

"Hold my hand and try to help me." I start to feel frantic. "Help you how, Kiar? Shall I fly us out of here?" My voice has reached a hysterical pitch, making me sound unrecognisable. Kiar is panting now. "Neve is the one with the strong air affinity, not me. "So please just take my hand." He is as frightened as I am. I grab his hand. "Close your eyes and picture our bubble expanding into the room until all the flames are out." Kiar's hand is slick with sweat. I try so hard, but when I open my eyes our bubble is getting smaller. Kiar collapses to his knees. "I can't hold it much longer." The strain is visible on his face. I pull Neve's heavy body closer with a serious amount of effort and it drains all my energy. I have to lie down as the bubble is caving in, making it hard to breath. *Oh God, we're going to die,* I think. Kiar's breath is becoming shallow and Neve is still unconscious. "Kiar... do... something." My own breath is hard to catch. The air is so hot now. Kiar lies beside me, still trying to hold the air around us, but it is starting to shimmer. Dots appear in front of my eyes. The heat is intense. My own body is covered in sweat. I lick my dry lips. *Water, sweet water,* I think.

Cracking noise erupts above us. I look at the ceiling and can see small cracks appearing. A drop of water trickles from the first crack. *Am I seeing what I want to see, or is this real?* Then more cracks start to appear, getting wider; water starts to sprinkle from the cracks, dousing the roaring fire slightly. Then I hear a thunderous crack just before a part of the roof collapses. I grab Kiar's hand as a wave of water pours out, rushing towards us. The impact bursts our tiny bubble and sweeps us against the wall. My back bashes against the wall, taking my breath away and filling my lungs with water. I am too weak to react. Darkness sweeps in.I wake to Kiar screaming at me. He rolls me on my side and I painfully cough up water. My back is in agony. We are still sitting in water, but it's reduced to small puddles. Kiar shakes Neve awake. I sit up carefully. My eyes fall on Morrick standing in the entryway. Neve grunts with pain from his hands as he examines them, but when his eyes fall on Morrick, he turns as white as a ghost. None of us move.

"What the hell happened here?" Morrick's anger at this moment reminds me of Tristan's. Deadly. I don't want Neve or Kiar to get into trouble. This was my idea, after all.

"The roof collapsed," I say while standing on wobbly legs. "We are lucky to be alive." My voice quivers, not with fear, but the cold. Morrick doesn't reply.

"Get up and go back to the main room," he says to Neve and Kiar. As Neve passes, Morrick touches his shoulder. "Get your hands looked at."

Neve's face pales even further. "Yes, sir."

Damn, I forgot about his hands. How too explain that one away?

Morrick doesn't seem interested in further explanation. He turns and leaves, calling back to me over his shoulder. "Come on, Sarajane."

I follow him back to the main room. My mother is rubbing ointment into Neve's burnt hands. When I arrive, she throws me a worried glance. "Are you all right?"

"Yes. Fine. Just need to change." I lie and make my way to my room. I can hear my mother telling Alana to help me. The last thing I need or want is her help. Slamming the door of my room, I hope Alana gets the message that she isn't welcome, but it doesn't stop her.

"So did you have fun?" Her words are laced with mockery.

I ignore her and start to remove my tunic. The ache in back is torture. Alana goes to throw me another smart comment, but the sight of my back silences her. Turning to the mirror, I glance over my shoulder. My back is a mass of colours. It looks like someone has splattered colourful paint all over an easel. *Jesus, it looks bad.*

Alana starts filling the bath quietly as I examine myself. "The bath will ease the pain and the lavender will relax you." I have to look at her twice, but she seems genuine.

She is right. The lavender soothes me.

Chapter Eleven
SARAJANE

Morrick keeps Neve and Kiar busy for the next two days so I never get to talk to them. My back is healing really fast. I wonder what Alana really put in my bath. I never ask, as she is back to being her usual obnoxious self. My mother has become distant and whispered conversations cease when I am close by.

Today it is only Alana and me left with Liber guarding us. "I'm going to my room," I announce. Alana continues her cleaning and Liber just nods.

The door across from my room is left slightly open. Normally this door is locked. On days of exploring I tried this door, but it was always locked. It's a study filled with really old books and scrolls. A writing desk is tucked away in the corner. After retrieving a torch from the hall, I place it in its holder, giving light to the room. A sheet of paper is lying on the desk. Two small stones keep it in place. I walk closer to take a look. My name is circled at the top of the page. I read down farther. The handwriting is squiggly and hard to understand, but I can make out some of it.

Shows signs of water affinity, level three. But uncontrollable.
Beside this is a list of five elements:
Air
Earth
Water
Fire
Spirit

Water is ticked off. Then it continues on to say, *She is not aware of her path yet, but in time, her destiny will be revealed to her.*

I look over my shoulder and listen carefully to make sure no one is coming. When satisfied, I continue to read. The handwriting changes. It's easier to read now, but more disturbing.

Experiment 1

Calm was influenced upon day three, five drops in tea. Successful.

I clutch the page, pushing the stones aside. I knew the tea tasted funny. The day my mother and I went for the walk, I knew my emotions felt suppressed. My mother was right; something was wrong, and now I knew Morrick was drugging me. For how long? And why?

"What are you doing?" I jump and let out a screech. Liber looks at me, full of suspicion.

"I was looking at the books." I hide the paper behind my back and lower it back onto the desk.

"You're not allowed in here."

I swallow. "Oh, I'll just go to my room now."

Liber stands in the doorway, but after a few nerve-wracking moments, he lets me pass. Sweat runs down the back of my neck. *Experiment.* The word sends a chill through me. I want to confront Morrick, but I know I'm better off just keeping an eye on my food and drinks. Morrick is our way home, and what if he denies it? Did my mother know? I bet Alana was involved. She's always organising my baths. Oh God, she's made the tea for us every night I've been here.

I refuse dinner that night and go to my room, complaining of a headache. I can't meet anyone's eyes without wanting to confront them. My mother says good night and offers me a hot cup of tea. I reject it. "I'll be fine in the morning, Mum."

She looks at me, worried. "Okay. I love you."

Guilt wells up in my heart. " I love you too," I say from under the covers. The door clicks closed and I'm alone.

Sleep comes and goes. The room is pitch black when I get up. My stomach rumbles from hunger. I make my way to the main room. Torches are still lit in the hall and main room. No one is in sight. I find some bread and cheese and sit down in one of the armchairs beside the smouldering fire and begin nibbling on it. My stomach stops grumbling when I finish everything.

"You must be Sarajane." I jump up off the chair, startled, and am faced with a young man. He has blond hair slicked back and a hard white face. He is handsome in an unusual way. He wears black clothes, but his robe is snow white, trimmed in gold with a high collar. The material looks like fur.

"Who are you?" My question makes his grey eyes squint.

"Prince Clive. Has my father, I mean our father, not mentioned me?"

I sit down on the arm of the chair. *I have a brother?* I can only shake my head. His eyes are the same as mine.

"Oh, I am very surprised." He looks anything but surprised.

"You're my brother?" I still can't believe this. Why did Mum not tell me?

He holds up one long finger and grins like the Cheshire Cat. "Half brother. You see, my mother is the queen and your mother is a servant." His face twists with disgust. "You are the result of a foolish king."

My heart breaks a little and then too much makes sense—the protection we are getting, the luxury of the caves. "Morrick," I whisper.

Clive laughs cruelly "They never told you? Well, they are very good at hiding things." I feel lightheaded and stupid. How could I not have seen this? "I am so sorry," I say without looking at Clive, and I mean it, but this seems to anger him. Before I know what's happening, Clive grabs me by my hair, throwing me onto the rocky ground, taking the skin off my knees and palms. The impact vibrates through my body and a squeal leaves my throat. I look up at Clive in horror as he takes out his sword

"You will be sorry." His blade strikes my arm, sending a searing pain though it. Blood starts to run down to my fingertips, trickling onto the ground. I get up off my knees and make a dash for the door, but he grabs me by the hair and drags me right back, until I'm on the ground again. When I look up at him this time, the hate on his face brings tears to my eyes.

"Why?" I ask as he raises his sword and swings it behind his back. It whooshes towards my neck. An arrow whizzes across the room in a blur and impacts with Clive's wrist. He drops the blade just inches before killing me. I follow the direction that the arrow came from and my breath catches in my throat. Tristan is lowering his bow, his cold eyes fixated on Clive.

Clive holds his wrist, screaming in pain, which soon turns to anger. He raises his other hand "*Lux*," he roars at me and a ball of fire comes rushing towards my face. I raise my hands to fight it off. I can hear the whiz of another arrow. My head swings in the direction of Tristan as he raises his hands, blocking the fire with a solid wall of air. The air engulfs the fire, extinguishing it.

Gurgling noises bring my attention back to Clive. An arrow is embedded in his neck. Blood gushes through his fingers as he tries to cover the wound. Another figure catches my eye. Morrick lowers his bow. Clive staggers, turning around. His face is one of disbelief and horror as he looks into his father's eyes, and then he collapses on the ground, blood pooling around him.

My stomach gives way. Placing my hand over my mouth doesn't stop the sick. I throw up;but it is just bile, as I have not eaten. My hand is covered in puke. No one speaks. I'm frozen with the horror of what just happened.

My mother, Neve, Kiar, Liber and Alana come into the room and halt when they take in the scene before them. My mother races to me, landing in the pool of Clive's blood. On her knees, she reaches for me. "Sarajane."

"Don't touch me." I push her away. "Don't come near me," I scream. Tears stream down my face. Morrick helps my mother off her knees. "You are a monster," I roar at Morrick.

"I just saved your life," he throws back through thin lips. I can't believe nobody is saying anything about Clive's dead body.

"You killed your own son." My words are cut off with sobs. I look at my mother as I stand on quivering legs. "This is your fault, taking another woman's husband." My temper flares. "You are disgusting."

Morrick's hand strikes my face, landing me on the ground again. No one has ever put their hands on me before. Fresh tears prickle my eyes, and no one seems to breathe. Strong arms wrap around my waist and lift me off the ground. I look up at Tristan, but he's staring at Morrick with a clenched jaw.

"The next time you do that, I will not stand by and do nothing, my lord." He looks so defiant.

Anger and humiliation cross Morrick's face.

I don't look at anyone as Tristan carries me from the room. He puts me down when we get to my room and helps me to my bed. I sit on the edge and sob. Tristan kneels down in front of me with a basin and cloth. He doesn't speak, just brushes my hair off my swollen cheek with a gentleness I would have never known he possessed.

My body goes rigid at his touch. He takes my stiffness for fear. "I will not hurt you." He dips the cloth into the water and squeezes it, releasing it of its contents before pressing the ice-cold cloth to my face. I flinch with pain. But he keeps it pressed against my cheek. Taking my hand, he places it over the cloth. "Keep that held to your face." After retrieving warm water and another cloth, he checks my arm. "

Is it bad?" I ask.

"No, only a flesh wound. You will be fine." After that he cleans my knees of ripped skin and blood. After inspecting my palms and putting a fresh cold cloth on my face, he tidies up.

"They drugged me," I whisper. When I meet Tristan's gaze, it is stone.

"King Morrick is the finest king we have ever had. Drugging you would be pettiness that is beneath him. Do you understand?" His words are ice.

"Get out now." I rise and point at my door. I don't know why I expected him to believe me.

Tristan doesn't move a muscle. "Sit down, Sarajane," he says as he moves towards me. I hold his fierce gaze for a moment. My stomach gives a little flip at his closeness, causing me to look away and sit down. "Morrick is your father."

I can't listen to this. "Stop. He drugged me." Tristan throws me a warning glare. "I have proof. In his study, I found a paper. He was writing it all down."

Tristan's fingers sink into my shoulders. "You broke into the king's study?"

I push him away, sick of being manhandled. "No, the door was open."

Tristan shakes his head and turns to the door. "Get some rest." And then he is gone.

I sit there dumbfounded for a while after he leaves. Lying on my bed, I cry myself to sleep. I only get about an hour's sleep; the commotion in the cave wakes me up. I get dressed in my travelling clothes, leaving my hair down. I hope it will conceal my swollen and bruised cheek. I take a deep breath before leaving the room. I need to be strong.

The main room is a bustle of activity. Neve is gathering supplies from the kitchen area. I look around the room, my eyes falling on the spot where Clive laid in a pool of his own blood. There wasn't a trace of last night's events. Everything is cleaned up, but I can still smell blood and vomit.

"What's happening?" I ask Neve. The sound of my voice makes the bustle in the room stop. "Everyone leave," Morrick orders. "Not you," he says while looking at me. I hold my head high to hide any signs of fear. Nobody seems to move. "That is an order." The room clears. My mother lingers as she walks past me, but I don't acknowledge her. I just stare straight ahead at Morrick, and then we are alone.

"Sit down, Sarajane," he says as he takes a seat.

"I prefer to stand." At least if anything happens, I can run. The feel of the dagger in my boot gives me some comfort, not that I know how to use it.

"I was trained as a guardian from the age of five in hopes that one day I would be king. Our training was harsh compared to now. The king at the time was into dark magic, always seeking more power. He brought darkness upon our lands. So many died of starvation or the plague. King Paulus held public hangings every week against people that had not committed crimes, but no one dared to question him or they might find themselves with a noose around their own necks." Morrick's face takes on a faraway look. "Nierra was head guardian at the time and he was to step up as king. Bellona loved him. She was still a princess, but soon she would be queen." Morrick's eyes are full of grief. "Nierra was my closest friend; he was a brother to me."

He takes a deep breath. "When it became King Paulus's time to step down, he wouldn't. Power, he ached for it. So he murdered Nierra, leaving his own daughter heartbroken. Bellona shut down after that and coldness crept into her soul. I became next in line to be king, so I knew Paulus would kill me or I must kill him first." Morrick rises and pours red wine into a goblet. He drinks it down in one quick gulp. He keeps his back to me while still holding the goblet. "We rebelled. In all the commotion, King Paulus got away, never to be seen again. But now rumours of him gathering an army have surfaced."

Morrick turns to me then. "I never loved Bellona. She wasn't capable of love, and she was rightfully my best friend's. I need you to know you were conceived from love. I truly love your mother."

Relief swells in my chest. I hadn't realised I was more upset about finding out I was born from an affair more than I had a different father. But I don't believe I could ever look at this man as my father. Not now anyway with my cheek swollen and bruised. The throbbing reminds me of what he did. We stand in silence. Maybe he's waiting for me to say something.

"Sir, the horses are ready," Legis says from the exit.

This takes Morrick out of his daze. "Thank you, Legis."

"We have to leave. Bellona is aware we are here and when Clive doesn't return, she will come," Morrick says to me in monotone.

"Where are we going?"

"Aquaterra. I have loyal friends there who will protect us."

"Protect us from the queen, Morrick?" She couldn't be that strong. Morrick is the king.

Morrick laughs drily. "The queen, King Paulus and an army of exiles, which I believe you have already encountered."

I shiver at the memory. "What are they?"

"Criminals who have been banished to the mountains for their crimes."

Disbelief ripples through me. "You're saying they once were human-looking?"

"That's exactly what I am saying."

Chapter Twelve
SARAJANE

Legis has the horses saddled and waiting when we all come out of the cave. Morrick informs Tristan that I will be travelling with him. Tristan pulls me up roughly behind him, and I am faced with his back, a wall of steel.

"There was no paper in the study," he whispers to me as we wait for everyone else. I saw it, read it and held it; someone must have destroyed the paper, But who? And why?"

"I made it all up," I say to Tristan's back.

He swings around, his eyes ablaze with anger. "You made it up?"

"No. But you think I did so what's the point in explaining myself when you've already made up your mind?"

His anger subsides. "I don't know what to make of you, Sarajane."

I flush. He is staring at me intently. His breath caresses my cheek. My skin feels too exposed. And then I'm faced with his back again. I let out the heavy breath I wasn't aware I was holding.

Mum doubles up with Legis and Alana with Liber. Kiar and Neve ride alone. Neve's hands are bandaged, but he doesn't seem to struggle holding the reins. We are moving slowly over the rocky area.

Neve rides up beside Tristan and me and gives me a mischievous smile. "How's your back?" he asks.

"Still stiff, but I'll survive." I glance at his hands. "Your hands?"

"Sore, but I'll survive." A big grin spreads across his face, making his nose look more crooked than usual. I can't help but laugh.

"You're a bad influence, Neve."

He tries to hide his smile. "It was your idea."

"No, Neve, it was your bright idea to show off," Kiar says, riding close to us.

Neve looks embarrassed. "Things go wrong, even with the best of us," he says, causing Kiar to laugh.

"Yes, I have heard of people with level three fire affinities sending rooms up in flames, nearly killing people." Neve's face is bright red. Kiar loves teasing him, but the reality of what could of happened plays on my mind.

"If you ladies are finished talking, we are going through the mountains soon. So try and be alert." Tristan's voice is like ice.

I roll my eyes at Neve, but his face is serious. "Yes, sir." He falls behind us with Kiar. I want to punch Tristan for ruining the only good thing I have in this godforsaken place.

Moving through the mountains is painfully slow. Everyone is on edge. When the creature attacked me in the desert, I remember Tristan saying he was a long way from the mountains, so this is where they must live. I tighten my grip on Tristan and he tenses but relaxes after a few moments. Darkness rolls in along with a cutting wind. I hang onto Tristan closer, soaking up his body heat.

"We will reach camp in one hour." Tristan's voice is low, but it carries along the wind. My teeth are chattering from the cold.

"O… k… aay," I reply through numb lips. The horse under us starts to get uneasy; it slows down suddenly. Neve's horse rears up behind us.

Morrick's booming voice renders me frozen with fear. "Exiles."

Tristan jumps off the frantic horse, leaving me with nothing to hold on to. The horse rears back and I try to grab its mane, but my fingers slip through and I go tumbling to the ground. Tristan grabs me just before I hit the ground. "Stay behind me." He pushes me back with his hand while withdrawing his sword and getting into a battle stance. My eyes shoot over and back, looking for the exiles. "Move in closer," Morrick calls to us from his horse. My mother and Alana are behind Liber and Legis. Neve and Kiar stay close to Tristan and me. I crouch down, removing my dagger from my boot, not that I know how to use it, but maybe I'll get lucky.

Everybody's breath is forming white clouds in the cold air. The horses have started to settle down. "Maybe they were just passing," Legis says up to Morrick. But we all move in closer.

My hands become slick with sweat, contradicting the bitter cold night. I rub my hands on my trousers to dry them.

An ear-piercing screech breaks the night's silence and then they charge. Running at full speed down the side of the mountain towards us. The first one to reach us literally runs into Tristan's awaiting hand where his neck is snapped. I crouch down, feeling sick, all I can hear every few seconds is their dying screeches, but they keep coming.

Kiar roars in pain beside me. One of the exiles is hanging on to his leg by its teeth. I run over against Tristan's protests and dig my dagger into its eye. The exile immediately lets go, squealing.

"Thank you," Kiar says, looking green.

Another one races for me. I have no dagger now. I back up and hit the stone wall of the mountainside. I can see all the exile's teeth; its mouth is wide open, ready to bite. He freezes an inch from my face and crumbles to the ground, an arrow sticking out of the back of its head. My eyes meet Morrick's. He just nods and continues to fire his bow. Neve fights two exiles as I help Kiar against the mountainside. Legis, Liber, Neve and Tristan tighten in front of us, while Kiar, my mum, Alana and I stay behind them. Morrick flanks to our right, firing arrows from his horse. There are too many; they will tire us out soon.

"Kiar, give me your sword," Alana says in a stern voice.

Kiar laughs through his pain. "You're a girl, not a warrior."

"Don't say I didn't ask nicely." Before Kiar can respond, Alana punches him in the face, knocking him out. She kicks his sword off the ground into the air and grabs it. If that were me, I would have lost all my fingers. She gives me a grin. "I will have to help protect you, princess." She pushes her way between Neve and Tristan and fights.

Neve is knocked off a bit by the sight of Alana fighting, but he recovers quickly. Tristan gives no reaction. Typical. I have a newfound respect for Alana. She is a quick and graceful fighter; she moves easily as if she knows their steps before they even attack. I watch as she and Tristan share a knowing look. Jealousy boils my blood. She is beautiful, sharp and can protect herself. I go right back to hating her.

I check on Kiar's leg; it is bleeding pretty bad. "Mum." She comes to assist me, pulling off Kiar's belt from around his waist, which holds five fighting knifes. He was really expecting trouble. She tightens the belt around his leg just above the bite to slow down the bleeding. Taking off her own cloak, she presses it against the wound. A chunk is missing from his leg, displaying shredded tissue. My stomach coils, but I manage to keep it down.

The fighting dwindles. Tristan and Alana finish off the final few. "You have quite a talent, Alana," Morrick says with pride in his voice.

Alana blushes, something I didn't think she was capable of. "Thank you, King Morrick." She bows her head.

"Saddle back up. We need to leave before more return," Morrick says while turning his horse. Tristan helps get Kiar up on Neve's horse. Since Neve's horse is vacant, I jump up on it awkwardly. I took riding lessons when I was younger so hopefully I can still remember. Once I'm up, I feel proud Alana isn't the only one with a hidden talent. No one passes any comment; only Tristan barks orders at me to stay in front of him. Alana glances around at me. I give her a grin and she snaps her head back around.

Riding is more exhausting than I remember. My thighs burn in no time from holding my body to suit the rhythm of the horse. Moving through all the exiles' bodies is disgusting.

Once we pass through the mountains, we hit the desert at full speed. Light shines in the distance; a camp is set up with two fires burning and several tents. As we race closer, a man stands, waiting on us. The closer we get, the faster my heart pounds. I know this man. He was in my head, talking to Adora, or Linda. It feels like a lifetime ago.

"What's wrong?" Tristan asks from behind me. My posture must have stiffened. We are too close to camp for me to explain. Even if I wanted to, I wouldn't know were to start.

Morrick reaches Mirium first and embraces him.

"Nothing," I reply to Tristan just as we reach Mirium. I slow my horse down and get off as gracefully as possible, which isn't graceful at all. Mirium is greeting my mother when his eyes fall on me. He has pulled off the wise old wizard perfectly, with his long white hair and beard. He holds a staff in his left hand and a long royal blue cloak frames his body.

"Sarajane." He bows his head slightly to me.

"Mirium." I bow back.

My mother looks startled. "You know Mirium?"

I don't know why, but I lie. "No, I heard you use his name."

My mother gives a relieved smile. "Of course."

I don't return her smile; I'm still too angry with her. Tristan and Neve pass me, carrying Kiar to the closest tent. They greet Mirium as they pass.

"Come. Food is ready," Mirium says to the rest of us.

A young girl no older than sixteen hands us a bowl of stew and a roll of bread each. She smiles and gives everyone friendly greetings. When she reaches me, her eyes focus on the ground as she stretches out my food towards me. "Princess."

I take it, feeling confused at her behaviour. "Thanks." Her eyes shoot up and she just stares at me in awe and fear.

"Navada, please join us." Mirium pats a space beside him. Navada bows to me and scurries over to Mirium.

I eat every bit of my stew and bread roll. Once everyone is finished, they trickle off to their tents. Morrick, Mirium, Tristan, Neve and I are all that is left. Tristan and Neve dig into their own stew.

"What do you make of all of this, Sarajane?" Mirium asks, catching me off guard. My thoughts had returned to home.

"Sorry, of what?"

Morrick looks annoyed with my response. "Saskia."

"It is different from my world."

Morrick's jaw clenches. "This is your world. You are not mortal, Sarajane."

I shoot Morrick a glare. I knew I wasn't mortal. Mum explained to me the day at the willows that we are partial immortals; our lifespans are longer. But this isn't what I meant. "I'm more mortal than Saskian."

Mirium looks amused by all of this. "And what does it mean to be Saskian?" Mirium asked me with a glint in his eye. This all feels like a test and for some reason I really don't want to disappoint him. "Loyalty to this world is what makes one a Saskian." I truly believed this. Tristan's loyalty to his king never faltered, and Neve and Kiar's to Tristan. It all trickled down, and their loyalty was unshakable, all for their world. I had given the right answer by the way Mirium's eyes sparkled. "And what does it mean to be mortal?" This seems a much harder question, but one image surfaces. I know this could cause trouble from Morrick. "Mortals value a life." I know we have wars, but in everyday life, a life has a value, unlike the way Morrick struck down his son so easily. Mirium considers this. I don't look at Morrick, but I don't have to, as his anger radiates off him, making its way to me. "Sometimes it becomes necessary to take a life; it does not mean we value it any less"

"Well, I believe you should try and disarm someone before killing them." This time I do look at Morrick, who looks fit to kill me. Mirium touches his arm gently to calm him down, which seems to work.

"If someone valued their own life, they would not attack you. Therefore, we wouldn't have to kill them." I look at Tristan in astonishment by how passionate and sure he sounds.

"But why try and kill me in the first place?" I ask Tristan. This is something that bothers me. Clive would have more of a reason to kill me than just that I was his half-sister or maybe he was crazy. Tristan remains silent.

"Because, my child, you are the biggest threat that some Saskians will ever face and the greatest gift to the rest of us." Now I feel double confused by Mirium's words, but he isn't finished. "Some of us are willing to give up our lives to save yours."

"But I don't want anyone to do that. I never asked for that," I say.

"It is not about what we want in life. We do not choose our paths or our destiny; they are already chosen for us." This is all getting very mythical and a headache is starting to brew.

"And who chooses our paths? Because I would like a word with that person."

Mirium laughs genuinely. "And tell me, what would you say to this person?"

"That I do not want anyone to die for me. I have enough on my conscience already." Not completely true, but I don't know if I'll ever forgive myself for Clive. He was killed because of me by his own father.

"One day you may have the privilege of meeting our maker to ask your question."

No direct answer so I ask a direct question. "And what is this maker's name?"

Mirium smiles. "God, of course, my child."

Religion, a very shaky subject that I'm not going to get into. "I'm going to check on Kiar." I excuse myself.

"I will come with you," Neve says while walking beside me.

When we reach Kiar's tent, he's awake. His face breaks into a huge smile when Neve and I sit down on either side of his cot. His leg is freshly bandaged.

"How do you feel?" I ask while checking his temperature by placing my hand on his forehead. It feels normal to me.

Kiar beams up at me. "Better now that you are here, nurse." I laugh.

"Don't fuss over him; he only got a little bite," Neve says, shaking his head in pretend disgust. We laugh and joke for a while. Neve and Kiar insult each other playfully. I yawn. The day's occurrences start to set in on me. I kiss Kiar's cheek and bid him good night, promising I'll be back in the morning to check on him. Neve walks me to my tent that I share with Alana. *Great, just what I need.* She's awake when I enter. My dagger is placed on the pillow on my cot. "Did you?" I ask, picking up the dagger. "I found it and picked it up. I was going to throw it away. It's a sorry excuse for a dagger." She turns her back on me. "Thank you, Alana." She doesn't answer. She's pretending she doesn't care, but she does. The dagger is clean and it shines in the torchlight from being polished. "Maybe you could show me how to use it?" I ask. She turns around; her face shows no emotion. "Ladies do not fight." She is one to preach. "You do," I throw back. She huffs and sits up. "I am a servant; you are a princess. Do you not get it yet? My life is to serve you. I am no more than your ghost." Sadness fills her eyes. I shake my head. "No, Alana." She laughs bitterly. "Don't be so naïve. Open your beautiful eyes and take a good look around you. This is not an equal society like the world you came from. It's about your bloodline, and you're more important than the rest of us." Her voice rises in frustration. I look at her, lost for words. "You are a sorry excuse for a princess." She storms out of the tent. Tears sting my eyes. Her words hurt more than I ever could have expected possible.

That night, I think about all Alana said. I think she's really upset over having to be a servant, tidying up after me when she's such a gifted fighter.

The next morning, I go to Morrick's tent. He raises an eyebrow when I enter. He's seated on a rug with Mirium, enjoying a platter of fresh fruit.

"Ah, Sarajane, please sit," Morrick says.

I sit crossed-legged. I don't feel as confident now that I'm here, but I'm not going to be a sorry excuse for a princess anymore. "Morrick, what decisions do I have as a princess?" I hold my head high as I speak.

"It depends what it is." He pops a grape into his mouth.

"What about jobs for people?" I ask.

"I would listen to your opinion." I feel disappointment. My opinion; that is all. "Why the sudden interest?" I don't blame him for questioning me.

"I don't want Alana as my servant anymore."

Morrick looks aggravated now. "Sarajane, we have important things to discuss." In other words, I am dismissed.

"This is important to me. Alana isn't happy running around after me when she was born to fight." I hold up my hand so he will let me continue. "I think she's worth more than my personal slave. She's bright and strong, so I request you make her a guardian."

Morrick looks livid. "Don't be so silly. Never in our history has a woman been a guardian, and most certainly one with no affinity at all."

This was news to me. I hadn't realised Alana had no affinity. "I understand, but never in your history has a mortal become a princess." I hope I have my facts right to prove my point.

"That is different," Morrick barks.

"Have you ever considered her gift is fighting?" I ask.

Mirium studies me. "What would you propose, Sarajane? That we throw our rules aside on a whim?" He has a good point.

"No, but I would hope King Morrick would at least consider my proposal seriously. I'm not saying to change your rules. I just think when extraordinary people are discovered, then extraordinary exceptions should be made."

Morrick seems stunned for a moment. "You feel very passionate about this?"

"Yes."

"I will consider it," he says. I rise to leave. "Sarajane, as for now, Alana is yours personally. Understand that you can command her to do certain things within limitations."

I never thought of this. I smile at Morrick and Mirium. "Thank you."

I rush back to my tent to tell Alana the great news, but it's empty. I can hear striking swords behind the tents. Are we under attack? I creep around, keeping my head down. Tristan and Legis are practising. Sweat soaks both of their tunics. Tristan looks overly attractive. I stand there watching his every move until Legis notices me.

"Princess?"

Tristan's gaze falls upon me. I can feel a blush rise in my cheeks. "Have either of you seen Alana?"

"She is with Kiar," Tristan replies stiffly. He returns to fighting. *Is he jealous of Alana being with Kiar?* I won't let that sink in or ruin my news for Alana. I find her in Kiar's tent as Tristan said. They are laughing when I enter. Alana goes quiet when she sees me.

"Have you come to check on your patient?" Kiar asks, smiling.

"No, I've come to borrow your visitor." I look at Alana; she doesn't budge. "Please, it will only take a moment. Without looking at me, she stands.

"I will only be a minute," she tells a worried Kiar. I roll my eyes and smile at Kiar to let him know it is nothing serious. His face relaxes. *Does he like Alana?* That would be something to look in to.

As we enter our tent, Alana crosses her arms defensively. "What?" she asks with a tone.

"I spoke to Morrick—"

She cuts me off. "You ran to Daddy because I upset you." Her words are laced with sarcasm.

"No, I requested you were made a guardian."

This knocks Alana off completely "What did he say?" Her eyes are wide with astonishment.

"He will consider it."

Her face falls. "Oh."

"But you are mine to do as I command for the moment."

Her face turns into a snarl. "You are enjoying teasing me, princess."

"Alana, I want you to be my personal guard. No more picking up after me. You're better than that."

"Oh... I don't know what to say."

I have to laugh. "That's a first."

She smiles back at me shyly. "Thank you so much." I return her smile. "You're welcome, but it comes with terms." She sits on her cot, beaming. "Name them." I smile at her beaming face. "I always want you to be honest with me, no matter what. You will always be with me unless I say so." She gives me a curious look. "That's it?" I shake my head. "No, one more thing. Don't call me princess ever again." Her face breaks into a smile. "Deal." she stretches out her hand and I shake it. "Deal. Now I think Kiar needs you." She blushes slightly and goes to leave. I feel pretty good about myself. "Sarajane." I turn around to Alana. "Thank you." She hugs me and races out of the tent. Maybe we can be friends. I leave the tent. I don't want to be on my own—my mind only wonders to home—so I go to the fire. My mother is sitting there, showing Navada how to make soup. I still haven't spoken to her properly since Morrick hit me, but if I walk away now, it'll look like I'm hiding and that is something I won't be doing anymore. My mother looks up at me with a pleading look in her eyes and Navada just looks terrified. *Why is she afraid of me?*

"I am showing Navada how to make soup," my mother says while cutting up onions.

"I can see." I know she's trying to make small talk, but now that I think about all her lies, I'm just not in the mood for pretending. Thank God Liber, Neve, Mirium and Morrick join us.

"We are leaving in an hour. A good friend of mine is going to shelter us for a few days in Aquaterra."

My mother looks surprised. "Musa is allowing us to stay in Aquaterra? Has that ever been allowed before?"

"He understands the situation we are in and I am the king. But no, we are the first guests they will ever have," Morrick says.

"Why?" This sounded weird, a place nobody was allowed into. It sounded like a cult.

"Because they are a very old tribe that like to be left alone." Images of warriors living in small huts with different colour paints on their faces come to mind, but soon I will find out.

Our group of eleven sets off through the desert towards Aquaterra.

Chapter Thirteen
SARAJANE

From the distance I can get a clear picture of Aquaterra. It is surrounded from the west and south by water. The desert surrounds the rest of the landscape. Tall wooden walls that have been erected rise into the air for miles around the settlement. The smell of seawater is refreshing after the heat of the desert. A large portion of the wall starts to descend slowly like a drawbridge. They must have seen us coming.

As we get closer I notice small insets cut into the wall that have a slot cut out of them with enough space to fire an arrow or to see people approaching. When the drawbridge hits the sand, it sends a cloud racing towards us. I pull my hood up and around my mouth and half close my lids to shield them from the sand. As we cross the drawbridge, I look behind me as it rises. It is pulled by six enormous men on either side pulling a heavy steel chain that is encircled through hooks attached to the wall. Sweat laces their bodies from the tremendous weight of the bridge.

We move slower once we are safely in Aquaterra, but the settlement looks like little dots in the distance. As we get closer, the settlement starts to take shape and the array of bright colours is heaven to my eyes. Lime greens, cerise pinks, turquoise blues, yellows, oranges, reds. All the women and children are dressed in striking colours, and their laughter and chatter matches what they are wearing. The women all seem to be very petite with long brown hair and chocolate eyes, but the tribesmen are huge. They're enormously built; it is clear to see as they only seem to wear white, black or brown trousers and no tops. They all carry similar features to the women, the long dark hair and brown eyes. It is intimidating at first glance, but their smiling faces put me right back at ease.

We get off

the horses and bring them to the troughs where they gulp down water. My legs feel stiff after the long ride. I shake them out to loosen them up.

"Trying to fit in with the natives?" Kiar asks, smirking.

"Ha, ha, you're just hilarious."

"Yes, I think I am a pretty funny guy." I nudge him playfully. His big brown eyes and kind heart remind me of Josh so much my heart gives a little squeeze at the thought of him. I push it away, knowing it will drive me crazy. "Sarajane?" Kiar gives me a questioning look.

"I'm fine, before you ask."

I trail behind everyone else, taking in the settlement. The huts are built in a full circle with what looks like bamboo branches that frame the walls and roof. A pipe sticks out of the roof that releases smoke; wooden shutters are open in the huts like windows that let the light in. A large well is right in the middle where wooden buckets lay against it, not in use. It looks like everything is made from the same wood, giving it a magical appeal. The huts are all different sizes, some the size of a room, others as big as a house, and there are two at the beach's edge that are the size of three houses. Large towers stand on the beach a mile or two apart. They run the full stretch of the beach. I shield my eyes from the sun to take a look at the towers. A man is perched on the top, sitting with his legs crisscrossed. He looks like he's mediating. A roof covers his head, but there are no walls surrounding him.

"Sarajane." The group has moved on, but Kiar has waited for me.

"Sorry." I hurry along, catching up with the rest. The people have all stopped what they are doing and are staring at us. "This place is amazing," I say.

"I agree with you. It is not what I was expecting," Kiar responds.

A tall man with old features embraces Mirium like an old friend would. A smile that's genuine is spread across his face.

"Musa," Mirium says fondly while embracing him. This must be the tribe's leader.

Musa is dressed in a long white tunic to his knees and sandals cover his feet. There are tattoos covering both sides of his face. Small circles and lines cover the corner of his eyes. His eyes sweep over our group and pause on me briefly, but I'm hiding in the back.

"Greetings, friends of Mirium's are friends of mine. Your huts have been prepared." A lady walks beside Musa with a shy smile on her face. They must be related. Her face is designed just like his, except for the dots and lines around the eyes. "This is Ndee and she shall show you to your huts."

Ndee bows, still smiling. Everyone else is watching us as if we're from another planet. Well, I suppose I am. We break up as we are taken to our huts. I watch as Morrick, Mirium and Musa walk towards one of the large wooden structures farther out.

Ndee places one arm above the other at chest level and bows. "Princess." She is practically beaming. I can't muster up too much enthusiasm towards her, as I am starving and really want a bath and change of clothes.

I try to copy her bow. "Ndee."

Someone coughs behind me. I turn to Alana. "She only bows to you, Sarajane. Do you want me to stay with you?"

I ignore her comment about not to bow to Ndee. "Ndee, this is my personal guard, Alana." The two ladies acknowledged each other. "And you have the day off." I give her a smile and follow Ndee into the hut.

The walls are covered in a red-brown clay just like plaster, only it isn't smooth, but it adds character to the charming hut. All the furniture is made of bamboo wood, just like the hut. On the table sits a large pottery bowl that holds lots of fruit. Ndee opens a door I hadn't noticed. I follow her into the room. The bedroom holds a bed and a large wooden tub that has taps running too it.

"Is that running water?" I ask Ndee with excitement. "Yes, princess, and we have hot water," she says proudly. I turn the tap on, not sure what to expect, and water pours into the tub. I dip my finger under the water. It's warm.

Ndee joins me and looks a little embarrassed. "Sorry, the kilns have only been burning for the last hour. That's how we heat the water."

I hug her with pure joy and start stripping off my clothes as the bath fills up. "No, Ndee, this is heaven."

She scurries across the room and closes the wooden shutters as I climb into the bath. She lights several candles around the room.

"Candles?"

She smiles. "We make our own, princess. Maybe tomorrow you would like to see how they are made?"

I lie back in the water; every part of me relaxes. "That sounds great, Ndee."

As I soak, Ndee moves around the room, picking up my clothes, and then she leaves. I just lie there enjoying the peace and quiet. When I am wrinkly and the water is nearly cold, I begrudgingly step out and dry myself off with a really fluffy towel. I wrap it around my body and examine my bed. The frame is made of bamboo and the mattress could only be described as a beanbag. A large square one. I let my hand sink into it; it's really soft.

"That is animal skin stuffed with feathers," Ndee says, making me jump.

"Animal skin?"

She giggles. "Yes, but it is cleaned and stitched together and stuffed with feathers." Loads of coloured material is draped across her arm. She raises them slightly. "Your clothes, princess." Two other women enter then, making me wrap my towel tighter around my body. "This is Ola and Dene." I smile at the two happy women. "They will help get you dressed." I don't get to respond. They start evaluating and discussing what colour would best suit me.

The women giggle as they wrap me in their own custom dress. They decide on a lime green material that they wrap around my body, covering one shoulder and leaving the other bare. They comb my hair out and weave flowers into the cascade of curls.

All the ladies study me. My eyes seem unusual to them as they all have brown eyes, and my skin looks pale in comparison to theirs. When I'm complete, Ola and Dene bow and leave, leaving Ndee and me alone.

"The celebration will be soon, but first Musa requests your company." Ndee leads me through the settlement. There must be a few hundred people living here. A lot of the women are getting ready for the celebration. The excited chatter sounds everywhere. The tall towers along the beach catch my attention. Once again I glance up; there are still men sitting at the top of them.

"What are they doing?" I ask Ndee.

"They are controlling the waves so we don't get flooded and for the water mill that helps us generate electricity."

I look at Ndee in surprise. "Electricity?"

She gives me a proud smile. "Yes, but it is only used in the main buildings. Follow me." She continues towards one of the larger wooden structures. "You will see," she says as she opens the door.

The inside is very like my own hut, wooden floors, brown plaster on the walls, only on a much bigger scale. The room must be used for meetings, as a large table is placed in the centre. Its surface is covered in maps. I take a quick peek at the maps as I follow Ndee and can see they are of Saskia. It's a lot bigger than I initially thought.

When we reach the back of the room, large red curtains conceal another area where Musa is. The air in the room is filled with incense. I'm not entirely sure what I smell, but it's familiar. Musa is seated on a lavish rug on the ground. Material of all bright colours hangs from the ceiling and is pinned to the walls. The centrepiece in the ceiling is a light, electricity. Pottery is scattered around the small room.

Musa smiles when I enter. "Princess Sarajane, please sit."

I sit on a vacant rug across from him and Ndee leaves. "Musa, my room is lovely." I'm not entirely sure how to address him or what to say.

"I am glad you like it, princess." Musa is only wearing trousers. Well, they look more like white linen pyjama bottoms. His chest is bare and covered in tattoos and old scars crisscross his chest. There are so many the further I inspected them. "Saskia wasn't always this peaceful," Musa says. Then his eyebrows crease. "I hope we will see peace for a long time."

I feel embarrassed I made it so noticeable, staring at his scars. "Sorry, I didn't mean to gawk."

He gives a smile. "You were just curious and you have every right to be; this is your history also." Guilt wells up inside me. I don't belong here. I never fought for it. I don't have as much as a scratch, yet this man destroyed in scars feels as if I have as much right as him. "We are having the celebration tonight in honour of our guests, and as part of our tribe, we each receive a tattoo that brands us."

My first thought was my mother would kill me. Then I smile. I wasn't talking to her anyway. "Do I get to pick?"

Musa studies me for a moment. "No, but if you could, what would it be?"

"I don't know. I've never thought about it before," I answer honestly.

Musa rises, the smell of incense following him as he crosses the small room. The smell washes across my face, making me a little lightheaded. He sits back down with a large bowl half filled with water. "Water is a powerful affinity to behold by anyone and it can show us who we really are." Musa dips his finger in the centre and small circular waves push towards the edge.

"You can see yourself in a mirror. It is no different than water," I say. I spent plenty of time looking at my reflection as I sat by the river at home.

"A mirror shows you as you are seen, yet water can alter and change us."

I just nod, clueless about what he is trying to say. His smile tells me he knows I haven't a clue. He takes his finger out. "Take a look." I bend over reluctantly and am not shocked when I see my own face stare back at me. "Really look," Musa says.

I study myself, my curly hair woven with flowers, grey eyes, long eyelashes, pink lips, a round chin—the same way I always look. The smell of the incense still lingers around my nose and I have the urge to sneeze but can't. My reflection grows smaller and I can see my body. I'm wrapped in a white gown, a smile spread on my face as I pick flowers. I look so happy. I bring the flower to my nose and inhale a sharp breath. The smell of roses fills the air. I bend down to examine the flowers more closely and a small pair of white wings emerge from my back.

I knock the bowl over, the image gone, and look at Musa. "What are you burning?"

"Beeswax. What did you see?" Beeswax, that was the smell I couldn't place. I was hoping he would say something stronger so I could explain the image away.

"I had wings. Did I see the future?"

Musa retrieves a cloth and dabs up the water. "No, you only see yourself." He meets my eye then. "Your true self. So we now know what your marking will be."

I raise both eyebrows. "We do?"

"Yes, wings. They will be done during the celebration, which you are going to be late for if you don't hurry."

I rise on shaky legs and look down at Musa's scarred chest. "Are all the men dead that hurt you?"

Musa looks surprised "Yes, they are."

That makes me feel better. "Good." I leave through the large meeting room. All the maps are gone. I hadn't heard anyone come in.

Ndee is waiting for me just outside. "Food is ready," she says the moment she sees me.

"Good, I'm starving."

She leads me back to the heart of the settlement where a bonfire is ablaze, lighting the night sky. Drums are the choice of music and the beating is almost hypnotic. Tribe members have gathered around the fire, eating and chatting, while some dance around the flames. Several children stare and giggle as Ndee and I pass by. I don't mind all the smiling faces. It eases my heavy heart a bit.

Everyone greets me with "princess" and bows as I pass through. It's overwhelming. I feel like royalty. Then my conscience slips in. *You're no princess.* But I banish the thoughts and try and enjoy this night.

My breath catches when I see Alana. "Wow," I say.

She blushes. "Really?"

I grab her hand. "Really." They have pinned all her hair including her fringe up off her face, letting everyone see it.

"You are just like a princess now," Alana says in a warm voice.

Ndee ushers us on through the crowd as children weave in and out with excitement. Laughter fills the air and then I can't hear anything as my eyes fall upon Tristan, who is looking at me from across the fire. His brown hair is loose, falling to his shoulders. He wears no top, just plain black trousers. His bare chest is muscular and the sight of it sends emotions through me that I wasn't aware I felt for Tristan. A look of shock passes his face and then it's gone. Does my face portray my feelings? He looks away and then the noise comes rushing back, along with Alana's voice.

"Sarajane, are you all right?"

I look at her, feeling embarrassed. "Yeah, sorry."

"You looked far away." She tries to hide a growing grin.

I give her a dirty look and close in on the bonfire where food is being handed out. I fill a plate of meat mixed with herbs and salad and sit down beside the bonfire.

Alana joins me and nudges my shoulder. "I shouldn't tease"

I nudge her back. "No, I was caught red-handed."

Her face becomes serious. "You really like him." It feels weird talking like this with Alana, but it feels really good at the same time.

"Yes and no. I like him, but I spend most of the time hating him." I shake my head. "Oh, I don't know. But what about you and Kiar?" I give Alana a grin.

Her face brightens at his name and then she looks sad. "I can't do anything about it. It is not my choice."

"Whose choice is it? Kiar's?"

She laughs bitterly. "That would be simple, but no, the king and queen choose who we will be matched with."

This sounds so stupid. "How would they know who you love?"

Alana gives me a *don't be silly* look. "They choose who they think would work well together and some people find love in it."

My heart breaks for Alana and Kiar. This sounds barbaric. "So the king and queen match everyone in Saskia, including here?"

"No. Saskia is broken up into four sections and the king and queen control two. Aquaterra and Hummus are ruled by different people with different rules."

My heart lifts slightly. "Then move to one of them with Kiar."

Alana shakes her head. "Oh, Sarajane, it is not that simple. You have to swear allegiance to your new ruler. We would never see Saskia again. We can't cross each other's lands. Too many wars started by one settlement crossing into the other. And anyway, even if I agreed, Kiar is loyal to Saskia and the king." Alana becomes silent, running her finger around her plate. Her words about Kiar make me think Alana isn't from Saskia.

"Are you loyal to Saskia?"

Fear runs across her face and she looks over her shoulder and then back to me. "Of course I am."

But I can see she isn't. I leave it alone. Neve and Kiar make their way over to us and I smile at them both. "Fun party?" I say to Neve.

"I lit the bonfire."

Kiar sits down beside Alana. "Neve, the whole place would be on fire if they let you near it," Kiar jokes.

Before they can start bantering, I jump up and grab Neve's hand, surprising him. "Dance with me?" Before he can answer, I drag him off, leaving Kiar and Alana behind.

"I never noticed how much you wanted me before," Neve says playfully.

"You wish, Neve."

He twirls me around repeatedly until I'm almost sick. When he stops, I have to lean on him; everything is spinning too fast.

"Feeling okay, princess?" I look up at his moving, grinning face.

"Shut up, Neve, and just stay still."

He laughs loudly. "I'm not moving."

Everything starts to settle and I can see Tristan making his way towards Neve and me and he doesn't look happy. "Neve," he barks, causing Neve to let me go and stand straight.

"Yes, sir."

"You are on duty. This is not a resting period."

"Sorry, sir," Neve says and walks away.

"What is your problem? He was only dancing," I say to Tristan, my temper rising.

He comes up to me, making me take a step back. He doesn't come closer. "They are here for your safety and your father would be angry if anything happened to you."

"What about you, would you care?" I ask, not quite sure where the courage came from. It knocks Tristan off for a moment. He takes a step closer and this time I don't move. My legs are like jelly and I figure if I move, they will give way so I stand on locked legs. "Yes, I would care." My heart is pounding at his words. All I can do is stare at him as he stares back at me. His eyes flicker to the left and back to me and his face becomes hard again.

"Your father would demote me if you died." He gives a quick bowing gesture. "Be careful, princess." And he walks away. I stand there fuming and then to make it worse, my mother appears beside me. Tristan must have seen her approach.

"Sarajane, I'm sorry. You can't keep avoiding me." Her eyes are filled with sadness.

"Mum, you took that man's side over me." She goes to defend him. "He hit me," I remind her before she says something that will do more damage.

"That man is your father and your king, Sarajane."

I stamp my feet with frustration, knowing this is a pointless conversation. "John is my father, and he is not my king." I storm off before she can say anything else. I find Alana where I left her, looking into the flames. I plop down beside her. She throws me a sideward glance. I shake my head to let her know I don't want to talk about it. So she returns to looking at the flames.

A group of children are watching us. A few of the older ones are egging on a young girl of maybe eight or nine to come over to us. She makes her way over, glancing back over her shoulder at her encouraging friends. "Hello, princess," she says shyly with her hands behind her back, swaying slightly. I push my anger down and look at the little girl; her eyes are huge and brown. She is adorable.

"What's your name?" I ask.

"Mei."

"Mei, that's a beautiful name." I pat a space beside me. She sits down and sticks out her tongue at her friends. I laugh. "How old are you, Mei?"

Her little face looks up into mine. "Eight years old now," she says very maturely. Alana is listening to us. "Mei, this is Alana, my personal guard."

Mei's face squishes up. "A girl can't fight."

Alana raises an eyebrow. "Really, and who told you that?"

Mei looks at her hands shyly. "My granddad said when I was fighting with my cousin that girls don't fight."

I suppress a laugh. "Well, Alana here is a great warrior." Her eyes light up as she looks at Alana.

"Your granddad has never seen me fight," Alana says proudly.

"Maybe you could show me. My cousin always fights with me." Her little face looks angry. I can't stand to see a child bullied.

"Did you tell your granddad about your cousin?" I ask gently, seeing as Mei is really upset and at eight years of age, this is a big deal.

"No, he is always busy."

"What about your mum or dad or have you any older brothers or sisters?"

Her big eyes look sad. "My parents are dead and my brother…" She dwindles off. "I am not allowed to speak about him, granddad said." The poor child.

I notice Musa moving through the camp with Ndee. They are clearly looking for someone. Ndee's face relaxes when she sees Mei. "Mei, your granddad was looking for you."

Musa approaches and Mei jumps to her feet. "Mei, I told you to stay close," he says in a stern voice, but love for this child radiates from his eyes.

"Sorry, Granddad, I was just talking to the princess."

Musa smiles at me and picks her up in his arms. "Bed time." She grumbles but curls into his arms as he carries her away.

"Time for your marking," Ndee says, full of excitement. I roll my eyes. Pain isn't something I look forward to, but I follow her to a makeshift tent where a man waits with a tray of ink and small look-a-like needles.

"Where would you like it?" he asks. Only one shoulder is bare, so I opt for there. It isn't as painful as expected and the tattoo is just two small, fluffy wings. They look really nice when they're complete. I retire to my hut afterwards, feeling the day's events heavy on me.

Chapter Fourteen
SARAJANE

The next day, Ndee takes me to the kilns as she promised and we are accompanied by Mei. She hops along beside us to keep up. The kilns are positioned near the beach, embedded into the large cliffs. The heat in the stone structures is intense, coming from two large ovens that are about six feet tall and six feet wide with large doors on the front. I can see pipes running from one side of the kilns and disappearing behind them, then reappearing on the opposite side.

"The water will be hot today?" I say to Ndee while wiping sweat off my forehead. She laughs at my red-hot face.

"Yes, indeed. This is where the pottery is made." She gestures to several wooden pottery wheels that are covered in dried bits of clay. "The pottery is shaped here." Across from the pottery wheels, wooden tables are positioned; they are only the width of two benches. "And here we use a knife to inscribe our designs. The pottery then goes into the oven. When it's baked, we leave it in the cooling area." She gestures for Mei and me to follow her. We leave and go through a wooden door that brings us into a smaller room, but it is much cooler. A woman is seated at a desk, painting a mug in a vivid red colour. The swirls that have been engraved on the side of the mug are painted white.

"And this is where we paint and glaze the pottery." Ndee seems so proud of what they did and she should be. "Do you want to make something yourself?" she asks.

"Yes, that would be great, wouldn't it, Mei?"

The little girl beams up at me at being acknowledged, and she has been so quiet throughout Ndee's talk. "Yes, princess." She's doing her cute little swaying thing again. I can't help but smile at her.

Ndee shows skills of a great teacher. Her instructions and patience make what I'm doing seem so easy. Once I have a bowl shaped, she sets it in the kiln. It isn't perfect, but I'm delighted with it, even though Mei produced a perfect vase.

"We will come back and check on them later," Ndee announces while putting Mei's vase in the oven. "But we better get Mei back and feed you, princess." My stomach grumbles on cue.

I tidy myself up in my room, making sure nothing has gotten on the beautiful blue wrap that Ndee left out for me. I return to the main room. There is nowhere for cooking, but a plate filled with food is laid out on the circular table. I sit down. The chair under me has a soft cushion. The plate is colourfully dressed with lettuce, baby tomatoes, and the rest I can't name, but I start on the fish. Ndee brings over a pottery jug and pours me out a mug of water. "Thank you, Ndee."

She smiles. "You're welcome, princess."

Ola arrives then with another plate of fish and a mug. She lays it out across from me. I stop eating. "Is someone joining me?" I ask.

"I am," Tristan says from the door. He has washed and changed into a simple black jumper and trousers. His hair is loose around his face. He dismisses Ola and Ndee, who scurry off as if they are afraid of him. Tristan pours himself some water and sits down as if it's normal for us to eat dinner together. I just sit there, staring at him. "What is this about?"

He chews the fish slowly and then looks at me. "Does it bother you?" He doesn't smile or grin, just keeps an impassive look. If I said *Hell yes, eating with you bothers me*, he would win. So I cut up my fish.

"Of course not, Tristan."

"Good," he says self-assured. We eat in silence. He didn't come here to have dinner with me—something is up. It's hard to eat with him so close. I feel weird; I didn't know what to say. I've never had a normal conversation with him. I know then he is looking at me; my skin tingles. "Your face is healed." My head shoots up and I search his green eyes for something, anything, but nothing shows. Morrick's angry face just before he struck me comes to mind. Then Clive's body. I get up abruptly, knocking the chair out behind me, trying to banish the image.

Guilt tightens in my chest. Tristan moves towards me, leaving only inches between us. "It is not your fault." His words sound so good. A tear of relief slides down my face and he wipes it away with his thumb. I close my eyes at his touch. He keeps his hand on my face and I rest into him, breathing in his scent, and he lets me take comfort against his chest. His heart pounds under my ear. Is he nervous? Maybe he feels the same way I do. I look up into his face placing my hand over his pounding heart. If I just reach up on my tippy toes, I can kiss him, but he moves closer, his lips brushing mine. Butterflies erupt in my stomach. "Why are you here?" I whisper against his lips. I keep my eyes closed, afraid of the answer. He doesn't answer straight away. Instead, we just breathe, no one wanting to make the next move in case it's wrong. "I don't know," he responds and then he kisses me gently at first. I cling to him, wanting more, needing more. He does as my body commands and deepens the kiss. I feel out of control. I push my body harder against his, running my fingers under his top. In one swipe he has it off, revealing a very toned and muscular chest. He kisses my neck, pulling my hair aside as I run my hands along his broad back. "You look beautiful," he says through kisses. His words make my urgency for him go up a notch. I direct his face back to my mouth and kiss him with everything I feel for him. He returns the kiss with the same amount of emotion. His hands fumble as he tries to get my wrap off, but the way it's tied only lets it drop off my shoulder and no lower. He kisses my bare shoulder, sending electricity through my body, and then I can't breathe.

Tristan freezes and looks at me. I try to pull air into my lungs, but nothing is happening. Oh God, my knees give way from under me, but Tristan grabs me in his arms before I fall. "Sarajane." I can hear the panic in his voice. I grab at my chest, horrified. Dots swarm in front of my eyes. A man steps out of the shadows. He must have been there all along. Tristan lets me down and reaches out his arms towards the man. I can see the man go numb and slump against the wall, a look of astonishment on his face. The air fills my lungs almost immediately. I take in large gulps. The man's astonishment fades and is replaced with anger. Tristan kneels down to me, holding my face. "Are you okay?" he asks. I cough and nod. The man behind us is now standing and an axe releases from his hands, coming directly towards me. Before I can scream, Tristan turns and grabs the axe in mid-air and flicks his wrist. The man seems to be frozen as panic runs across his face. Tristan flings the axe and embeds it right between his eyes. Before I can react, Tristan scoops me up in his arms and hugs me to his chest. "Are you all right?" he asks while kissing the top of my head. I am speechless from the urgency in his voice, but I answer to calm his trembling body. "I'm fine." My voice betrays my assurance by quivering. Tristan leans back and his green eyes search my face and then his gaze falls on the dead man. His jaw becomes hard with anger. Another one dead and all to save me. The door bursts open as twenty men pour in. Tristan pushes me behind him and breaks a leg off the nearest chair as a weapon. The first three men attack. Tristan uses the wood like a sword, hitting all three men with such force they lie unconscious and bleeding on the ground. They are down before they even realise what hit them. Every man that comes for him, he disarms, and they join the rest on the ground. I've never seen anyone so fast. At least ten of them are down now. The others can see there is no point coming in threes so they surround him, moving in. He takes out another three before the rest overpower him.

Tristan throws his head back, breaking the man's nose behind him. The man grabs his face and howls in pain as blood pours through his fingers. I can see one move up slowly behind, but I don't get to warn him in time. The man smashes Tristan in the back of his head with a chunk of wood. Tristan falls to his knees and the rest jump on him, knocking him completely to the ground. He still struggles under them, but they finally overpower him. The men are huge' there is nothing I can do to help. But at least he didn't kill any more. I'm still in shock by how easily he
    fought.

Morrick and Musa walk in then, taking in the room. "Let him go," Morrick commands.

The men look to Musa and he nods. "Leave us."

Tristan gets up, touching the back of his head. It comes away sleek with blood. The room empties; the others help carry the ones that are unconscious out of the room. I just stand there, dazed.

"What happened here?" Morrick asks, absolutely furious.

Tristan looks at Musa. "One of your men tried to kill Sarajane so I disposed of him and then we were swarmed." Tristan doesn't even flinch.

"You did more than dispose of him. I felt the pull. We are all connected in this tribe."

Morrick steps towards Tristan, trying to control himself. "You didn't use your powers? Tristan, tell me you didn't." There is a pleading in Morrick's voice.

"He tried to kill her, Morrick. What else could I do?" Tristan's own anger is rising.

"You managed to disarm fourteen of Musa's best warriors, yet you had to drain one."

Tristan holds Morrick's gaze. "He caught me off guard, a mistake that will never happen again."

Morrick steps closer to him. "You said that after Alana."

Tristan flinches at this as if it is a blow. "That was different—"

Morrick cuts him off. "Yes, it was. You didn't know what you were doing then, but you were fully aware this time." Everyone becomes silent and Morrick's gaze falls on me.

"What is this all about?" Musa asks calmly.

Morrick takes and deep breath. "Tristan has unusual gifts. He can take anyone's powers once he intercepts where it is coming from." I couldn't believe what I was hearing, but it explained why the man had gone limp when the air filled my lungs.

"Anything else, Tristan?" Musa asks, still calm.

"Yes, I can shield all powers used against me." His gaze flickers to Morrick, but he doesn't say anything else.

"How could you, Tristan? I don't understand. You could have disarmed him."

Tristan looks at me for the first time. "He was going to kill her, Morrick."

Morrick grabs Tristan's arm. His voice is low but laced with torment. "Don't look at my daughter like that." His voice rises. "You have no right to her."

Musa clears his throat. "Morrick, this is my land and you came here as I guest. You didn't feel this was important enough to tell me?" Musa is angry now.

"Musa, I swore I would never use these powers again, so therefore, Morrick had nothing to tell."

Musa approached Tristan. "Yet you used them. Stay right here until I decide what to do." He turns and leaves the hut. "And you, fix your dress." Morrick's face is red with rage. A blush rises in my cheeks as I retie my dress at my shoulder with shaky hands. "This might be acceptable behaviour in the mortal world, to fling yourself at a man…" Morrick stops as Tristan stands beside me. A muscle twitches in his jaw with his temper.

"This is my doing. Leave her out of it."

Morrick's eyes become wide with anger, but his voice is no more than a whisper. "Be careful, Tristan, you're not the king yet. I am still your king and don't you forget it." Morrick turns his back on us, his shoulders heaving with anger. Tristan's hand squeezes mine gently. I look up at him and he gestures for me to leave the room. I squeeze his hand back before I go to my room.

I inhale deeply, willing myself not to cry. That's all I seem to do in this place. At moments like this, home seems so far away. A life I lived a long time ago.

It feels like forever I pace my bedroom floor before the door opens. Morrick looks over my shoulder, not meeting my eyes as he speaks. "Musa thinks it's best if you come out to hear what he has to say."

My legs begin to shake with each step I take towards the door. My stomach turns with nerves. What will happen to Tristan? Everyone is seated. Musa and another tribe member sat on the couch while Mirium and Tristan sit on armchairs across from them. A third armchair is vacant beside Mirium.

Musa gestures towards the chair. "Princess, please sit." Mirium gives me an encouraging look as I sit down stiffly. Morrick sits at the table where I had dinner, all signs of my earlier meal gone. This feels like court.

"This is Kia." Musa introduces the man beside him. He looks nervous; a sheen of sweat coats his bald head. His eyes are focused on his feet. "Ziar was the man that tried to kill you. This is his cousin," Musa explains to me.

"I am sorry."

Musa acknowledges my sympathy with a nod of his head, but Kia just keeps his head down.

"Tell them what you told me, Kia."

Kia looks at Musa, startled "But…"

"No buts. Kia, tell them."

Then Kia meets my eye. "He was ordered to kill you." He holds my gaze; a hardness shows on his face. He turns to Morrick to explain his case. "King Paulus threatened his family's life if he didn't kill the princess."

Morrick stands and approaches Kia. "Are you positive he said King Paulus?"

Kia sinks farther back into the chair. "Yes, sir."

"How did he get into Aquaterra?" Tristan asks. He doesn't look like he's buying this story. I don't blame him. Aquaterra is very well guarded.

"When we were on a routine trade with Hummus, we passed through the mountains and it was Ziar's shift to gather water." Kia smiles at the memory. "He was so angry; he hated chores. When he returned with no water and looking pale, he wouldn't tell me what happened. The men laughed, saying he was trying to get out of it, and Ziar laughed along with their jokes, but I could see he was afraid. The whole journey he was looking over his shoulder and at night he never slept.

When we got home two days ago, just before you arrived, I questioned him."

Morrick's body is rigid in front of Kia. "You knew this for the last two days?"

Kia's eyes shoot to the door nervously. "Yes."

Musa pats him on the shoulder. "You can leave now, Kia"

Morrick blocks his way. "He knew my daughter was being targeted and you pat him on the shoulder?"

Musa isn't intimated; he rises too. "Morrick, this is my land. I will deal with Kia as I see fit, not you." His last words rise slightly.

Morrick stands aside, but he watches Kia until the door closes. "How did he know my daughter was here?" Morrick looked at us all. "Someone has betrayed me."

"Yes, it does seem that way, but accusing your men will not get answers. You must test them." Mirium says wise words from a wise man.

I don't see the need for me to sit here; there is too much testosterone in the room. I get up and head for the door.

"Where are you going?" Morrick demands.

I turn back around. "To get some fresh air."

Morrick looks at me as if I am dumb. "You want to walk around alone and defenceless after someone tried to kill you? Remarkable."

"Alana will stay with me."

"Tristan, go get Alana and then come back here. We are not finished" Morrick gives him a warning look.

Mirium is watching me. "Are you all right, Sarajane? You must have gotten a fright." The understatement of the year.

"A little one, Mirium."

Tristan returns with Alana. She must have been close by. She is dressed in another beautiful dress, not her fighting clothes. Morrick shakes his head at the sight of Alana and me standing together. "Maybe if someone attacks, you can smile your way out of it." Then he turns his back to us, visually giving up.

Tristan pulls a dagger from his boot and places it in my hand. "Take this." I go to object, but he tightens his hand around mine. "Please." Is he trying to push Morrick?

"Fine." I wrap my fingers around it and leave with Alana.

We walk a while. Alana doesn't ask anything. She lets me be and I appreciate that. "Alana, what did Tristan do to you?" She freezes. "I'm sorry. Never mind."

Her body relaxes. "No, it's fine. What did you hear?"

"Just Morrick had said something about him using his powers on you."

"Come on." I follow her back to her hut. It's the same as mine, only hers looks like nobody has even sat in it. I sit down, glad for a rest without Morrick watching me disapprovingly.

"I am not from Saskia." She sits down and takes a deep breath. This isn't going to be good. "I come from the Enola Tribe, near Saskia, but we have our own ways. I had a sister, Noria, and parents and friends." Her face takes on a faraway look. "We never gave any trouble to anyone and we kept to ourselves. At the time, we didn't even know who the king or queen of Saskia was. We lived off the land completely."

"You were happy?" I ask, but I can see by her smile that she was.

"Yes, but then we were invaded by King Paulus and his men. They slaughtered us." Tears run down her face. "I tried so hard to stop them, but they wouldn't. She was only twelve." She looks at me as the tears pour down her cheeks. "My sister didn't deserve such a death. And then it was my turn. Nearly our whole tribe was dead so I was faced with a large group of men." My stomach turns. "They took turns beating and raping me." The tears stop and Alana's face becomes stone. "But they let me live. I don't know why. Maybe it was because I could live in my own torment for the rest of my life." I could feel my own cheeks wet. "I stayed in our home with my family and just sat there for seven days." The smell must have been unbelievable from the dead after that long and she must have been terrified. "At the time, Morrick had overthrown King Paulus and he sent out his own army to find survivors in the smaller settlements. There weren't many left. When they came for me, I was disorientated, still protecting my family's bodies from any vultures. That's when Tristan arrived. He was a man so I thought he would hurt me." She paused to take a breath. "I attacked him with fire and he took my gift away by accident. He never knew he could do it. He tried to calm me down, but in the end the only thing he could do was knock me out. They kept me in that state for three days until I arrived at Saskia, where I was treated by the maidens." She looked up at me then. "I took loyalty to King Morrick, and Tristan taught me how to fight so I would be able to defend myself if anyone ever attacked me again."

"Alana, I am so sorry." I know my words can't come close to what she went through.

"Thank you. I am lucky to be alive." Then she gives a bittersweet laugh. "But sometimes I wish I died with my family." I wipe at my own tears, feeling weak for crying in front such a strong person. Alana looks at me and gives me a genuine smile. "Your tears for me are not a weakness, Sarajane. It just shows you have a kind heart." I go to her and hug her so tight, feeling so angry at this world to let such horrible things happen, yet they happen everyday in the mortal world, but just never to anyone I know.

Chapter Fifteen
SARAJANE

I stay with Alana that night. I just can't bear to leave her. The next day we spend helping out in the kilns. I have to check on my bowl anyway, and Mei and I paint our pottery together.

I meet my mother once. After Alana's story, it makes me want to forgive her.

We both pause before passing each other.

"I want to forgive you so much, but I know I will never forget." I look up at my mother. "Does that make sense?"

She embraces me. "Perfect sense. I'm not sure I will ever forgive myself, either." She kisses my forehead. "But I love you no matter what and will never stop. You are my daughter." She says this with such fierce pride.

I give her a hug back. "I love you too, Mum." Some of the villagers have stopped and are watching us. We both laugh a little and wipe our tears away. "I need to help out in the kitchen so..." I feel a bit awkward.

"Okay, love." She squeezes my hand before I leave.

That evening, we eat in one of the big indoor rooms. It's like a large canteen. It houses over three hundred people at once. I sit with Alana. She is quiet all day, even when Neve and Kiar come to join us. I can see Liber and Legis sitting with Tristan and the other guardians. Neve and Kiar keep the chat flowing at our table as they always do with their light-hearted banter.

"What is wrong? You are awfully quiet." I look up at Neve and feel bad I wasn't even listening to anything he was saying.

"Sorry, was just thinking." Kiar gives me a look that says, *Continue*. I wasn't going to say anything about Alana so I decided to tell them about me. "Someone tried to kill me last night."

Alana drops her fork. "And you are only telling me now, Sarajane?"

I give her the best sorry look I can muster. "It was nothing really. Tristan sorted it."

Kiar smirks. "Oh he did? And where was this when you were attacked?"

I can feel my cheeks burning as all eyes are on me now. "My hut."

Kiar continues. "Oh, so you and Tristan were in your hut?"

I throw a piece of lettuce at Kiar, but it doesn't reach him. Instead, it flops down halfway across the table. "Whatever, Kiar."

He looks confused. "What does that mean?"

I get up with my plate. "Since you're so smart, you can figure it out." I leave then, leaving my plate beside the large tubs that act as sinks.

I stay with Alana for the rest of the night, just wandering around the settlement. It's nearly dark, but there are lots of people still around. Then I see Mirium, Morrick, Musa and Tristan moving through the crowd. They are heading for the large barns that I met Musa in. I grab Alana's hand and drag her with me.

"Sarajane, what are you doing?"

I give her a mischievous smile. "Finding out what they're up to."

Alana lets out a groan. "Sarajane, you cannot follow them if they—"

But I keep moving, leaving Alana with no choice but to follow me. I stand in the crowd until they have all entered the building and then move towards it slowly. I can see a wooden shutter open at the side of the building to let in air. I move around the building slowly until we are out of sight and then turn to Alana. "Stay low." I crawl along the ground until I'm directly under the window.

"Who else is involved?" That was Morrick's voice

"Bellona?" Musa asks.

"No, she won't. She hates her father." Morrick seems adamant on this point.

But Mirium seems to disagree. "Morrick, she is allied with Lucian, and King Paulus could be also. We have to look at every possibility."

"What about Carew, then, since we have to look at every possibility?" Morrick says smartly

"He has never been seen since." Sadness fills Musa's voice, but it doesn't sound genuine; it sounds forced.

Alana tugs on my arm and gestures back towards the huts, but I shake my head and continue to listen.

"But he will be. I just cannot say if it is for good or bad." Mirium's words are gentle. This must have been someone Musa cared about or pretended to. "Lucian wants Sarajane alive so King Paulus must not be with him, since he wants her dead, but the images are foggy and unclear." I freeze at Mirium mentioning my name.

"Have you heard any more on the girl?" Morrick asks, but he sounds like he couldn't care less.

"Yes, Bellona has her, but she is alive." Mirium pauses. "You need to tell Marta, Morrick. It is her daughter."

My heart stops beating and my body becomes rigid. They can't be talking about Jessica. That isn't possible. I calm myself and listen. Alana grabs my wrist, her eyes pleading with me to leave.

"She is not my daughter. She is from a mortal man and none of my concern." Morrick's voice is cold and hard. He's talking about my sister. *Oh God, this isn't happening.*

Alana pulls on my arm again and I crawl numbly behind her. Their voices start to fade. When we stand, I can't even speak, and Alana veers me off towards the sea. The wind is a lot stronger the closer we get.

"Oh God, Alana, they're talking about my sister."

Alana grabs both my shoulders. "Calm down. We will think of something."

I look at her, shocked. "Are you going to help me?"

"I can't come with you, but I can find out where she is."

I nod my head several times. "Oh God, I can't believe they're going to let her die." I can feel the rage towards Morrick rising in me. How could he? But I need to stay calm. If they won't help save her, I will have to do this myself.

"They said Bellona has her, so she would be in Saskia."

I look at Alana, bewildered, and then I start to feel hysterical. "I don't even know where that is, Alana."

"I will draw you a map."

"This is not happening." I grab Alana's shoulder and shake her. "Tell me this is not real," I scream.

Alana's face becomes stern and a look of determination crosses it. Her words make their way through my fear. "Calm down and think of your sister." She is right; this is not helping.

"Tell me what I need to do"

"Okay. Go back to your hut and act normal. Change into your travelling clothes and arm yourself. When the settlement becomes quiet, sneak out to the back of your hut. I will meet you there."

"And then what?" I ask, seeing too many holes in this plan.

"Just trust me, Sarajane." We leave the beach and go our separate ways. I meet no one and make it to my hut. Once I'm changed and armed with my own dagger and Tristan's, I just sit in the main room, waiting for the settlement to go quiet. It feels like days. I sneak out as Alana said and stand behind my hut. Alana is there. I hug her. I know she's breaking a lot of rules and taking risks. But she's all business. "Here is the map. It is easy to follow. I will get you out of Aquaterra, but you have to do exactly as I tell you." I don't get to answer. We move from hut to hut, using them as cover until we are back at the sea. The fence that surrounds Aquaterra runs a good mile out to sea, but Alana keeps making her way into the water.

"We can't swim that far," I call to her.

"We are not swimming; we are diving." She disappears under the water. I follow her about four feet under the water. A large section of the fence is cut out enough to let a person fit through. We swim through it and come out the other side, but it makes me wary of Alana. Is she the traitor? Did she cut this out so she could move freely from Aquaterra? It doesn't matter. I just need to get to Jessica so I have no choice but to trust her. She runs out into the desert away from the fence and keeps moving at a fast pace, but her footsteps make no noise. When we are out of sight, she stops and I try to catch my breath.

"I can't stay much longer, but in the next five minutes you will come to an old building that looks like it is not used. Inside is a horse, saddled and carrying water and food."

"How do you know all this, Alana?" I ask, praying she isn't the traitor. I really like her.

"I just do." She hugs me. "I can't keep them off long. They will question me the minute they realise you are missing. So at best, you have until morning."

"Okay, thank you." I give her one more quick hug and follow her directions to the old building. Inside, I find a horse saddled and equipped.

Chapter Sixteen
SARAJANE

Once I'm on the horse I make my way towards the mountains. Alana's map is easy to follow. When I hit the mountain, there is a pass about three miles in that will take me straight to Saskia. I kick the horse, pushing its body faster and harder. After a few hours of intense riding, the sun is starting to rise. I know I don't have much longer before they notice I'm gone. I kick the horse again, willing it to reach the mountains in the distance. The temperature drops the closer we get to them. I can't think about what I'm doing; it just terrifies me too much. So I focus on Josh's face. I think of his smile and kind words. A sense of safety and peace washes through me. "I miss you." Thinking of him pushes me on and I finally reach the mountains. We slow down, our pace almost at a crawl, as the ground is uneven and rocky. Goose bumps pop up all over my arms. I wrap my cloak tighter around me to shield myself from the cold. The horse starts hesitating at every step we take. At this rate it will take forever to reach Saskia. I tug the reins. "Go faster." He throws his head back and sighs; a cloud of cold air leaves his nostrils. I kick his side. "I said go." He rears up, nearly throwing me off. I grip his neck to keep myself on the saddle. My heart is pounding. Something is spooking him. I look around me, but it is still dark in between the mountain. The horse starts moving back slowly. I let him. I'm not risking being thrown off again. I keep looking around to see what is scaring him. Stones fall down the mountainside. I squeal. The horse panics, moving back too quickly. "Shhh, it's okay." I try to calm him, rubbing his neck, but he is freaking out. He moves quicker, fumbling over his own legs. I know he's going to fall. I jump from his back at the last minute and land awkwardly on the ground. I roll out of the way just as the horse falls on his side. He would have crushed me if I hadn't moved. He is still kicking his legs wildly, his head thrown back, showing eyes that are nearly all white, and as quick as he falls, he gets up on his knees and then stands. He is facing the way out and he races off. "Hey, come back!" I roar after him, but he is racing like his life depends on it. I stand on shaky legs and brush gravel off my clothes. Looking around doesn't help. I can't see more than ten feet in front of me. It looks like the shadows are moving all around me. I move back slowly and hit the stone wall. How the hell do I get myself into such stupid situations? Here I am alone, in the dark, stranded. "Okay." I let out a deep breath and wipe my hands on my trousers.

I start walking. Light shines in different areas wherever the mountainside has collapsed, allowing sunlight to escape through. It is now morning. I try to walk in the light as much as possible. I know I'm being followed, but I can't stop. I reach the next area of light and bend down, pretending to tie my lace. I slip the dagger with shaky hands out of my boot and hold it at my side. The movements are strong up ahead, but there is nothing I can do, only stay calm until I reach that area and then run. This is the best plan I can come up with. The distance starts closing in, and whatever is just a few feet away doesn't move, but I can feel their hungry eyes watching me. Shivers run all over me; the hairs on my arm and neck sand up.

They slither out of their hiding places and surround me. "Breathe," I remind myself. Oh God, this was a bad idea. I grip the knife. If I can take out the two in front of me, I might have a chance at running. They circle and hiss around me. I turn in a full circle to watch them as best I can. Now is my chance. I run at the one that's in front of me, sticking my dagger in its neck. The exile crumbles to the ground. The rest seem frozen and I run with everything I have. I can hear their howls behind me as they take chase.

"Don't look back," I tell myself and then I look over my shoulder just as one of them leaps off the side of the mountain, taking me tumbling to the ground. I try to stab him, but he hits my knife away and it crashes to the ground. I crawl back and kick him in the face. He growls and reaches out with long talons, tearing my cloak, ripping some of it off. I crawl on my knees to get away. Then I'm pushed down, scraping my cheek as he leaps on my back and rolls me over. His breath smells like rotten meat.

The other exiles were cheering, but now they are all silent. A giant of a man is standing behind the exile. My eyes widen at the sheer size of him. He looks like a warrior from some jungle movie. He is definitely over seven foot tall with jet-black straight hair that hangs down his back. His chest is bare and I've never seen such black eyes. He places his hands on the exile's head and twists, snapping his neck like a twig. He pulls the dead exile off me and throws him against the side of the mountain. I can hear his bones crunch as his lifeless body hits the wall. All the other exiles hunch farther down to the ground, looking afraid.

The giant looks at me then and speaks. "My name is Carew Warrior." I just nod, afraid if I speak I'll say something wrong and end up like the exile. "No others will attack you. You have my word." This guy could kill me in seconds

"What about you? Do I have your word?" My voice shakes uncontrollably.

He inclines his head. "Of course, princess." He reaches out his hand and pulls me off the ground. He is handsome in a manly animal way. I look around at the exiles. They are still bowing low to the ground.

"Why are they following me?" I ask.

He turns, fixing the creatures with a fierce look. "You have encountered them before?" The creatures look afraid. Good.

"Yes, one attacked me a few days ago."

He shakes his head. "Our king will be very unhappy to hear that. He will punish the one who attacked you, severely." A grin spreads across his face, making me squirm.

"It is dead." The image of him throwing himself on Tristan's sword springs to mind.

Carew looks surprised. "You killed it yourself?"

"No, my protector did." That sounds impressive.

He looks around, standing on alert. "And where is your protector? I did not smell him."

"Smell him?" He looked at me angrily. "I asked you a question, princess. I expect an answer." "Sorry, I'm on my own." My voice is stuttery. His name is niggling at me. I've heard it before. Then I remember Musa saying his name. But I don't mention it. I look at the exiles and back at Carew. "Are you their master?" I ask. "Yes. Enough questions, princess. You may pass." I gather my scattered cloak around me and walk past Carew, and the exiles part for me. I turn around. "Thank you." His face falls a little as if no one has ever thanked him before. Then it fills with hate. "Go before I change my mind." I run. I don't stop until my lungs are burning, and then the settlement comes into view, with a large castle sitting right in the middle. That's where my sister will be. I take off my tattered cloak and sit a rock on top of it. I will come back this way and can get it then. I forgot my dagger, but it doesn't matter. Tristan's dagger is in my other boot. Seeing Saskia from this point is amazing. The kingdom is huge, stretching for miles, but I don't have time for sightseeing. I still have to get into the castle. I move down the hill towards the settlement. When I reach the village/city, everyone has taken to the cobbled streets, bartering with goods. It feels for the first time that I have been transported back in time. The smell of home baking tantalizes my senses, but there is still an undercurrent of sewerage seeping through. I move through the village with my head down, but I can't see the castle from ground level. I just know to keep moving straight. Once I find the main square, I find the castle. There are no walls surrounding it. It just stands huge and daunting before me. There are a lot of people moving towards the castle so I join in with the crowd. As we get closer, I can see guards are scattered everywhere. Four of them block the main entrance. This could be a harder task than I first thought. The crowd makes its way to the left of the castle. I follow until a huge wall comes into view. Everyone seems to be moving that way. I break off and move down the wall that is facing the castle. A side door is slightly open. I can hear the hustle of a busy kitchen coming from behind the door. Steam pours out into the street. I keep my back to the wall, trying to slow down my racing heart. A stout man with a washcloth slung across his shoulder comes out the door with a large pot. He sloshes it down an open gully. No wonder the place smells of rotten food and sewerage.

When he turns to go back in, he stops at the sight of me. "You new?" he grumbles. I nod my head. "Get to work, then. The pots won't wash themselves." He pushes me roughly through the door while mumbling about how useless his staff is. I move through the hectic kitchen, keeping my head down. I can see a door just up ahead.

"You." I stop as the man comes after me. "The pots are over there," he says through gritted teeth while pointing. I go to walk away and he hits me with a wet cloth across the arm. It stings like hell. I want to grab the cloth and hit him back, but I have to act afraid, which isn't too hard. "Don't wear clothes like that in my kitchen ever again."

I nod. "Yes, sir." I race to the pots and start scrubbing them. They are stacked in rows on top of each other, all caked in different foods. Hopefully he will leave or take a break soon; then I'll have my chance to escape. I wash the pots while trying to keep an eye out. Steam rises from the large pots and flames jump from pans; the heat is hard to tolerate. Then I see the man going out the door again with another pot. It is now or never. I make a beeline for the door. Just before I reach it, a woman grabs my shoulder, spinning me around "Are you dumb? Boss said to wash the pots so wash them." This woman is a bully. I can see she is enjoying this. She grabs my arm when I don't move. "Don't touch me." She's wasting my time. I push her away and try to leave again, but she grabs my wrist roughly. The kitchen staff has gone silent. My anger flares. I grab her arm. "Get off me," I say. She starts to scream, startling me. I wasn't hurting her. Then the smell of burnt flesh makes its way through the cooking aroma to my nose. I pull my hand off her arm; a handprint is burnt into her flesh. She is hysterical, jumping from foot to foot. She makes a dash for a sink of water and sticks her arm in. I can hear the sizzling of her flesh.

I look at my hands. *What am I?*

"You!" The stout man is back. No time. I need to get out, so I run. "Stop her!" he roars, but nobody tries. Instead, they stand out of my way. I push through the door. The fresh air brushes my skin. I gulp it down, erasing the stench of burning skin. I keep going, not even sure where I am, but I can't afford to move slowly. The man will more then likely pursue me. Nobody pays any attention as I make my way through the halls. I keep my head down and stay close to the wall without getting in anyone's way. I look over my shoulder, but the man never follows me.

"Watch where you are going." I smack into a young girl. She's walking beside a beautiful blond lady that is dressed differently. Wealth radiates from her. Another simply dressed girl stands on the opposite side, staring at me with disgust.

"Sorry," I mumble and try to pass. Outrage passes over the blond woman's face.

The girl I smacked into looks at me with disbelief. "You bow to Princess Luna, you stupid girl." Princess Luna? Oh God, this must be Clive's sister, my half-sister.

I push that complication aside and bow. "I apologise, Princess Luna."

"Servant, what are you doing walking down the corridors without looking?" Oh Christ, this couldn't get worse.

"Sorry, but my boss asked me to get clean cloths for the kitchen, Princess Luna." I bow again, hoping I'm not overdoing it.

"I hope you were not preparing my food in that array?"

I look up at her as she takes in my appearance with distaste. "No, I just wash pots, Princess Luna." I try to pass again, still bowing, but she just stands there.

"Wait." I freeze. I am sprung. "Tie your lace before you fall." She flips her blond hair over her shoulder and walks off. "She smells like rat poop." The two girls on either side of her laugh, but it is forced. *Rats' poop, bitch.* I think.

When she moves around a bend, I get up and move faster through the halls, this time looking where I am going. I don't know what to look for along the way. There are several doors on either side of me so I start peeking in as I pass, making sure no one sees me, but they are all bedrooms. I come to a stairway and climb. I end up on the main floor. There are no servants around and the corridor is wide and quiet. I can hear voices coming from a room farther down, but they are muffled through the heavy wooden door. I press my ear against the door and fall flat on my face onto a marble floor. I look up and smile at two guards.

One grabs me and drags me off the floor. "What were you doing, listening for information?"

I shake my head. He drags me into the room. I dig my heels into the marble floor, but they just squeak the whole way until he throws me back onto the floor. "It seems we have found a traitor, my lady." I look up and into the hard white face of the queen. She sits upon a large gold throne at the top of the room. She wears a blood-red dress that flows all over the marble floor. Her hair is pinned back severely, making her face look stretched.

"Are you a traitor?" she asks, tilting her head to the side.

"No, my lady."

"Of course not." She gives me a frightening grin and then flicks her hand towards me. My breath catches. It feels like my soul is being touched. It is the most unnatural feeling I've ever felt. I push it away with all my strength and it stops. The queen stands up, her pale blue eyes fixated on me. She walks towards me. Her dress is like a pool of blood flowing after her. "What did you just do?" She seems horrified yet excited at the same time.

"Nothing." I lower my eyes to the floor. She slides a dagger out from her sleeve. My hand rests on my boot, not that I will get away if I harm her.

"Tell me now and I will not hurt you." Her voice is like a thousand snakes squirming around me.

"I did nothing."

She gives me a pleasurable look. "We will see." She stretches out the knife towards my neck. "Are you sure?"

I swallow; panic and fear start to rise. I really don't know what happened. "I pushed you away." She looks at me, studying my features. "Do I know you?" I drop my head. "No, my lady." I say. "Look at me while I speak to you." I look at her ice-cold eyes and recognition flashes across her face. She strikes out with the dagger but freezes just as it is a hair's breadth away from my neck. Sweat drips from my forehead onto my cheek. She pushes the dagger with all her force, but it won't move. The dagger goes sliding across the floor and she starts laughing. "Sarajane, welcome," she says with a psychotic smile on her face. "I should have known it was you." Her face turns into a snarl and then she returns to her throne. "I have been waiting for you," she says. "Where is my sister?" She ignores my question. The guards around the room are closing in on me slowly, but Bellona holds up her hand and they stop. "Life is full of hard decisions. Sometimes they are made for us." She shrugs her shoulders slightly. If I'd blinked, I would have missed the motion. "And sometimes we must make them ourselves. Would you not agree, Sarajane?" I don't know where she is going with this so I just remain silent. She takes my silence as whatever answer she wanted. "My son was struck down too young." Her eyes grow colder, which I didn't think was possible. "A life, what is it worth?" I squirm under her stare but straighten my shoulders. I can't show fear or she will eat me up. "Bellona, your son tried to kill me," I say in the strongest voice I can muster. Her roar silences the room. "Enough. I will not listen to your lies." She composes herself into a statue-like stance while wiping spit from her chin. "It does not matter. He is dead. I would kill you if I could, but I gave an oath not to harm you." Relief fills me. "So you are free to go." My muscles tense. She will kill Jessica. Her lip rises ever so slightly and then falls back into its hard, straight line. Fear rushes through me. "Do you like games, Sarajane?"

I answer with an abrupt no. The queen moves towards me. "Pity, because I have one for you, but you don't have to play it." She circles me, making the tension in my body increase. My palms are slick with sweat. "In the forest of Eden, south of the Amour Caves, there is a small hut where two guards hold a young lady." My heart rate quickens. "You have two days and then your time is up. The thread of life shall be cut."

I want to kill her and my voice makes it clear how I feel. "If you harm my sister..."

Bellona stares at me and her guards move closer. "What will you do, Sarajane? Your time has started; you have two days to rescue her, so I suggest you leave." I don't understand why she is giving me time.

I told my feet to move and they obeyed.

"But you also have another choice." I turn back to her. "It will take two days to leave Saskia and cross to the mortal world where your father John is being held by guards. So you choose who lives and who dies." Angry tears leave my eyes. "Why? They have done nothing wrong." My nails dig into my palms as I try and control my anger. "Life is not fair. I realised that when you took my innocent son's life. So I am being rather kind telling you in advance. You must show up to the forest or the mortal realm. No one else can stop this. The guards must see you." This time the queen leaves with her guards trailing behind her. I stand frozen only for a second and then my limbs catch up with my brain and I run from the room out the main doors of the castle. Nobody stops me as I run back through the village. Just on the outskirts beside what looks like a memorial garden stands a man with a horse. I slow down as I pass him. "Sarajane," he whispers. I stop. "I am Dominic, a friend of your mother. The horse has water and food in the side packs." This seems a little too convenient. "Corrona, my wife, works in the castle and she overhead you and the queen." He stretches out the reins towards me. I take them and he helps me up. "Tell Marta that we said hi." Then he lowers his head. "And sorry."

I don't ask why. "Thank you, Dominic." I kick the horse and make my way towards the mountains. I stop before entering, retrieving my cloak that still lays under the rock and tying it around my neck. My body shakes with adrenaline. I have no idea how to get to Eden Forest, but I have to try. I take a steady breath and make my way through the passage in the mountain. I am not far in when I can hear the hooves of horses coming in my direction. I pull on the horse's reins, directing him into an indent in the mountainside, hoping the shadows will give me enough cover.

As the voices get closer, they become clearer. A smile breaks across my face at Neve's and Kiar's voices. It isn't their usual banter; if anything, they sound worried. I pull the reins, gesturing for the horse to move out. Mirium, Morrick, Tristan, Liber, Neve and Kiar stare back at me. Big, relieved grins appear on Neve's and Kiar's faces.

"Did you miss me?" I can't help but ask.

Tristan rides up alongside my horse. He is livid and trying hard to control his face, but his eyes tell the truth. "You." He clenches his jaw, unable to find any words that can match how outraged he his.

"She has my sister," I tell him, my own anger rising. He knew this but didn't care.

"Then where is she?" Tristan questions, but his words are uncaring, his annoyance still too high.

I turn from him and face Morrick. "She has her in the forest of Eden, held by two guards. I have two days to rescue her."

Morrick tuts. "Her stupid games." He lets out a heavy breath. "Fine. Liber, escort Sarajane back to Aquaterra." Morrick cuts off my protests. "We will get her." As if he cares, but I rein in my anger.

"You can't. I have to show my face to the guards or they kill her."

Morrick looks to Mirium for inspiration. "I do not know the outcome, but I feel the truth in her words."

Morrick's face darkens. "It is too dangerous."

"She's my sister; I will save her. I'm not asking for your permission, Morrick"

Neve and Kiar look alarmed at my tone toward their king. I know I have maybe gone to far, so I soften my voice. "I need your help, please."

Morrick doesn't reply. I look at Tristan now. He hasn't moved a muscle. "And if we do not help, Sarajane, will you come back to Aquaterra with us?" he asks.

"No, I will get her myself."

He looks back at Morrick and then returns his hard gaze to me. "I thought as much. Okay, we will help." Relief courses through my body. I knew I couldn't do this alone. But Tristan isn't finished. "If you disobey me again, I promise you will regret it. Understand?"

I still have to tell them about John. I can't save both. My voice sounds drained when I speak. "She has my father too." I direct this to Morrick, praying to God my words hurt him. "He is being held in the mortal world so I have to choose between my sister and my father." Morrick stares at me with icy eyes, picking up on the emphasis I put on the word father, but it isn't a lie. He reared me as his own, loved me. He was everything a father should be.

Mirium has a faraway look on his face and then he snaps out of it. "Morrick, you must go with Sarajane and help her sister. I will go to the mortal world for her father." He hesitates on the last word.

"Mirium, it is only my face that can save him."

Mirium moves to the opposite side of me, his grey eyes full of wisdom and kindness. "Do you trust me?" I haven't known Mirium long, but I do trust him.

"Yes."

He smiles gently. "I will go to the mortal and do my best to save him."

I just nod. It seems impossible if I'm not with him, but I focus my mind on Jessica.

Before leaving, Mirium turns to Tristan. "Aim high."

Tristan nods as if he understands what Mirium means. Maybe he does.

Liber leaves with Mirium and the rest of us take off with Tristan leading in silence. After an hour's riding, Tristan speaks. "What is the exact location?"

I meet Tristan's unattached gaze. "South of the Amour Caves. There is a hut in Eden Forest."

Tristan gives me a curt nod and we start moving again.

"Will it take two days to reach Eden Forest?" I ask Neve as he rides just a little up ahead of me.

"A day, but it is a forest and we are looking for hut so that will take time"

"Not if we split up," I say.

Tristan stops abruptly and turns his horse to face me. "For once, do as you are told. No one is splitting up." My cheeks light up with rage. *How dare he!* "I am future king and you will obey me, Sarajane Anderson." At that he whips the horse back around and continues riding, his back stiff with anger. We follow. I am breathing heavy with anger. Neve chuckles beside me. It is quiet enough so that only I can hear.

"What's so funny?" I don't like being laughed at.

He clears his throat. "Nothing is funny." He moves a little ahead, out of my line of vision. I could bet my life a grin is still plastered on his skinny face.

After a few hours of travelling, I start to feel exhausted. It has been a day and a half since I've slept or eaten and it's catching up on me.

"We will stop here for a rest," Tristan announces to us all. We are still in the mountains. They seem unending. But I don't want to waste any time.

"No, we need to find my sister."

Tristan climbs off his horse and the rest follow suit. Morrick seems no longer to be in charge. I wonder what had happened last night. They have reversed roles. Kiar comes over to help me down, but I sit stubbornly on the horse.

"Bellona said two days." I can hear the panic in my own voice.

"Today is the first day," Tristan says. Then his eyes study my face. "And you can't defend yourself in this state. You need rest."

Kiar reaches out his hand to me once again, only this time I take it. I know Tristan is right, not that I would ever tell him.

Kiar pulls out a bedroll and lays it down behind a large boulder that is only a few feet away from the mountain's edge. I sit down on the bedroll with my knees tucked up to my chin. Kiar sits on his haunches so we are at eye level "How are you holding up?" His kindness and brown eyes remind me so much of Josh I feel I can talk to him.

"Not good, Kiar. These things keep happening that I can't explain, and no matter how much I push them to the back of my mind, they always manage to push themselves forward." I know I'm not making much sense, but Kiar sits there patiently. "I see colours around people. I think I made that water pour into the caves the time Neve set it on fire. I burned a woman with my hand, and I pushed Bellona away from me using my mind." That's it. I blurt everything out.

Kiar sits for a second, staring at me. Then he smiles. "Maybe you have lots of affinities." His eyebrows furrow. "But we usually have one or two." We sit there. I don't know what else to say. Kiar pats my leg. "Get some rest. We will figure it out."

"Thank you, Kiar," I say while squeezing his hand.

"That's what friends are for." My face falls. Josh always said that to me. "What's wrong?" Alarm sounds in Kiar's voice.

I shake my head and smile. "Nothing, Kiar. I'll get some rest." I lie down.

The wind can't get to me in my cosy little space. I don't get to think too long. My mind slips away into a deep sleep.

Chapter Seventeen
SARAJANE

When I wake I'm in a pool of sweat. It's still bright. Pushing back my bedroll and stretching, I can smell food. A fire is burning and a rabbit is turning above the flame. "How did you catch a rabbit up here?" I ask Neve, who jumps at my voice and then smiles.

"Sarajane. The forest is only an hour's ride away so Tristan caught dinner." I sit down. Tristan was nowhere in sight. Neve turns the rabbit at regular intervals. Kiar is slumped against a large rock, his eyelids closed, yet I don't think he's asleep.

"Why stop here when we're only an hour away?" I ask Neve.

Morrick sits across from me, rubbing his face "You were exhausted." I don't reply to him. I just can't right now.

Tristan returns, looking grumpy. He never looks any other way. He ignores me. That suits me just fine. At this stage I just want to get my sister and go home.

The air is cold. I pull my cloak tighter around me, but it is shredded from my run-in with Carew and the exiles.

Morrick stirs across from me and examines my clothes through narrowed eyes. "What happened?" he asks. For some reason, I don't want to tell anyone about Carew.

"I fell into a bush." Morrick's eyes narrowed even more at my blatant lie, but I don't care. As if I would trust him ever again. I return my focus to Neve. "Is the food ready yet?"

"Nearly. Would you like a leg?" My stomach turns. I know he's trying to be nice, but if I see the little white paws, it will be enough to finish me altogether. My green-looking face must portray my horror, as Neve hurries on. "Or maybe not."

I give him a weak smile "Just the meat, no bone. Thanks." Neve smiles back, making him look younger. "How old are you?"

"Nineteen, but everyone thinks I look older." I would've thought he was maybe my age, in his early twenties.

Kiar's eyes open and a look of amusement passes over his face. I knew he wasn't asleep. "It's all the lines on your face, Neve."

Neve's hand immediately goes to his face to check for lines. When he feels none, he relaxes. "No, Kiar, it is because I act older," he says proudly with a boyish grin on his face. Kiar laughs heartily and I can't help but laugh with them. Neve's face breaks into a huge smile as he shakes his head, turning the rabbit.

I look across at Tristan. He watches me with a serious expression on his face. I don't look away this time but remember what it was like to have his lips on mine, his hands running through my hair. He looks away.

Morrick leaves during our exchange. I can't believe he hasn't even tried to apologise to me. I banter on with Neve and Kiar. They would raise anybody's spirits. They always seem to see the glass as half full no matter what they are faced with.

After our food, Morrick pulls Neve aside to speak to him before we leave. When Neve returns, he doesn't say anything and we never ask. We move out. Within the hour, we reach Eden Forest. Standing on the edge of the forest, I can see it stretching for miles. My optimism drops to the floor. This will be like looking for a needle in a haystack. Neve jumps off the horse and sinks to his haunches with his hands pushed deep into the soil.

"He has an earth affinity, but it is a level one," Morrick says to my confused look. But that means Neve has three affinities, which they all say is rare. I hold my breath until he rises, rubbing the dirt off his hands.

His face tells all before he speaks. "Nothing, sorry." He looks so guilty. I try to give him a reassuring smile, but I can't hide my disappointment.

"We move south through the forest," Tristan says, giving us all a pointed stare. "And move as quietly as possible." Once his little speech is over, we all follow behind. My heavy boots seem to crush everything under my feet. I'm the only one making noise. After a few hours my thighs burn from walking and sweat soaks my tunic. My footsteps sound louder as my feet are heavy to lift.

"We will take a break," Morrick says, much to Tristan's annoyance. I don't protest. I throw down my knapsack that holds water and some bread and rest against a tree. Removing my beaker of water from my knapsack, I gulp it down.

"Thirsty?" Kiar asks with an amused smile on his face. I notice Kiar, Neve and Tristan look like they haven't just trekked through the forest for the last few hours. Their tunics are dry, no sweat. At least Morrick looks a little breathless, and I mean a little.

"Do you guys run miles every day or something?"

Neve sits down beside me. "Yes."

Kiar laughs. "Don't worry. Give me a few months with you and I will whip you into shape."

"I hope you don't mean literally?" I give him my best mock horror look, causing him to laugh. Looking at Kiar, it is uncanny how, when he smiles, he looks more like Josh. The laughing settles down. "What age is your sister?" This is the first time anyone asks me about her, but I know Kiar is being as gentle as possible with his words. This sobers up all my humour, bringing me back to what I am here for. "She is eighteen next month, but going on thirty." Neve looks confused, again. "I mean, she acts older than she is," I explain. "Oh, she is like me, then." Kiar and I exchange amused looks but don't laugh. Neve just looks too sincere. "Does Jessica have any extra abilities?" Morrick asks, nearly making me jump. He and Tristan are always sneaking up on me; this is something I will have to work on. Well, I knew that they were going to check the area, but they never made an entrance when they returned.

"No." I gave him a hard look. Why show any interest in her now when before she was not his concern? Neve and Kiar don't speak. They seem to suddenly be intrigued with the forest floor. That means Tristan is back also.

I look up from Morrick and meet Tristan's cold gaze as he leans against a tree, watching us. He holds my stare as he comes over, throwing a leather pouch on the ground while sitting down with us. He throws each one of us an apple. "Found an apple tree not far from here," he tells me. I didn't ask where the apples came from, but it is tasty, extra sweet. Nobody speaks. The only noise is me munching on my apple. I look at Neve and Kiar, who haven't taken as much as a bite.

"What's wrong?" I spit the bite that's left in my mouth onto the ground. Then the world shifts. *What the hell?* Tristan is at my side, holding my head, resting it on the ground. Everything is starting to lose its colour.

"What did you do?" Morrick asks with alarm in his voice.

But Tristan just whispers in my ear. "Sorry, but it is for your own good."

"Tristan, you answer me!" Morrick's voice is at a peak, but he is swaying form side to side.

I look back at Tristan, who is still on his knees. "You bastard." My words are slurred as if I have drunk a brewery dry so I'm not sure if he can make them out, and then everything is gone.

I awake with a pounding headache, my hands are tied behind my back, and I am leaning against a tree. I open my eyes. Streaks of sunlight break through the trees, blinding me for a second. I lower my gaze. A pair of boots comes into view, then legs. Neve is seated not far from me.

"I am sorry, Sarajane. Don't be mad." He does look sorry.

"Just untie me, Neve, and I will forget all this," I say in the best friendly voice I can muster. I will kill Tristan.

Neve looks away, conflicted. "I can't. I have orders."

I don't have to ask from whom. It's still bright so maybe I wasn't out long. I can still catch up, but I need my hands untied. I sit quiet for about twenty agonising minutes and then when I think enough time passes, I take my chance.

"I need to use the bathroom." I give him an *I'm sorry* look, but he stands, shaking his head.

"Oh no, he said you would try that."

I growl in frustration, then regret it. "Neve, I'm fine about this. I understand everybody is worried about my safety." He isn't quiet sure whether to believe me. "But I really need to go."

I cross my legs in a really girly way, pretending I just can't wait much longer.

He takes a few sharp breaths through his nose. "Fine. You have one minute." He helps me up and unties my hands, but never takes his eyes off me.

I put my hand on my hip and tilt my head in what I hope looks like girly expression. "Neve, I can't go with you looking at me."

He blushes slightly. "Oh yeah," he says and turns his back to give me privacy. I kneel down and remove the dagger from my boot. I'm not going to hurt Neve, but I need him to believe I will.

"Hurry up," he says, his voice sounding anxious at having me untied. I take two steps towards his back and hold the dagger to his throat.

"Don't try anything or I will kill you."

He goes to move. "Sarajane." But I push the blade harder against his throat. A trickle of blood runs down his neck. He inhales a sharp breath, his face turning red with anger.

"Now put your hands in the soil and see if you can find them."

"Sarajane, think about what you are doing."

I push a little more. It's only a knick, but I still feel horrible. "Now, Neve." He gets down on his knees. I move with him to keep the dagger against his throat so he won't try anything.

He pushes his hands into the soil and concentrates. "Nothing," he says. Panic rises. This is my only plan. I grab his arm with my free hand, shaking him slightly

"Try again." Then I am zoomed forward at an incredible speed through the forest. We stop at a hut. My heart is racing. Five guards surround my sister. I watch this from above. "Jessica," I scream in terror, but nobody seems to hear me. She's covered in bruises, a swollen eye, split lip; her arm is twisted at a horrible angle. I'm pulled from the hut. Ten men surround the area. *Oh God, it's a trap.* As I am pulled again against my will, I move back at an incredible speed, seeing all the treetops, and then I slow down. Tristan, Morrick and Kiar walk slowly with their swords drawn. Tristan's eyes scan the area. He looks dangerously beautiful.

And then I'm back in my body beside Neve, finding it hard to breathe. He looks at me in shock. I twist away from him and puke. "We have to warn them?" Neve still sits still. I shake him by the shoulders "We need to move now, Neve."

He comes out of his daze. "No, I have strict orders." He grabs my arms.

"Neve, please. They will die and you saw my sister." The look he gives me is pity. "We need to warn them. Just warn them, I promise." I meet his eye. "Please."

He lets my arms go and runs his hand across his bald head. "Okay, but you do everything I say."

I nod. "Yes."

He gives me a stern look. "I mean it, Sarajane."

"Yes, okay, Neve."

He hands my dagger back to me. A blush of embarrassment progresses along my cheeks. "Sorry."

He just checks his armour, obviously not forgiving me yet. "They are about two hours ahead of us," Neve says as I remove my boots and cloak.

"What are you doing?" he asks as I leave them under a bush.

"We need to move fast and with as little noise as possible."

He shakes his head, knowing he's disobeying orders "Fine, lets move." I follow him, branches poke into my feet, but I just picture my sister and push on. My noise level is a lot lower. We move at a fast pace and after two hours, I stop. "We should have met them. They were moving a lot slower."

Neve nods his head in agreement. "I will try to see them." He kneels down and digs his hands into the soil. I stand guard, keeping an eye around us. "It is not working," he says after a few moments. He tries again. "Nothing. Maybe it was you?"

I give a little laugh. "I don't think so." Then I sober. "Just try again."

He reaches out a hand for me to take. "It won't hurt. Just to try, Sarajane."

I roll my eyes. This is a waste of time, but I take his hand and kneel down, uncomfortable nobody is watching our backs. The minute we lower our joined hands into the soil, I'm pulled from my body again. I can see Neve and me. It looks like we're praying. Then I do a full rotation from this height. Tristan is watching us from a tree; his face displays his anger, but there's also a glimmer of admiration. Morrick is watching from a bush on our left; he looks intrigued by what we're doing and a little annoyed at seeing us. And Kiar is to our right, smiling.

Then I pull back into my body. I don't feel sick this time, as we didn't move through the forest at full speed.

Neve whispers beside me. "It is you, not me." I'm not convinced I had anything to do with this. We stand. Morrick is the first to show himself, then Kiar. He's fighting to hide his smile.

"You couldn't even guard a girl with her hands tied," he says to Neve in a low voice.

Neve's face turns bright red. "She had a dagger to my throat."

I have the good sense to look away, mortified. Tristan jumps down from the tree and saunters over to us at his own leisure. His movements of confidence annoy me. "You will never learn." That's all he says to me. "Move."

But before he can, Neve clears his throat. "Tristan, we came here to warn you." Now he has everyone's attention. "There are fifteen guards in total. It is an ambush."

Tristan looks at him suspiciously. "And how would you know that?"

I'm afraid, in case he tells him it was me, so I rush in. "Does it matter? I saw it too, when he used his affinity. *So* we just need to think of how to take out fifteen guards."

Tristan gives a sarcastic laugh. "And what will you do? Kill them all with your dagger?" He glances down at my feet. I have only socks on and they're darker in some areas from bleeding, but I don't care. I just need to get to my sister.

Tristan moves away and speaks to Morrick, who hasn't even acknowledged me. Kiar is smiling at me with pride that I managed to escape Neve. I smile back, causing Neve to nearly cut me in two with a look.

"All right, we're splitting up." Tristan gives me a look that says, *Say anything and you will be sorry.* So I gloat silently. "Kiar, you're with Morrick and you two are with me." *Great.*

Kiar leans in. "Wish I could go with you to see what you will do to Neve this time." He walks to Morrick, all signs of his smile gone.

We follow Tristan at a painfully slow rate. I want to tell him to hurry but know he might end up gagging me and tying me to a tree. He motions for us to get down. I can see Morrick and Kiar on the left have stopped moving too. We hunker down.

I try hard not to move a muscle as a guard walks past us. Tristan rises slowly and pulls the guard behind the bushes where he breaks his neck. He has it snapped before we can blink an eye. The man's dead eyes stare up into the sky. I feel sick. I gawk at Tristan in horror; he meets my horrified stare with a fierce gaze as a muscle tenses in his jaw. Then he returns to scanning the area. I can hear low moans to the right as Kiar and Morrick pick off another guard. All ten are dead within a few minutes. It is frightening to think Tristan could kill someone in seconds. I shiver with this knowledge.

We are still twenty feet from the hut, but there is no growth around. If we move into the opening, we could be picked off one by one. Tristan moves towards me slowly, still on his haunches. We're all behind a large cluster of bushes.

Once he's near he grabs my wrist roughly. "Listen to me. You stay here and don't move." When I go to protest, he puts pressure on my wrist. The pain runs through me; it feels like my wrist will snap. I bite the inside of my mouth to stop from crying out; blood soaks my tongue. "I mean it, Sarajane." He meets my eyes. There is a wildness in his. He reduces the pressure and I pull my arm away. I swallow the blood in my mouth and then regret it as my stomach churns.

"You think inflicting pain on people is the only way to get them to do what you say." It seems that way to me.

He grins, but it is unsettling "It is the only way to control you."

A door slams, drawing our attention to the hut as two guards are walking towards where we are hiding. "Where is Cura? He should have reported back fifteen minutes ago." They walk past.

"Stay here," Tristan says and leaves soundlessly. Seconds feel like minutes. Neve hasn't moved at all. Then I hear a small groan, then another. Tristan slides back in as if he never moved. That leaves three.

We sit there, hoping someone else will leave and hopefully we can just walk in and get Jessica. No such luck. No one comes out. Tristan creeps on his belly over to Morrick and Kiar, leaving Neve and me. I grab Neve's hand and we see in the hut, only three guards left. I look around the room for another door or window, but there is only one way in and out. Jessica is freshly cut along her forehead. Blood runs into her already swollen eye. I want to kill them all.

Then I am just hovering above Neve and me. *Why am I not going back to my body?* I look around. Nothing? I can see leaves fall behind us. My eyes shoot up and I honestly can say my heart stops beating. There has to be thirty men in the trees, watching us. Then I am back beside Neve. He is pale. The only advantage we have is they don't know we know they are there. We both crawl over to the rest.

Tristan turns to me. "What are you doing?"

I grab his arm, digging my nails in. He doesn't even flinch. "In the trees. Men. Maybe thirty," I whisper in his ear. He acts calm, which makes me wonder if he even heard me. I pull his arm again.

"Aim high," he says. I'm unsure what he means and then it sinks in. Mirium told Tristan to aim high before we left for Eden Forest.

Before I can say more, leaves and men rain from the trees, but they've lost the element of surprise. Neve, Kiar, Morrick and Tristan are on their feet and make a circle around me as they fight. I stand on shaky legs. Tristan, who is fighting two men, roars at me to get back down. I do just as an arrow cuts off a lock of my hair and whizzes past Neve's shoulder. I stay low, taking deep breaths to try and calm myself. A man falls at Tristan's feet, but he has no head. I close my eyes, blocking out the horror. *This isn't real, this isn't real,* I repeat to myself. Neve's scream makes my eyes shoot open. An arrow is embedded in his shoulder, but he keeps fighting.

"Get back into the forest," Tristan commands while dragging me by the arm. They move in a full circle until the trees surround us thickly. Tristan grabs me and pulled me against a tree, saying nothing at first. I peep out. There are only three men left fighting Kiar and Morrick so we've won.

Tristan draws my face back to him, making me meet his eyes. "Listen, this time I really need you to stay here." His eyes are pleading with me, making me feel bad.

"Or else?" I ask boldly.

"I don't want there to be an or else. Just do this for me."

I hold my breath. I'm taken back by the sincerity in his voice. "We're winning, Tristan."

He rests his arm against the tree alongside my head. "That was only ten so there are still twenty left, and if you haven't noticed, they have a distinct advantage." He doesn't say anything else, just stares at me intently, sending my heart rate into overdrive. My feelings towards Tristan are jumbled and confusing. He touches my cheek so gently, running his thumb down my face. "For me," he whispers and then he's gone and I'm left breathless.

I look around the tree. He has withdrawn his bow and arrow, aiming into the trees. Men scream as they crash to the ground. Neve and Kiar have taken to the trees while Morrick battles on the ground. My hands tighten around the dagger as I wait.

The screams of a men dying are starting to grind on me and then I hear a scream that I recognise. When I look out, Neve is on his knees, blood pouring out of a stub that is left of his arm. I can see his arm a foot from him. The guard raises his sword again, and I run with everything in me and jump on his back. He tries to throw me off, but I stick my dagger into his neck. He falls to his knees. I plunge the dagger three more times until he's motionless. My hands and clothes are soaked in blood.

Neve collapses on the ground. He's losing too much blood. I tear my tunic along the bottom and wrap it tightly around his stub to slow down the bleeding. "Stay with me," I say while tying it as tightly as I can.

A blade is placed at my throat. "Get up," a guard orders and pulls me against him as he turns to the fighting scene before us. "Surrender or I kill her!" the guard roars. The sounds of battle stop as Morrick and Kiar drop their weapons almost immediately. Kiar's eyes go straight to Neve; a look of anguish crosses his face. Tristan drops from a tree. He is breathing heavy. He told me not to move and I disobeyed him again. "Drop your weapon, Tristan," he says while pushing the blade harder against my skin. Tristan throws down his bow and arrow. "Move to the clearing." We nearly won; there are only five men left. Neve is left lying on the ground, but he's unconscious.

The door opens and the remaining guards leave the hut. One stands out from the rest. He has a bald head and is a large man, but there is a look of savagery and cruelty about him. He claps his hands as he walks towards us smiling. "You came, Sarajane." He looks at the guard. "Release her." The blade is taken from my throat. *How does he know who I am?* Then again, everybody seems to know me. "I will take great pleasure in killing you slowly."

I swallow. "The queen said if I showed my face my sister would live."

The bald-headed man smiles with pleasure. "Bring the girl out."

A guard goes to the hut and carries Jessica in his arms. When he reaches us, he lays her at my feet. I fall to my knees and run my fingers along her neck, checking for a heartbeat. It flutters under my fingers; she is alive.

"No one said anything about you living." The bald man looks down at me. He is really enjoying this.

"Taurus, Bellona gave her word that you or any of her men would not harm Sarajane. Or maybe you are willing to disobey your queen," Morrick says in a king's voice.

Taurus laughs cruelly and looks at Morrick with hate. "She is not my queen. But I do enjoy her body every night."

Morrick's face remains impassive at this comment. "This is your last warning, Taurus. Call these men off now or you will feel my full wrath." Morrick's voice is as hard as steel. I would be afraid if his threat was towards me, but it just seems to anger Taurus.

He grabs me by my hair, dragging me off my knees. My scalp burns with pain. I let out a screech. He looks at Tristan then, smirking. "Maybe I will have her body before I kill her." He runs a rough hand across my chest. Fear rolls through me. I feel repulsed by the motion. Tristan's jaw clenches, his hands balled into fists at his side.

I look down at Jessica. At least I've saved her. Her eyes open and she looks up at me. She reaches her hand towards Taurus's foot. *What is she doing?* Before she touches him, she smiles at me through bloody lips. Taurus screams and wheels back, but it only lasts for a second. Then he looks at Jessica and kicks her in the stomach so hard her body moves a foot away. I scream with anger and run for Taurus. When I touch him, his body is flung into the hut. I can't stop. Only one thought runs through me. *Kill him.*

Arrows are fired at me, but seem to bounce off an invisible shield. I don't look left or right but move straight into the hut and grab Taurus. He looks afraid. It is my time to smile. I feel as if my hands are on fire. I push them against Taurus's chest. He screams in pain as the smell of burnt flesh rises. I don't care. I just want to destroy this man who has hurt my sister. The hut is vibrating around us. I let my hands sink farther into his chest. The roof rips off in a gale-force wind and the walls are being torn apart around us. Taurus is roaring, but I can only see his mouth moving. His face is twisted with pain as tears flow from his eyes. I don't stop. I look at him through hair that is being whipped across my face with the wind. I can see something purple shine under my hand. I pull it. I know it's his soul and I want nothing more than to crush it.

"Don't, Sarajane. You are not like him. Let it go," Morrick says so softly beside me it knocks me out of my zone. The wind reduces and I open my hand, releasing Taurus's soul.

I sit there on top of Taurus, shaking. Someone pulls me off. Then I'm in Tristan's arms. He smiles at me. "You scared me. I thought I was going to lose you." I expected him to be angry.

I never get to answer, as I pass out.

I open my eyes slowly, feeling weak, and my head throbs. Jessica is beside me. I sit up quickly. Blood rushes to my head.

"Not so fast. She will be all right." Morrick reassures me.

I look at Jessica's battered body. *Oh God, what did she endure?*

"We heal quickly, Sarajane. She is partially like us."

I look around for Tristan and Kiar, but I can't see them. "Where is Neve?"

Morrick's face saddens. "He won't make it, but he has been asking for you."

"Take me to him." Morrick nods and lifts Jessica, taking her with us.

Tristan and Kiar are on either side of Neve. I can see by his colouring that he hasn't much time left.

He forces a smile when he sees me. "Sarajane." Tristan moves so I can sit with him.

"Oh, Neve, I'm so sorry."

"Don't be sorry. You brightened up my life when you walked into it." A lump rises in my throat. I am the cause of his death and we both know it. His hand squeezes mine. "Promise me you will look out for Kiar."

I look at Kiar, who is crying. Tears slide down my own face. "I promise." And then Neve is gone.

Tristan is beside me then. "You were a good friend, Sarajane."

"Don't. I got him killed."

Kiar looks at me with anger. "He died in battle, the way we will all go."

I start to cry harder. Tristan pulls me into his chest. I let my body give in to the horrors of today and silently beg Neve and Kiar to forgive me. I caused so much.

Morrick carries Jessica and Tristan insists on carrying me, but I refuse. I deserve the throbbing in my feet. It's my fault Neve has died. Kiar won't leave Neve's body behind. He slings him over his shoulder and carries him as silent tears run down his face.

Nobody speaks after walking for what feels like days. I stumble and fall; my feet are too badly cut. Tristan scoops me up. I don't object, and he carries me the rest of the way. We reach the edge of the forest an hour later. It's easier leaving. We don't have to be quiet. When we reach the horses, Kiar removes a bedroll and wraps Neve in it. He ties it at both ends and slings him over the horse. We take off.

The next two days, we ride towards Aquaterra. The silence isn't uncomfortable, as everyone is lost in their own thoughts. For me, Neve's death takes the most. No matter what he said, I still feel responsible. I'm feeling responsible for a lot lately. My sister would never have been taken if not for me. My dad is in danger. It feels like everyone was hurt because of me. Morrick killing his son to save me. It makes no sense.

My powers—that is something I push to the back of my mind. I can't comprehend it. I need to focus on getting to Aquaterra and speaking to Mirium to see if my dad is all right.

We stop for food and rest and nobody speaks, not even Jessica, even though she is healing fast. On day two, we reach Aquaterra.

Chapter Eighteen
SARAJANE

Once we arrive at Aquaterra, I go straight to my hut without speaking to anyone. I just need time to myself. Everything is too much right now. I lie down on my bed. My tunic is crusted in dry blood from the guard I killed. A knock sounds at my door. I take my face out of the pillow. "Go away."

"Sarajane, it's me," Jessica says. I sit up straight. She hadn't spoken one word the whole way from Eden Forest.

"Come in." Jessica stands in the doorway, her face nearly fully healed, but she is scared on the inside. I can see it. I open my arms and she races into them. I pull the quilt over the two of us and we curl up as she cries in my arms. I rub her hair and let her feel safe in my arms.

We must have fallen asleep because when I wake, it was dark. I sit up and rub my eyes. Jessica lies fast asleep. A shadow in the corner stirs. I light the candle beside my bed. My mother sits in the corner, her eyes raw from crying, deep circles running under them.

"Mum."

She comes to me and sits on the bed. "Thank you, sweetheart, for bringing her back safely." Jessica stirs then and Mum rubs her arm. "How do you feel, love?"

Jessica gives a big stretch and smiles at me. "Better now that I'm here," she says.

Mum looks away. I know she has bad news by the way her shoulders are set. "Mirium wants to see the three of us in the main barn." My stomach tightens. This is about dad. We walk to the barn, hand in hand. Jessica looks petrified, but this is her real dad. I give her hand a little squeeze before we enter the barn. Mirium sits alone at the head of the table and gives each of us a kind smile as we sit down around him.

"Hi, Jessica, it is lovely to meet you." Mirium reaches out his hand, causing Jessica to flinch in her seat. Her reaction startles us all. Then she straightens and takes his hand in hers. "You have very unique talents, my child," Mirium says while still holding her hand.

"They helped me when I got myself in sticky situations." Jessica sounds so much older than eighteen.

Mirium gives her another smile before returning his attention to us all. "Sarajane, Marta." I swallow. This is it. "I went to the mortal world and indeed, they had John held in the house by two guardians belonging to the queen." He pauses briefly. "I am so sorry." My mother lets out a strangled cry. "He was dead by the time we reached him." My mother sobs into her hands and Jessica just looks frozen in her chair. Mirium stands. "I will give you time alone." He squeezes my shoulder as he passes me before leaving the barn.

This is all too much. "Jessica." I take her hand in mine.

She looks up at me and tears stream down her face. "They killed Dad." I nod my head. I don't want to speak in case I burst into tears. And Jessica has been through enough.

Mum takes her head out of her hands. "My baby girls, I am so sorry."

Jessica curls into Mum, letting my hand go. "It's not your fault, Mum." And they cry.

I leave the barn for my hut after an hour of tears and memories, feeling like my soul has been pulled out of me. Jessica is staying with Mum tonight. When I arrive in my main room, Alana is waiting on me. I don't say anything. It feels so good to see her face.

She hugs me. "I am sorry."

I look at her. She's done so much for me. "Thank you, Alana—for everything."

She looks me up and down. "You stink."

I laugh through tears. "Thanks for that."

She links her arm with mine. "Come on, you need a wash and food." She has the tub filled and I strip robotically. I didn't want to think about anything. "You had a visitor today," Alana says from where she sits on the bed.

I stir in the tub, looking over at Alana. She looks tired. "Who?"

She raises an eyebrow. "A little girl around eight with big brown eyes."

"Mei," I say fondly.

"Yes, she called here every day looking for her princess."

The poor little child. "I will see her tomorrow." I lie there and let the water relax me.

"What happened to Neve?" Alana asks, her voice cracking on his name. I get out of the bath and wrap myself in a towel. "Here, I will brush your hair."

I sit down as Alana untangles the mass of curls. "He died in Eden Forest. He lost too much blood." Alana keeps brushing my hair. "How is Kiar?" I ask.

Her hand freezes. "Not good, Sarajane. But in time he will heal." She continues brushing the knots out.

"It is such a mess. I wish..." I stop speaking. I don't know what I would prefer. If I never came here, then I would've never met Alana, Tristan, Neve and Kiar. I would've been blind to who I was.

Alana stands back. "All done."

I turn and face her. "What happens now?"

She purses her lips in thought. "Now we bury Neve and look out for Kiar."

She is right. Kiar will be hurting the most. "Yeah, you're right."

I get dressed in clean travelling clothes. I don't want to be in a dress. Alana and I eat in my main room. The early hours of the morning are creeping in.

"You need rest, Sarajane."

I give her another hug. "Thanks again, Alana." I go to bed, but my dreams are haunted by too many dead faces, taunting me the whole night long.

When I awake a few hours later, I feel as if I haven't sleep at all. Banging on my hut door awakened me.

I open the door. Mei stands there, swaying back and forth, looking up at me. She is adorable. "Hello, Mei, come on in." I open the door farther. She looks around and then climbs up on a chair, her legs tangled from the height.

"I couldn't find you, princess," she says.

I sit across from her. "I had to do a job, but I'm back now."

She bobbles in her little head in understanding. Then she twines her hands together, looking shy. "Granddad said you are sad."

A lump rises in my throat, but I push it back down. "Yes, my dad died." She bobbles her head again. "But he's in heaven now with God." I'm not too sure if the child understands what death was.

"My mammy and daddy are in heaven too. I will ask Mammy to take care of your daddy." She sounds so matter of fact.

"Thank you, Mei. That would be lovely."

She beams and climbs off her chair, coming over to me. I don't know what to do, but she climbs into my lap and curls into me. Her little hands wrap around my neck. "Don't be sad, princess. I will be your friend." My hands hang loosely at my side, but I hug her back, her words giving me strength.

"Mei." I hear Ndee calling her name.

I take her off my lap. "Come on, we better get you home." She places her little hand in mine as we leave my hut. I have to face the world; I can't hide out forever.

Ndee gives Mei a stern look. "Mei." And then her eyes fall on me, full of sadness. "I am so sorry, princess."

"Thank you, Ndee." The settlement is quiet. "Where is everyone?"

Ndee picks up a reluctant Mei. "It is our day of mourning for the dead."

I am touched by this act of kindness. They didn't know my dad or Neve that well, yet they mourn for them. "Thank you, Ndee."

"Princess, Musa requests your company in the main barn."

I nod and then give Mei a kiss on the cheek. "I will see you later, Mei." She waves until her hand nearly falls off.

"Okay, princess." Her little face makes me smile as I cross the settlement to the main barn. Everyone is waiting inside—Mirium, Musa, Morrick, Tristan, Alana, Jessica and Mum. They sit around the large table. Mirium has taken the head chair and to the left of him, Musa sits with Tristan, Jessica and Mum. Morrick is to his right with a space beside him. I sit down, Alana on the other side of me.

"Now that we are all here, we shall get started," Mirium says. I'm unsure what all this is about, but I will find out soon. Mirium turns to me. "I know this has been very hard on you, Sarajane, and you have not been told the reason you are here, but…" He looks at Morrick and Musa. "We spoke and agreed that you are strong enough for the truth." I shift in my chair before Mirium starts. "This world was created by four fallen angels. It was their punishment. But after centuries, they were forgiven. So God allowed them passage back into heaven, but they still remain here." There is an intake of breath from everyone around the room. Obviously, not everyone knew this. That makes me feel a bit better. I'm not the only one in the dark. "The four of them can only return to heaven when they join together, but there is one angel missing that will not complete the circle." This all sounds like a child's story. "So God created a vessel that he filled with great powers beyond our beliefs. This vessel would vanquish Lucian, the angel who has turned to the dark world, and help the other angels return to heaven, giving Saskia back to the people that now live here." Mirium stops to let this all sink in. I was following perfectly, but just don't get what this has to do with me. "The vessel would come in the form of a young lady who would not live in this world, but would pass through fire to get here. The door would be closed to her until her destiny is complete." I squirm in my chair, feeling uncomfortable with the way Mirium is looking at me. "You, Sarajane, are the vessel."

I am finding it hard to breathe. It makes too much sense; I can do too much. "I'm only a girl, Mirium. I'm emotional, and I can't fight or make sense of a lot of things. I can't be…"

Mirium gives me a sad smile. "You are the one, Sarajane."

I look at my mother, who looks absolutely horrified. "You expect my daughter to go up against Lucian? Mirium, you know what he is like. I won't allow it." My mother rises, her body visibly shaking. "Sarajane, Jessica, we're going home." Then she looks at Morrick. "I won't loose her, Morrick. I'm sorry."

Morrick stands then. "Marta, Saskia will no longer exist. The longer the angels are here, everyone will die."

My mother lets out a tortured scream. "I don't care! I will not lose my daughter. No."

Morrick really loves my mum. I can see by how torn he is when he looks at her. "Marta, she can't leave."

My mother moves around the table, grabbing my arm. "You can't stop us." She tugs me to get up.

"Marta, she can't leave because the door is closed to her. You can try, but she has to stay here."

Fear runs all over my body. My mother lets me go and hits Morrick. "How could you do this to her?" He stands there as she repeatedly hits his chest, and then she crumbles in his arms. "How could you?" she whispers.

Everyone says nothing and stays perfectly still. Jessica and I are standing. I feel so far out of my depth, but the only thing running through my head is that I would never see home again. Josh. What about my dad? Would I get to bury him?

"Marta, please sit. This isn't helping," Morrick says gently and carefully. My mother sits beside me, taking Jessica on the other side, and holds our hands. She dries her face with the hem of her skirt.

"Sarajane, I know this is very overwhelming, but it is your destiny," Mirium says.

"I can never go home?" I ask.

Mirium's grey eyes look sad. "Not right now. No, but we are all here to help you." As if that will give me comfort.

I feel too shocked. "So I have to kill an angel and help the other three back to heaven or else everyone dies?" Mirium only nods. "So I must save the world?" The irony is a joke.

"Yes," Mirium replies.

"And this is why either everyone is trying to kill or capture me or use my family against me?"

"There is far more to explain, Sarajane. Deception runs deep, but there are lots of people willing to help you. But later I will try and educate you on, let's say, our political front in all of this." I nod my head, not sure of what else to do.

My mother looks at Mirium with hate. "You knew this and still took my daughter from her home and dropped her here?"

Mirium looks tired. "Marta, the clock has started to tick. We left Sarajane as long as we could. If we didn't bring her here, someone would have tracked her down and killed her, leaving us all with no future. You have seen that yourself with Bellona and Lucian."

I look at Mirium. "Why kill me if it will kill this world?"

Mirium lets out a deep breath. "Because you are too powerful and fear of something greater makes people want to destroy it. They do not see beyond their own personal goals or greed. They see only what they want to. And then others do not believe that the angels will destroy us. They haven't so far, so you are just a threat they must eliminate or use for their own personal gains. Sarajane, we will continue this conversation later, but first, Musa would like to address us all."

Musa rises, nodding at Mirium. "I will be brief. Firstly, I am truly sorry about Neve and John. You have my deepest sympathies. Neve will be buried here tonight." He looks at my mother. "You will return to the mortal world."

My mother hugs Jessica. "Yes, with Jessica." Then she turns to me. "But we will come back to you." I can't reply. The pain is too much so I just nod.

Musa continues. "Secondly, I can not house any of you much longer." Morrick and Mirium look at Musa in outrage, but Musa raises a warning hand. "I am sorry, but I cannot put my people in any more danger. Your traitor was already too much of a threat."

This shocked me. They had found a traitor. "Who was the traitor?" I ask Musa.

"It was Liber, Sarajane." Alana looks at Tristan shyly "That's how I knew about the fence and the horse when I…" She let the rest die. I didn't blame her for not finishing.

"I will house you for a few more days, but that is it. I cannot put my people in danger," Musa says.

"Musa, think about what you are saying. She is our vessel." Morrick objects, but Mirium puts a hand on his shoulder

"It is the way it is meant to be, Morrick. We need to leave anyway and make our way to Hummus." So not only do I find out I have to save the world. I have to leave to another unknown place. "That is all, my friends. I will leave you now, and, princess, God is gracious." *Very insightful.* Then Musa leaves.

"We will leave it there for now," Mirium says. You would think we were just chitchatting, but everyone starts to get up and leave. I'm the last to make my way from the room.

Mirium walks with me through the settlement. "I will come to your hut tonight and you can ask me any question you want. I will answer them to the best of my ability."

"Thanks, Mirium." We part then and I go to the main dining room. Everyone is there, but only a few whisper and talk amongst themselves. Conversations cease as soon as I walk in. *Just great, now I'm a freak.*

I get a bowl of soup and a roll and sit down beside Alana and Kiar. Alana tries to muster up some enthusiasm when I arrive. "So you are our saviour."

I give a small smile. Kiar doesn't look up at me. All he does is cut his fish into tiny little bits. "Kiar, how are you?"

When he finally looks at me, his eyes are bloodshot. "How do you think I am?" He gets up and leaves.

Alana shifts over so she and I are face to face. "He does not mean it, Sarajane. He is just upset."

I bite my lip to hold back my retort. "Alana, what do I do about everything?"

She shrugs her shoulders. "I really don't know, but it will come to you. You are smart."

Yeah, really smart, getting everyone killed around me.

"Princess." I look at Mei as she smiles up at me. Ndee walks over to take her away, but she is a welcomed distraction

"It is fine, Ndee, really." She gives me a sceptical look. "Cross my heart," I say and Ndee helps Mei up beside me.

"Now be good, Mei," she says before leaving.

"She never lets me have fun." Her little grumpy face causes Alana and me to laugh.

"She cares about you, Mei." But I know that is a hard thing to understand at such a young age.

"I wish you were my mammy." That would mean I had her when I was sixteen.

"Maybe sister would be better?" I smile at her thoughtful face.

"Can I tell you a secret, princess?" I wink at Alana, and she looks away as if the wall is so interesting. I bend down so she can whisper in my ear. "My brother would really like you." She looks around once she has it said.

"Why is that a secret?" I whisper back to amuse her.

Her little face looks bewildered that I didn't know. "We don't speak of excels."

I a, taken aback. I know she means exiles. My heart is pounding. "What is your brother's name?" I look at her sad face.

She doesn't whisper in my ear this time. She just whispers his name while looking in my face with her big brown eyes. "Carew."

Oh God, he looked like this tribe, but what did he do to be exiled? I couldn't ask this child. Alana clears her throat and Mei sits up straight, looking a little frightened. I give Alana a scowl. "Don't worry, Mei. Your secret is safe with me." I kiss her forehead, the poor child.

She sits with us, telling us all about her friend who can make water balls they fire at other kids. The more I spend time with this child, the more I know I am going to miss her.

Alana pulls me away. It is time to bury Neve.

Kiar, Tristan and Morrick are already there and Neve's body is tied to a wooden raft, ready to be set free into the water.

"Would anyone like to say anything?"

Kiar moves beside Morrick. "Yes, I would." I bow my head as he speaks. "You were the best guardian I have ever worked with, Neve. You were more than my friend; you became my brother and I will never forget you."

My heart breaks for him. Tristan speaks briefly then, saying he died an honourable death in the path of war. Alana shakes her head when she is asked if she wants to say anything.

Then it is my turn. My stomach tightens. I feel I should say something. "Neve, you made me laugh at times it felt it was impossible. You put your life in danger for my sister, and I will always be grateful. I will miss your big smile and crooked nose, and I'll always keep my promise to you." I nod at Morrick that I'm finished. It doesn't seem enough, but it's the best I can do.

Alana squeezes my hand as Morrick, Tristan and Kiar push the raft out and light it on fire. His body drifts out to sea. Kiar stands looking out. I can see by his shoulders he is crying. I rub his back, but he shrugs my arm off. "Go away, Sarajane"

I am taken back by his anger. "Kiar, please."

He turns to me. "Because of you I have no brother, so just leave me alone."

"You blame me?" I ask him.

Tristan gives him a warning glare. "Nobody blames you, Sarajane. He died at war, the way most of us will go. Kiar knows that. Isn't that right, Kiar?"

Kiar doesn't turn around. "Yes, that's right." But his body language says it all. I don't feel mad at Kiar. I blame myself.

"Don't do that to yourself." I look at Tristan and smile sadly. "I can't help it."

He goes to move closer, but I don't want his sympathy. I take a step back. "I have to meet Mirium so I better go." I turn my back and leave. I don't wait for a reply.

Mirium is waiting for me in my hut. "That was tough?"

I pour myself a mug of water. "Yes, but I don't want to talk about it." Mirium's presence will be a good distraction. "So I ask any question and you answer it?" I take off my boots and sit cross-legged on the couch.

"I will be as honest and exact as I can."

"Okay, so there are really three angles here, right now as we speak?" I ask.

"Yes, they are in Hummus." This is hard to believe.

"Real life angels with the wings and all?"

Mirium smiles. "Yes, they are very much real."

"Can everyone see them?"

Mirium considers this. "No, they are kept safe, as they are dying, and if they die, we die. Not many people even know they're still here. If everyone knew, how would we keep them safe?"

"So this fourth angel, Lucian, he is like a bad angel that I have to kill?"

"You can't kill him. You must vanquish him to the underworld, and yes, he is bad." Mirium finishes.

"So explain to me how Bellona ties into all of this and why she wants me."

"As far as we have gathered, Bellona is working with Lucian to capture you. She must be getting something in return to do this deed with Lucian. We are not sure if Lucian knows who you are or if he just wants your power. None of that is clear to us," Mirium says

"What have the exiles got to do with this?" I ask.

"We believe the exiles are being used by Lucian, but they are soulless creatures now, so they do not always follow orders as they should, but he seems to have recruited them."

This makes me think of Carew. "Will Carew become like them?"

Mirium's eyes widen briefly; then he smiles a little. "Ah, I should have seen this coming. So you met Carew?" I nod. "When someone is exiled from their community, they have committed a crime so they are banished to the mountains, never to return. They live, sleep and eat whatever they can scavenge. As you know, we live a long life, as in a couple hundred years, but the exiles can live to be a few thousand years old. That is why they take on the form of a creature, from the harsh weather and conditions. They usually go mad from the lack of living amongst people, and then we believe with their dark thoughts they lose their souls so they live forever as soulless and tormented creatures. The more intelligent ones can still communicate." I feel sick. Why not just put them in prisons? "So if Carew carries on the path he is on, yes, one day a long time in the future he would become one of them." My stomach tightens at the possibility of someone like him turning into one of them. "But if he has a reason to fight for his soul, he will remain human."

I look at Mirium. "How do you mean fight for his soul?"

"If he truly asks for forgiveness for his crimes."

This sounds simple. "He seemed nice, well, kinda. So why would he not?"

"Carew would never ask for forgiveness. He would do it all over again if he had to. You see, he killed his own father by stabbing him twenty times in the heart and then strangled his mother." I am shocked. *Jesus, he could have killed me. What a monster.* "So I do not believe there is any way to save Carew. How did you meet him?"

"He saved me when his exiles tried to kill me."

Mirium rises. "What do you mean his exiles?"

"He said he was their master. Why?"

Mirium sits back now "Sorry. Nothing. We will leave it there for now. I have other matters to discuss with Musa." Mirium's abrupt departure rattles me. It has something to do with Carew. "Oh, I have chosen Tristan and Alana to be your guardians until you have fulfilled your calling."

"What about Kiar?" I ask

"Do you want him as one also?" Mirium looks ready to leave.

"Yes, please."

Mirium waves his hand. "I will inform them all straight away. I must go. We shall talk tomorrow."

Not five minutes later, Kiar bursts in my door with Tristan and Alana trying to calm him down. "I will not guard you." Tristan is fuming, but I shake my head to let him know I can handle this.

"Yes, you will."

Kiar walks up to me. "Why are you doing this?"

I try to act calm, even though his hate for me is tearing me apart. "I want to be protected by the best people, Kiar, so your one of my guardians."

He moves in circles, breathing heavy. "I won't protect you."

"Though, Kiar, you are, so we're done for now." He leaves and Alana chases after him. I flop onto the couch, feeling overwhelmed.

Tristan is still here. "Why do you want him to protect you so bad?" I look at Tristan; he's angry.

"I just do Tristan, okay."

He kneels down in front of me, his hands in fists on either side of my thighs. *Too close,* my mind is screaming. "He reminds you of that boy from the ball?" Tristan accuses me.

I can't look him in the face. This is too close for comfort. My heart races. "So what about it?"

Tristan grabs my face, making me look at him. "You love this boy, do you?" Why was he so angry. I push his hand away.

"Maybe I could have, Tristan, but I never got the chance. As I remember, you dragged me out of there before I knew how I felt." My own anger at the injustice of all of this starts to boil. But Tristan doesn't look satisfied.

"So you want Kiar because he is like the boy?"

I am taken back by his tone. "Tristan, are you jealous?" I feel foolish saying it in case he isn't. His answer is abrupt. "Yes." He rises then, running his hand through his long hair. "You know how I feel. I make it perfectly clear, yet—" He cuts himself off, looking frustrated. My heart is in overdrive. "How do you feel about me?" My voice shakes. He turns to me, looking defeated. "I don't want him near you, Sarajane, or any other man." He runs his hand through his hair again. "I don't like Kiar like that. I just made a promise to Neve to look out for him so what better way if he is always with me?" I confess, even though I am really enjoying seeing him jealous. He looks thrown off for a second and a little lost for words. "Good, that's good." I raise both eyebrows. "Yes?" He kneels back down and smiles at me, a real smile. I think I might pass out. He is divine. "Yes," he says and then kisses me. It isn't gentle. The kiss feels urgent and full of need, but I return it with my own urgency. He is the first to break the kiss, both of us breathless. "You need your rest." He kisses my nose and smiles his full-watt smile, making my heart pound at my rib cage. "Sleep, princess," he says before he leaves.

I sleep, but the faces keep haunting me—Neve, Clive, Taurus and the guard I stabbed, who calls himself Ovid. When I awake, his name circles in my head. It isn't possible for the dead to speak in your dreams.

I change into fresh clothes and wash my face and teeth. Mum and Jessica are leaving today and I need to put on a brave face. I leave my hut and find Alana waiting outside for me.

"Good morning." She throws me an apple.

"Is it poisoned?" I ask before taking a bite.

She bats her eyelids innocently. "Would I?"

I laugh and take a bite. "Yes, you would."

We make our way through the settlement. It is back to being full of people, but there is an undercurrent of unease. "What's going on?" I ask Alana.

"I don't think we are welcome anymore," Alana says, but she sounds like she doesn't care.

We make our way to the main barn where Morrick, my mum, Jessica and Legis are waiting. I haven't seen Legis in a long time. I feel bad that I haven't missed his presence. Tristan and Kiar arrive after Alana and me, and then Mirium follows. I don't sit down, but lean against a wall, eating my apple. Every bite I'm finding it hard to swallow, as Mum and Jessica's departure shadows over me, so I give up.

"Legis and myself will take both of you across," Morrick says, holding my mum's face. I look away, feeling like I'm invading a private moment. Alana must have felt the same. She comes over and stands beside me.

"Really, you will come with me?" Astonishment sounds in my mother's voice.

"But I can't stay, Marta." He sounds like he wishes he could.

"I understand," my mum replies.

"How are you holding up?" Alana asks while nudging my side.

I shrug my shoulders, not sure how I feel. I'm trying not to allow myself to feel anything. "Fine."

Alana raises one of her pointed eyebrows. "Yes, you look the picture of calm." Her sarcasm is always there.

"Sarajane." Morrick's voice makes me look up. "Tristan, Alana and Kiar are now your personal guardians, I believe?" he asks.

"Yes, they are."

"Good, they will stay with you at all times as I cross over. On my return, we will leave for Hummus."

I just nod and look at Jessica and my mum. Bad idea. My stomach tightens with fear. What if I never seen them again?

I am allowed to go with Morrick, Legis, Jessica and my mum to the front gates to say my good-byes. My mum is in a flood of tears and she won't let go of me. "Mum, it will be fine. I am safe. Please don't worry."

She kisses my forehead. "My brave child, how did you become to be so brave?"

I smile back at her, "From you, of course." But tears sting my eyes. I hug Jessica "I wish I could come, Jess. I really do."

"I know, Sarajane. I will miss you." I give her another hug, but we can't wait much longer. The drawbridge is being let down.

"Mum, will you do something for me?" I ask before she climbs up on the horse.

"Anything, sweetheart."

I swallow the lump in my throat. "Tell Josh I'm safe and that... Tell him I'm sorry." My mother races back over to me, grabbing me, and I cling to her for dear life. "Please don't forget him, Mum."

"Marta, I am sorry. We must go," Morrick calls from the horse.

My mother kisses both my cheeks. "I will see you soon. This isn't good-bye, Sarajane." And she leaves, sobbing. I don't watch as the horses leave. I just can't.

Tristan is waiting a short distance away. "Are you all right?" His face is tense with worry.

"Distract me, Tristan." He looks at me so seriously. "Okay." He takes my hand, leading me to my hut. Once the door is closed, he stands right in front of me, just looking at me. "You are so beautiful," he says while stroking my face. I look away. I don't feel very beautiful. He moves my face around, forcing me to look at him. "Look at me, Sarajane," he says just as he kisses me gently.

I keep my eyes open and stare into his deep green eyes. My body buzzes from his touch, his kiss. I push against him, letting him know I want more. He picks me up while still kissing me and carries me to the bedroom, where he lays me down on the bed. His gentleness still amazes me.

Our kisses turn more urgent. The more I realise what we're doing, the more I want him. I pull at his top and he takes it off in one quick movement and lies on top of me. I pull at his trousers and he doesn't hesitate to remove them. He stands there naked. I don't have it in me to speak, only stare. He is so powerful and manly looking. He moves down over me and unbuttons my tunic, revealing my breasts. He sits back and just looks at me. It feels so surreal to have Tristan look at me like this.

"I love you, Sarajane." He doesn't shy away after saying it but keeps his eyes locked with mine.

My heart pounds in my chest and neck. "I love you too."

His face breaks into his rare and divine smile and I melt as he bends his head down and kisses my neck, his hair tantalizing my skin. It takes a second to strip me down and both of us get under the covers to explore each other's body with our hands. And then we make love, the most passionate and amazing thing I've ever experienced.

I lie in his arms afterwards, the covers tangled around our naked bodies. He sits up, leaning on his elbow, looking down at me as he wraps curls around his fingers. He is smiling, and my heart is still racing every time I snatch a glance at him. He lies down and tucks me into his chest protectively. I don't know why, but this makes me think of Liber.

"Tristan, what happened to Liber?"

He raises my head by lifting my chin with a finger. "Don't worry. You have my word nobody will ever harm you."

I feel like laughing at his serious expression. "I'm not worried. I mean, is he dead?"

Tristan's expression softens. "No, but I will kill him once I find him." I can see he means it.

"Would you not hesitate because he was one of your men?"

"No." That seems harsh.

"What if I was a traitor? Would you hesitate?"

Tristan looks mildly annoyed. "Don't joke, Sarajane."

I give at little laugh. "Please just answer me."

He lies back fully on the bed, placing his hands behind his head. "I would hesitate for a couple of hours."

I look up and can see a smile on his face. "Who's joking now?" I say and poke him in the side.

He grabs me, nuzzling my neck, making me laugh. When he stops, he brushes the hair off my face. His face is serious once again. "I give you my word, I will love you always."

I sit up straight. "Tristan, you can't swear something like that."

He grins at me and pulls me back down. "I just did."

Mirium arrives later to go through our agenda about what will happen once we reached Hummus. We call the meeting at my hut. It is only Alana, Kiar, Mirium and Tristan. Kiar is still pissed, but I don't push him for any more. Tristan and I decide to keep what we did a secret for the meantime.

Mirium starts by explaining that I will have to be trained in fighting and most importantly, trained to use my powers and discover exactly what I can do. "We will not announce our arrival. I have friends who will keep us in safe houses for as long as necessary, and the Nevaeh society will help us, of course."

I look at Mirium. "Nevaeh society?"

"They are the protectors of the angels. Their sole purpose will be to protect you also. So when Morrick comes back, we will leave for the city of secrets."

I laugh. "Very mythical."

Mirium smiles a little, getting my humour, and then his eyes roll back in his head, showing off the whites of his eyes. We all race to Mirium together. He is having a vision.

"Don't touch him," Tristan tells us.

So we wait until he comes out of it. He does slowly, with a look of fear and devastation on his face.

"Mirium, what did you see?" I ask.

He looks at us all. "War awaits us in Hummus.". Mirium tries to rise on shaky legs. Tristan and I help him. "We must leave and start our journey to Hummus" Mirium says looking at me. "But the war?" I ask shaking my head. Mirium pats me gently on the arm. "The war we will fight another day. But now we must leave and start your training". Everyone leaves to pack., Tirstan pauses as if to say something, then changes his mind and leaves. Mirium stays behind with me. "Pack light, we will get garments and equipment on the way" Mirium says.

I grab my sachel and stuff a few pieces of clothing into it. I don't have anything really so I am packed in minutes. When I return to the main room, Mirium is still there. "Mirium are you not going to pack?" I ask gently. He must still be disorientated after the vision. "No I have all I need here" he says tapping his staff on the floor.

We gathering at the main gates of Aquaterra and say our goodbyes to everyone. Mei breaks my heart, as tears roll down her little face, I hug her and promise her I will see her again. Ndee has to pull her off me, as she won't let go.I face the gates unable to look at Mei, as Ndee holds her tightly. I am releived when the gates open and we can leave. I hate Goodbyes. Musa stays at the gates. I look back a few times until the gate rises, and I can see him no-more. Mirium leads the way, as Tristan, Alana and I follow. Kiar and Legis stay behind to wait for Morrick. We will all meet up outside Hummus. I take a deep breath as I walk, yet once again into the unknown.

Acknowledgements

To my parents, Veronica and Hugh, without you this book wouldn't be possible. Thank you so much for your support through this. I hope I make you proud. I love you both. To my Nana, I remember you giving me my first book (Mills & Boon) and I never stopped after that. Love you and miss you.

Secondly, I would like to thank my boyfriend Dermot. Your endless inspiration and encouragement will never be forgotten. Love you. To Shannon, Luke and James, who listen to my monster stories, I hope this story stays with you always. And last but by no means least, Pat and Eileen, thank you for everything.

Also, I would like to thank my siblings. To my sister Amanda, thank you for listening and being so enthusiastic. You're a wonderful sister. And to my brothers Mark, David and Nigel, thank you for your support. Also to my niece and nephews Alana, Jack and Jake, Love you all very much. To my Nana Sheridan, all my aunts, uncles and cousins, thank you all for your support.
To my friends and support group, Rachel, Sarah, John, Eimear, Paul, Bernie, Tara, and Lisa anyone I have forgotten to mention, thank you all so much.
Happy Birthday to Jack Brady from John and Dermot.
Love, Aoife Marie

Remember, too, I can be contacted at

www.aoifemariesheridan.com or on Facebook at

www.facebook.com/Aoifemariesheri

CITY

OF

SECRETS

Part two of the Saskia Trilogy

Coming soon